Cowboy Cool

Cowboy Justice Association
Book Five

By Olivia Jaymes

www.OliviaJaymes.com

Chapter One

Reed Mitchell turned his truck into the quiet, middle class neighborhood and suppressed the urge to gun the engine loudly, just to rile up the residents a bit. It was clear it wasn't that kind of place with its manicured green lawns, box-shaped hedges, and cookie-cutter homes all painted various shades of beige. He refused to think that people had actually chosen these colors of their own free will.

Driving slowly down the sunny street with the window down to let in the crisp autumn air, he shuddered inwardly at the thought of living here—like this. The houses were too close together and the conformity too rigid. Reed wasn't the biggest fan of society telling him how to act, think, or feel. Especially feel. So far in the last fifteen years or so he hadn't felt anything really and it was working out well. Not giving a shit about almost everything made his life much easier and stress-free than the alternative.

The only thing he ever worried about was the safety of his town, and he took that very seriously indeed. So seriously he hadn't taken a vacation in over five years, a little tidbit of information the new mayor had come across and almost stroked out over. Now here Reed was on a forced holiday from the only thing he cared about and at the same time doing a favor for one of his best friends. Life was a merciless bitch with a strange sense of humor.

He pulled into the driveway of 1309 Violet Road and reached under his leather jacket to his shirt pocket and pulled out the folded scrap of paper. Ava Wright, Logan's wife, had written down the address and he matched it to the house numbers on the mailbox before he pounded on the wrong door.

A quick glance told him he had the correct house, and if he played his cards right he could be out of here and back on the road toward his real destination in a couple of hours. Not that he was all that excited about Florida. He'd chosen the destination because he had a buddy there and it sounded like a place people went on vacation.

He pressed the doorbell and waited on the porch where the homeowner had placed terra cotta pots of bright red and yellow flowers. Reed didn't know shit about horticulture so they could have been tulips or roses or maybe something else for all he knew, but they managed to brighten up the deadly dull facade of the home and personalize it just a little. The door swung open and a pretty but frowning woman with auburn hair stood there clad in jeans and a black t-shirt with white lettering that read "Writers Do It With Imagination".

Yep, he was at the right place. According to Ava, her friend Kaylee Blue was also an author.

"Kaylee?" he queried. "I'm Reed Mitchell. Ava sent me."

Her knitted brow immediately smoothed and she stepped back with a sigh. "Hello. I guess you better come in. I told Ava that she didn't need to do this. I'm fine. Really."

"I'm sure you are," he replied smoothly, hoping it was true. The more fine Kaylee was the sooner he would be on his way to his friend's place in Vero Beach. Reed stepped through the doorway and into her living room. "Why don't you tell me what's been going on? Ava said you've received some disturbing emails."

Whatever Reed had been expecting the inside of Kaylee Blue's home to look like based on the dreary exterior, those thoughts were blown completely out of the water. The large great room that encompassed the living, dining, and kitchen space was a tasteful riot of color and bold personality. A bright red couch and loveseat with gold striped throw pillows were placed in front of a stone fireplace complete with photos and flowers on the mantel. The furniture was a dark cherry and the lighter maple flooring gleamed in the light of the old-fashioned ceiling fan whirring above the room. Everywhere he looked there were plants, paintings, and an entire wall of floor to ceiling books.

His own home in Montana was a bastion of bachelorhood with Spartan furnishings and the requisite big-ass flat screen television that he hardly ever watched. He was too busy working.

"Please sit down." She indicated the sofa and Reed lowered himself into the comfortable cushions. "Can I get you anything? Ava said you were on vacation and headed down to Florida. Have you been driving all morning?"

He had actually and his throat was parched. "I wouldn't mind something to drink. I've been on the road since dawn."

Kaylee bustled into the kitchen that opened onto the living room and peered into the refrigerator. "I have milk, ginger ale, water, and iced tea. With sugar."

Reed liked the sound of her voice, soft and a little husky but still firm and sure. So many women seemed to make everything sound like a complaint or a catastrophe. Or maybe it was just the ones he came across as a peace officer. He didn't meet people on their best days for the most part.

"Ginger ale, thank you." He noticed the kitchen was well-equipped with everything a foodie would love. At one point he'd dated a professional chef so he knew quality when he saw it. "Do you like to cook?"

Her eyebrows shot up as she handed him a glass and sat opposite on the loveseat. "How on earth did you know that? Do I have part of my lunch on my shirt?"

Kaylee looked down with a scowl and brushed at her clothes.

"I'm a cop. It's my job to notice things. You have a six burner gas stove with a double oven, a marble-topped island the size of your sofa, and a set of copper pots. You either like to cook or you want people to think you like to cook." He took a sip of the ginger ale and tried not to notice how her t-shirt pulled tightly across her full breasts when she moved. She wasn't very tall but was extremely curvy. Reed had never liked the stick-figure look so many females starved themselves for. A woman was supposed to have boobs and an ass. "So I'd like to get a look at those emails if you don't mind."

Kaylee folded her hands in her lap, her expression conflicted and a little stubborn. "There's really nothing to see. I told Ava that when I talked to her yesterday and again this morning. I've received nasty emails before. Not everyone is going to like what an author writes. You have to have a thick skin in this business. Ava gets them too, just not this type."

"What type would that be?" If Reed didn't see these emails for himself he'd never hear the end of it from Logan, and Logan would never hear the end of it from Ava. So Reed needed to see the damn emails.

"The 'you're going to burn in hell' emails." Kaylee shrugged as if getting them was an everyday occurrence. "Ava doesn't get those like I do."

Reed scowled as he studied the woman's body language. She didn't seem upset in the least which was strange. At least to him it was. "Why would someone send you something like that? Is your work controversial?"

Maybe she wrote political or religious stuff. That could get a crowd twisted into knots pretty quickly and without much trying.

Her cheeks flushed a pretty pink and she looked down at her fingers, now twisted in her lap. "I write erotic romance. The sex can be—how do I say this—quite graphic in my books. I don't use euphemisms."

This was a fascinating turn. Reed loved books but he had never ventured into what he considered to be women's territory—romance. But if they had hot sex then he might just make an exception.

"I'm not sure what you mean by euphemisms." He knew what the word meant, he simply wasn't sure why this was so different than other books.

Kaylee shifted uncomfortably on the couch cushion and looked up at him. "What I mean is I don't use flowery language—purple prose, so to speak—for body parts. I use–" she broke off, obviously noticing his ever-widening grin and groaned in exasperation. "For heaven's sake, grow up."

"Sorry, I just don't think I've ever read a book like that," Reed countered, not feeling remorseful in the least. The girl could probably dish it out as well he could given half the chance based on how she'd come right back at him. "Listen, I'm sorry about that. So you write some sexy stuff and every now and then someone takes offense. They shoot off an email telling you that you're tunneling your way straight to hell to sit at the right hand of Lucifer. Is that about right?"

"That's it." Kaylee nodded in agreement, her temper already calmed. She didn't appear to hold a grudge. "I get them from time to time."

"But Ava's freaked out about these emails," Reed observed. "What's different?"

"Other than her pregnancy has put her on bed rest and she's bored as hell? I have no idea," Kaylee declared. "She's letting her rioting hormones rule her common sense. Logan should run for the hills while he can."

Reed couldn't argue with that sound logic but also knew his long-time friend wouldn't do it. Logan Wright was so damn in love with Ava he'd do anything to make her happy, especially now that she was stuck in bed all day awaiting the birth of their twins. That's why Reed was here, after all. Ava was worried about Kaylee and Logan was stuck in Montana dealing with his wife. Getting drafted for this assignment had been inevitable.

"Nothing else?" he pressed. "Same old, same old?"

Kaylee sighed heavily and got up from the couch, crossing over to the kitchen island where a laptop sat on the counter. "The only difference is I've received two from the same person. Normally I get one, ignore them, and they quietly go away."

She came back and sat next to him on the couch and flipped open the laptop, tapping on the keys. "You can take a look for yourself. Boring stuff."

Reed scrolled through the vitriol spewed on the screen feeling slightly sick that anyone could send that to a person, let alone a female. For someone concerned with Kaylee's eternal soul, they'd used some hateful speech to get their point across.

Your whorish writing is the work of the devil and will sentence you to eternal damnation. Repent now and perhaps you will not be tortured and incinerated in the bowels of Hell. Fornication is a sin and your books lead good people down an evil path.

Then Reed opened the second.

Sin peddler. Slut. Fornication with beasts will send you straight to Hell and I will laugh as you are impaled on pitchforks and your flesh burned by flames. An eternity of pain and torture await you and I look forward to that day with glee.

"Fuck, this is one sick bastard," Reed muttered, setting the laptop on the coffee table in front of him. "You get these all the time? Shit, what kind of books do you write again?"

"Erotic romance. It's not even erotica. It's always about two people falling in love with a happily ever after at the end. They don't sleep around. They're committed to one another."

Reed could hear the impatience in Kaylee's voice as if this wasn't the first time she'd made that explanation. He hated to make her do it again but he needed to know what he was dealing with.

"This one talks about bestiality." Reed pointed to the screen and Kaylee rolled her eyes.

"I have a shapeshifter series. The men are part of a wolf pack and they can turn into wolves. But they never have sex in shifted form."

"Shapeshifters?" Reed repeated, not even sure what that meant. "Are you saying that the humans in your books can change into something else?"

This time she smiled at his confusion. "Sure can."

"Whenever they want?"

"Yep."

"Does it hurt?"

"No."

"And people like to read about it?"

"They think it's hot."

Reed sat back on the couch and stroked his chin. "This I have to read."

Kaylee's smile grew wider. "I can hook you up. I have some paperbacks in the spare room."

Reed had a "To Be Read" list that he'd probably never be able to finish but he'd put her book at the head of the line.

"I may take you up on that, although I usually read on my e-reader."

"I can handle that as well." Kaylee gave him a questioning look. "So that's what has Ava's knickers in a knot. I think she's overreacting."

It was clear this woman wanted Reed to agree. While the emails were venom-filled there was nothing all that *personal* about them. The writer didn't make any threats, nor did they seem to know Kaylee's address or phone number or any other identifying characteristics. While nasty, they could have been to any author.

Still, Reed wanted a little more information.

"When did you receive them? And how do these people get your email address anyway?"

Kaylee sighed and got up from the couch and headed into the kitchen, pulling open the refrigerator door and grabbing a can of soda.

"My email address is on my website. For the most part I en-courage my readers to contact me to talk about my books. As for when these arrived? The first on Monday of last week and the second one the beginning of this week."

The timing didn't seem urgent. Reed had seen stalkers flood their victims with communication every hour of the day and night, their obsession that great.

"Can I see some of your other emails like this?"

Her forehead wrinkled and she shook her head. "I don't keep them. They're not exactly souvenirs."

"You delete them?" he persisted, dragging the laptop closer. "Could they still be in your deleted folder?"

"Maybe." Kaylee shrugged and came back to sit next to him. "I don't get a lot of these, Mr. Mitchell. When I do I just hit the 'X' and move on. That's it."

"Call me Reed," he said absently as he combed through the deletes, not seeing anything of interest. "Does the originating email address mean anything to you?"

"If you're asking if I know anyone named 'bookchiller' the answer is no."

Reed studied the sender's address but it was a generic email host that anyone could sign up for without identification. Honestly, the email could have come from anywhere if the person had some technology knowledge, or even basic search engine skills. Instructions for spoofing an email address were available on the web.

"Listen, I don't think this is a big deal. From what you're telling me this happens from time to time and you ignore it. Which by the way is a good practice. Don't give people like this any attention."

"So you'll tell Ava that I won't be bludgeoned to death in my sleep?"

Reed chuckled at Kaylee's spunk "I don't know your neigh bors or the crime statistics of Champaign, Illinois but I will say that I don't think these two emails ring any warning bells. Now if things escalate, that's a whole different story. I would, however, report these emails to the police. Just in case you get more and this becomes an issue."

Kaylee groaned and slumped back on the cushions. "You have got to be kidding. What are the police going to do?"

"Probably nothing." Reed closed the laptop and turned so he could look into her eyes. "But—and this is important—if this continues they'll have a record of the harassment. They could also have a computer expert find the source of the emails."

Jared could definitely do it, and Reed could as well if given enough time.

"Fine." Her arms crossed over her chest and it made Reed wonder if she would really make the call. She definitely had a negative vibe about the entire situation. "I'll call them but they're going to think I'm wasting their time."

"Speaking as a lawman, I'd rather people waste my time every now and then. There's nothing wrong with caution."

Her lips tightened and her eyes narrowed. Apparently this stubborn miss didn't like being lectured. Too bad. He wasn't done.

"Before I leave I'll check your home for any vulnerabilities. That way you...and Ava...can feel safe." He pointed to the front door. "You can help by not opening the door to just anyone. Next time ask me who the hell I am before you open the damn door."

"I knew you were coming," she countered. "Besides, this is a safe neighborhood."

"You didn't know me from Adam." Reed wasn't going to let her wriggle out of this. "I could have been a serial killer for all you knew. Once you open the door someone can get in. So don't do that anymore. You have a peephole and a bar latch. Use them."

"Do you talk like this to everyone, ordering them around?" she asked indignantly. "We've only just met."

"I'm here as a favor to Logan and Ava. How you feel about that really doesn't concern me," he answered and watched as her cheeks turned an angry red. This one had a temper on her, and damn if Reed didn't want to poke at it. Just a little. He was on vacation after all.

Sparks practically flew from her bright green eyes. "Then by all means check the house. I think you'll find my home is quite secure, Mr. Mitchell."

"I will." Reed stood and started for the front door. "I'll begin here if you don't mind. I'll be checking doors and windows so feel free to go back to what you were doing while I work."

Kaylee huffed but lifted her laptop and tucked it under her arm. "I'll be in my office if you need me."

Reed didn't know where that was but the house wasn't that big. If he needed her he was sure he could find her. He chuckled as she strode down the hall, her shoulders straight, her gaze looking anywhere but at him. Her stiff posture didn't stop the gentle sway of her generous hips as she walked away and he watched until she disappeared at the end of the hall.

Kaylee Blue had grit and sass combined with a fun and fiery temper. Too bad he wasn't planning to stick around for awhile. A woman like that would be a delight to tame—in or out of the bedroom.

Scratch that.

She was Ava's best friend and that meant she was off limits. Logan would kick his ever-loving ass if Reed upset his wife by loving and leaving her BFF. Friendship meant more to Reed than a tumble in the hay any day.

He would secure the house and hit the road. Better for him, better for her. He doubted Kaylee was the no-strings type anyway. She had husband, kids, and white picket fence written all over her.

No way he would ever do that again.

Chapter Two

"This is a nice restaurant," Reed observed as they sat down at a table near a window. "Do you come here often?"

"Not too often. I'm usually working so I just cook for myself, but I thought it would be good to get out of the house since the weather was so nice."

The fact was Kaylee couldn't have stayed cooped up in the house with Reed one moment longer. When he'd started to investigate her windows and doors he'd decided that her security was woefully inadequate. One trip to the hardware store later and he'd been stripped to the waist, a tool belt around his lean hips replacing hardware and screws on her doors and locks on her windows. He'd even installed some motion triggered lights around the house and a camera for her front porch. She could now see who was at her door from her laptop. It had taken him all afternoon but she had to admit she did feel safer with all the work he'd done.

She also felt a little guilty.

He'd busted his very nice looking ass to help her and, especially at the beginning, she'd been less than appreciative about it. She'd decided the least she could do was be a good hostess and take him out to dinner. After all the work he'd done he deserved a good meal.

And she deserved to burn in that hell the email sender had talked about for the thoughts that had skipped through her mind as she'd watch Reed work. Despite every effort to the contrary her gaze had been drawn over and over again to his flexing muscles, wide chest, and flat abdomen. There ought to be a damn law against men as hot and sexy as Reed Mitchell. Even now sitting across from him she could smell the citrus tang of his aftershave mixed with his yummy male scent. He'd run back to his hotel for a quick shower and fresh clothes before picking her up for dinner. It might have been better for her sanity if he had stayed dirty and smelly.

Fuck, she needed a drink. And they needed to turn up the air conditioning. It was warm in here.

"Something from the bar?" the waiter asked as he handed them menus.

"Cosmopolitan," Kaylee answered quickly. A little alcohol would settle her nerves. She was acting like she'd never seen a man before, which of course she had. It was just that it had been a long time. Before she moved back to the area.

Since she worked from home she didn't get out much and didn't meet a lot of people, unless you counted the nice UPS guy that delivered something to her house at least twice a week. He was a nice man but married and not really her type anyway.

Reed Mitchell, on the other hand, embodied the sexy, handsome, alpha male that Kaylee wrote about on a daily basis. She simply never thought she'd be having dinner with one. She'd always thought they were strictly make-believe and that thought had given her some comfort. If they were as real as a unicorn she couldn't feel badly about not having one.

So much for that theory. Her proverbial Bigfoot was sitting right across from her.

Shit.

Reed ordered a draft beer and the waiter disappeared, leaving them alone. Kaylee fidgeted in her chair, crossing and re-crossing her legs. It had been months since her last date.

Not that this was a date.

"So, um, how long have you been a cop?"

"About seven years. How long have you been a writer?"

Kaylee immediately noticed that Reed turned the conversation back to her. Ava had said he was something of an enigma and it looked like he intended staying that way.

"Always, really," she replied, used to this question from people. "I wrote stories, mostly short stories, in high school and college. After I graduated I moved to Portland with my boyfriend and wasn't able to find a job right away. That's when I tried my hand at longer works. I never really stopped from that point on."

"That's where you met Ava?"

Kaylee nodded as the waiter slipped two large martini glasses in front of her. She looked up, alarmed at the amount of alcohol and the waiter seemed to understand her distress.

"It's Happy Hour. Drinks are two for one."

"Oh okay, that's fine." Just because they gave her two gigantic drinks didn't mean she had to actually imbibe them. She took a sip of the pinkish-red liquid and nodded in approval. The bartender knew what he was doing. The drink was strong, tart, but still a little sweet due to the cranberry juice.

"Are you ready to order?"

They ordered and she fiddled with the stem of the glass. "In answer to your question earlier, I did meet Ava in Portland. We belonged to the same writer's group."

"But you moved back here?"

"My grandmother died and left me her house, plus Ava had already moved to be with Logan. There wasn't much holding me in Portland. I can work anywhere."

"What about your boyfriend?"

Kaylee frowned, not understanding the question for a moment. "You mean David? He and I broke up about a year after we moved there. I found him in bed with a friend. Well, former friend now. She was welcome to the lying, cheating bastard. They eventually married and from what I hear he cheats on her too."

Reed whistled and shook his head. "Sounds like a real jerk. You're better off without him."

"I'm well aware," she snapped. Talking about her romantic past wasn't exactly pleasant. "I suppose you've never done anything wrong with a woman. You're like a choir boy."

She sounded waspish and bitchy and that wasn't what she'd intended. At some point in the conversation she'd drank the better part of a Cosmopolitan. She needed to slow down; already she was beginning to feel the effects.

But if she'd offended Reed he didn't show it in the least. He simply leaned back in his chair and smiled indulgently as if she was a recalcitrant child. "The women I date know up front that I don't do love and relationships. I don't do commitment. My job is the number one thing in my life and everything else comes a distant second. Very distant."

"So it's just about sex?" she challenged him. He was probably hot in the sack if his women put up with that shit and she couldn't deny the voice in the back of her head that was urging her to find out just how good Reed Mitchell really was.

"They are mainly sexual relationships, yes," he replied mildly. "Two people satisfying mutual desires. Does that offend you?"

Somehow her glass had emptied and she'd started in on her second drink. Her brain was buzzing a little but not in an unpleasant way. She was feeling warm and a little tingly sitting across from this sinfully sexy man talking about sex.

"No, it doesn't offend me. Actually I think it's smart. I don't do relationships either if you must know. A sexual thing is fine but a man in my life day in and day out just isn't going to happen."

She didn't mention why it wouldn't happen. Because men couldn't be trusted to hang around when things got tough. They always cut and run. She'd seen it so many times. It was better to be independent, self-sufficient. Her mother had depended on Kaylee's father and it had destroyed her.

Bowls of pasta were slid in front of them along with a basket of garlic bread. Kaylee breathed in the heavenly scent before picking up her fork and digging in. Her small lunch of cheese cubes and a few crackers seemed very far away.

They didn't talk much as they ate. Reed had a healthy appetite and concentrated on his food, but Kaylee found herself picking at the delicious pasta. Normally she would have enjoyed the balance of flavors in the Bolognese sauce but tonight she was instead uncomfortably aware of her dinner companion.

Every move he made drew her attention, from drinking his beer to biting into a piece of bread. His frame was powerful but he wasn't musclebound in an obvious way. His dark hair was trimmed short but a little fell over his forehead, giving him a boyish quality that didn't match the rest of his manly facade. His eyes were hazel with flecks of gold and green and his lips full and sensual. She had to resist the urge to reach across the table and trace them with her fingers.

"Another cocktail?" the waiter asked, appearing out of nowhere. She shook her head absently, noting her second glass was empty and continued studying her dinner companion. He reminded her of the handsome alpha males she wrote about in her books. Now she had a real live one sitting across from her. What were the odds of this happening?

It might never happen again.

She felt warm, relaxed, and a little giddy. Reed Mitchell was a man out of a fantasy and she only had tonight. One night to live out a dream. Or two, if he was willing and able.

She wasn't normally a woman who would sleep with a man she'd just met but this was completely different. She rarely left the house, rarely dated and now she had God's gift to women right here. She'd be a fool to pass up the opportunity. It was… kismet.

He'd already said he only dealt with females at a sexual level. He didn't seem repulsed by her although she was sure he could do better. She wasn't ugly but she wasn't a beauty either. Too short, too heavy, and hair too thick and wild. She was what people called "full-figured," although David had told her she was "fat." She'd told him his dick was too small. Eyeing Reed's large hands currently gripping his beer glass, she didn't think that would be an issue.

"Do you want dessert?" she asked huskily, their gazes locking for a moment across the table. She leaned forward and let her lips part slightly so her tongue could wet her mouth while sliding her hand closer to his. He could easily reach out and touch her but instead he sat back in his chair, his eyes narrowing as he regarded her steadily.

"I think I'll pass. You didn't eat much. Are you feeling okay?"

"I'm fine," she answered, a little disappointed that he hadn't said yes. Perhaps she was being too subtle. Men often didn't get small hints. "I'll get the check if you're ready to go home."

She signaled to the waiter and he set the check down nearer to Reed than to herself. Reaching for it, Reed's hand came out and snatched it from the tray even as he was digging into his pocket for his wallet.

"Dinner is my treat," she protested, trying to reach for the slip of paper but he held it just out of her grasp. "You did all that work on my house."

"Where I come from ladies don't pay when having dinner with a gentleman. It was nice of you to offer but I've got this."

His tone was firm and her first instinct was to capitulate but then she remembered that he wasn't the boss of her. She was an independent woman who made a good living all on her own.

"I invited you," she said and held out her hand for the check. "Where I come from that means I pay. When in Rome…"

"I should be Roman?" Reed grinned and a dimple pierced his cheeks. Dammit, he shouldn't be so handsome. And charming. He pulled his credit card from his billfold and held it up along with the ticket as the waiter walked by. In an instant he was gone and so was her chance to show him she could pay the check. "I really do think it's sweet but I'm old fashioned. I'd be uncomfortable if I didn't do this."

The whole point of taking him to dinner was to thank him and make him welcome in her town. If she didn't give in gracefully she was going to look churlish.

"Then thank you," she said reluctantly. "I didn't invite you out so you could buy me dinner."

"Never thought you did." Reed smiled as the credit slip and a pen were placed in front of him. The waiter thanked them and then once again melted away. "Are you ready to go?"

She nodded and picked up her purse from where she'd tucked it next to her feet and stood on shaky legs. The room tilted and spun and she had to grab onto the back of the chair to keep from falling over.

"Steady there." Reed's callused fingers wrapped around her arm for support and she shivered at the contact as electricity pulsed through her veins. "Are you alright?"

"I'm fine." The walls righted themselves and she pushed a few stray hairs out of her eyes. "It's just warm in here, that's all."

Let's not mention the two Cosmos I drank. What the hell was I thinking? One would have been enough to get me tipsy.

"Then let's go outside and get you some air. Do you need me to carry you?"

One look at his concerned expression and she knew he was totally and completely serious. No man had ever in her entire life offered to carry her an inch, let alone all the way to the car. Hell, had any man she'd ever dated been capable of it? Doubtful. They would have thrown their back out and ended up in traction.

Not very sexy.

Kaylee looked up into those hazel eyes and shook her head. "I'm fine."

Reed's arm slid around her shoulders so she could lean against his sturdy frame. "Let me help you. Just lean on me."

They walked slowly out of the restaurant and into the chilly air of late October. Her hand clutched at his butter-soft leather jacket as she carefully navigated the pitted parking lot.

"How many of those drinks did you have?" He scowled and carefully placed her next to his truck.

"Just two," she admitted. "I don't drink very often. Just a few times a year."

"It shows." Reed unlocked the door and helped her up into the seat before pulling the seatbelt across her body and buckling it. His warm hands brushed her skin and left a trail of fire everywhere he touched. She reached out and ran her fingers up his broad chest, feeling the steady beat of his heart under her palms.

"I know just what we should do when we get home."

She lifted her face for a kiss but once again he didn't take what was offered, taking a few steps back instead.

"You need to get to bed."

Reed turned on his heel and slammed the door behind him as he walked around the back of the truck to the driver's side. Kaylee giggled as he swung into the seat next to hers and let her fingers rub his muscled thigh.

"That's exactly what I had in mind."

Chapter Three

What had Reed gotten himself into?

When he'd told Kaylee he dealt with women purely on a sexual level it hadn't been an invitation or even a hint. It was simply a fact. But now he had a tipsy woman on his hands who had rubbed up and down his thigh the entire way home ensuring that his cock was at full attention and in the go-mode.

But it wasn't going anywhere.

Reed plucked the keys from her wandering fingers and opened the front door to her house, all the while trying to keep her steady on her feet and her hands out of his pants.

"Why don't you have a seat and I'll make us some coffee."

Kaylee tossed her purse on the dining room table and wrinkled her nose. "I don't drink coffee at night."

"I thought all writers drank coffee. Ava loves it."

"I'm not Ava. Haven't you noticed?"

Kaylee giggled and sailed into the kitchen, kicking off her shoes on the way. "We can have ice cream instead. I love ice cream."

Reed grimaced at the thought of any dairy product on top of the alcohol she'd had earlier. He didn't need her puking in addition to trying to seduce him.

Although it was kind of cute since she obviously didn't do this very often. Sexy in an innocent way.

If Kaylee had been anyone else…and sober…he wouldn't have hesitated to take her up on her offer. She was a beautiful woman and he was only a man. But as things stood she was the best friend of his best friend's wife. Nothing was going to happen between the two of them. He'd put her to bed—alone—and that would be all.

"I don't think ice cream is what you need right now. I think you need to get some sleep. You'll feel better in the morning."

Now that was an outright lie. Since Kaylee didn't drink often she was probably going to feel much worse tomorrow. The least he could do was try to head off as much of the inevitable hangover as he could.

"You need a glass of water and some ibuprofen."

Reed remembered where she kept her glasses from earlier today and quickly filled it with cold water from the refrigerator door. Kaylee had perched on one of the stools at the island and was watching him as he moved around the room. Not in a creepy way but in a warm, admiring way. A man could get used to a woman looking at him like that if he wasn't careful.

"Drink. Now where do you keep your medicine?"

She dutifully started drinking the water and pointed to a cabinet in the corner of the kitchen. Reed rummaged through the various first aid supplies and found the bottle behind some nighttime cold liquid. He shook two from the container and held them out.

"You aren't allergic or anything, are you?" He doubted she would have medicine she was allergic to in her cabinet but he had to be sure.

"No, I'm as healthy as a horse." Kaylee giggled and had to set her glass down. "Get it? Horse? There are horses in Montana."

Trying to keep from laughing at her fuddled antics, he nodded and placed the pills in her palm. "I get it. Cute joke. I bet you've never even ridden a horse in your life."

Tossing back the tablets, she took a gulp of water. "You'd be wrong. I've ridden, although not a lot." Her shoulders slumped and her lips turned down. "You don't want me, do you?"

Well, shit. He didn't need this tonight. All because he'd agreed to do Logan a favor and now look at how things were turning out. Logan was going to owe him big after this. It was all Reed could do not to grab her hand and guide it to his very hard cock pressing against the fly of his jeans.

"You're a beautiful woman, Kaylee Blue, but you are also a little drunk. I don't think it would be right to take advantage of that."

Her eyes narrowed suspiciously. "Are you just saying that to be nice? A lot of men say I'm too fat."

A lot of men needed to get their heads out of their asses. Kaylee was a gorgeous woman with curves in all the right places. Like a pinup girl from another era, she had a tiny waist with round breasts that begged to be worshipped, lush hips, and an ass that made Reed's palms itch to spank those bottom cheeks a bright red.

"You look just fine," he assured her. "That doesn't have anything to do with why we're not going to have sex tonight. You've had too much to drink, honey. You need to sleep it off.

Tomorrow you'll be glad you didn't jump into bed with some cowboy who will be gone in the morning."

"That's what I mean. I only have this one chance to sleep with a man from one of my books," she insisted, but her eyelids were already starting to get heavy. He could tell the alcohol was making her sleepy and she yawned just then to prove it.

"I have no idea what you're talking about, but finish your water and then I'm going to put you to bed. Alone."

She slugged down the rest and sighed as he placed the glass in the sink. "You're no fun."

"I hear that all the time," he agreed. "You need to get some sleep."

"It's only nine o'clock," she argued. "Eight year olds go to bed at nine."

"Eight year olds and grown women who have drank too much and should have known better do too," he retorted, liking the fact that she didn't give in to him too easily. Most of the women he knew were happy to let him boss them around. Sometimes because they liked having someone tell them what to do and sometimes they hoped he would fall in love with them. He moved the ladies who believed the latter out of his life at the speed of light.

"Can I have a kiss goodnight?" She was peeking at him from under her lashes, a sly smile curving her lips. Before he could say no she was winding her arms around his neck and pulling his head down to hers.

One kiss wouldn't hurt anything. He'd give her a quick one and then pat her on top of the head and send her upstairs to sleep. Running his hand down her spine, he pulled her a little closer and brushed her lips with his own, once and then twice. He tried to pull away but she pressed herself closer so he could feel her full breasts mashed against his chest and the warmth of her breath on his skin.

"I want a real kiss," she said huskily, pulling his mouth to hers. The kiss was hot, slow, and way too much with a woman he barely knew. She had his breathing ragged and his heart pounding all with the way she seductively played with his tongue. He didn't even want to look down at his groin, knowing his cock was painfully hard and ready for action.

He reached up and unwound her arms from his neck and took a step back, placing some much needed distance between them.

"This is a very bad idea, Kaylee. You'll regret this in the morning."

He was already regretting it. This woman had a potent effect on his libido and he needed to get the hell out of her home before he did something really stupid.

"I won't regret it." Her lids were drooping though and her voice was soft. "I'm glad you're here, Reed."

Was she lonely living here all by herself? The last thing she needed was a man like himself gumming up the works of her life.

"Do you need me to carry you up the stairs?"

Her chin was propped up on her hand and she was definitely fighting sleep. "No, but will you carry me anyway? I've never had a man carry me to bed before."

Reed inwardly cursed the asshole men she'd dated in the past. Obviously she was due for someone who truly appreciated her. That man simply wasn't him. He would put her in bed, head back to the hotel for a good night's sleep, and then in the morning get back on the road and start enjoying his first vacation in over five years.

He lifted her into his arms and she curled up trustingly, laying her head on his shoulder. By the time he found her bedroom up the stairs and at the end of the hall she was snoring softly. Balancing her weight on one arm, he pulled back the covers before laying her on the bed.

He scraped his fingers through his hair and sighed in resignation. He couldn't just leave her like this. Bending over, he slipped off her shoes and tucked her under the covers. Her features were soft and angelic in sleep, so unlike the independent and stubborn woman during the day. He brushed a stray strand back from her cheek and tucked it behind her ear. Her skin was soft and warm and...fuck if he didn't need to get the hell out of this bedroom right now.

Bounding down the stairs, he stood in the middle of the living room, torn in two. The logical part of him knew she'd be fine and he should just leave. Maybe he could write her a note. The other part didn't like the idea of leaving a semi-drunk woman on her own. She might wake up and stumble down the stairs, hurting herself.

With a sigh of resignation he kicked off his boots. He wasn't going anywhere until she was a hundred percent. He flicked off the one lamp she'd left on from earlier and then stretched out on the couch with a groan of relief. He was tired and in the military he had learned to sleep anywhere, but he would keep an ear cocked in case Kaylee decided to take a midnight stroll.

Just a minor change of plans. He'd still get on the road in the morning.

Chapter Four

Kaylee opened her eyes and quickly shut them again as a sharp pain pierced her skull. The light streaming in the windows was too fucking bright. Why had she left the drapes open last night? Slowly she lifted her lids again, wincing at the pounding in her temples and the back of her head. Shit, even her hair hurt.

Groaning as she pushed to her elbows, she looked down at herself still fully dressed from dinner last night. Her foggy brain tried to make sense of the evening before and she sat up, swinging her legs off the bed.

Dinner. Drinks. Oh fuck a duck.

Drinks explained the cottony dry taste in her mouth this morning. The small amount of dinner she'd eaten explained why she'd managed to get herself north of tipsy. And being nervous about having dinner with a handsome hunk from one of her books explained why she hadn't eaten in the first place.

It all added up to a nightmare.

Resting her head in her hands, the night before began unfurling in front of her like a really bad movie. She'd had too much to drink—something she hadn't done in years—and thrown herself at Reed Mitchell. Whether he was being a gentleman or simply wasn't interested, he'd turned her down which was probably for the best. She didn't need a man that good looking staring at the cellulite on her thighs.

She stripped off her clothes and stepped into the shower, scrubbing off the shame of the night before. Pulling on a pair of yoga pants and a t-shirt, she went down the stairs rubbing her forehead and swearing to never drink again.

She needed ibuprofen and coffee. Perhaps a mental eraser as well so she could forget her embarrassing behavior from last night. She wasn't in the habit of trying to lure unsuspecting men into her bed, despite what people might think because of her occupation. Reed probably thought she was a real slut.

"You're awake. I made coffee."

His deep voice was unexpected and she gasped in surprise, her heart skipping a beat with shock. She had to lean a hand on the kitchen counter to catch her breath.

"You scared the ever loving fuck out of me."

Reed was standing in her kitchen drinking coffee from a mug that said 'organized people are just too lazy to look for things' and munching on a piece of toast. He chuckled at her consternation and pulled down another mug and filled it. She wished she'd taken the time to dry her long hair instead of leaving it wet and loose around her shoulders. Paired with her pale features without a speck of makeup and she probably looked like Dracula's sister.

"You have a potty mouth in the morning. Do you want some toast with that?"

Her stomach lurched at the thought of putting food in it but bread might soak up some of the acid that was currently eating away at the lining.

"Thank you, maybe one piece," she conceded. "And I have a potty mouth all day long. I was just hiding it because you were a guest. Why are you still here? I thought you would have gone to the hotel last night."

He'd obviously made himself at home in her kitchen. He popped a slice of bread into the toaster as she sipped her coffee and rummaged in the cabinet for a few tablets. This headache wasn't going to go away by itself.

"I couldn't leave you when you were like that. What if you tried to get up in the middle of the night and hurt yourself? What if you got sick and choked?"

She leaned her forehead against the cool wood of the cabinet and sighed. "Wow, you're a real optimist aren't you? None of that even occurred to me. I got drunk. I passed out. If I'd woken up puking I guess it would have been a fitting punishment."

"Are you looking for these?" Reed held out the bottle of ibuprofen. "As for being punished, I think the way you feel is punishment enough. I tried to make it not so bad by making you drink water so you wouldn't wake up dehydrated."

"It helped." Kaylee tossed back a couple of tablets with a gulp of scalding hot coffee. "Thank you, by the way. I'm mortified but grateful you were there."

She kept her gaze firmly on her coffee cup. The mind-blowing kiss they'd shared was sadly still front and center in her memory. It would probably end up in her new book.

"You're welcome," he said, refilling his own mug. "You said you don't drink much."

"I think the last time was probably New Year's Eve. I had a couple of glasses of champagne and woke up with a headache. This headache."

"What made you drink last night?"

Reed snagged the now golden piece of bread from the toaster and placed it on a plate before handing it to her. She bit into it—no butter or honey—and let it melt on her tongue. She was surprisingly hungry. She was also not so naive that she was going to admit that he reminded her of her male characters. Her best course of action was to pretend nothing happened.

"I know you need to get on the road," she said instead, still avoiding eye contact. "I shouldn't keep you any longer. You have places to go. I do thank you, though. For everything. My home is like Fort Knox now."

"A single woman living on her own should be careful." Reed placed his mug on the counter. "You do seem fine so I think I will get going. You sure you'll be okay?"

"Positive." She lifted her head so he could see her give him a reassuring smile. "Once I finish this cup I'll be as right as rain. Do you have far to drive?"

"I'm heading to Florida." Reed tipped his head back and drained his coffee. "By myself it will probably take me a couple of days. I don't like driving sleepy. When I stop I'll just try for a place that has some local flavor. Do some sightseeing. I'm in no hurry."

"That's smart," she said, trying to sound more pulled together than she actually was. "Driving tired—that is when accidents happen."

He placed his cup in the sink. "I know. I'm a cop, remember?" he teased. "I'll call Logan and Ava this morning and let them know that everything is fine. Be sure to call the police and file a report. Today."

"Yes, Sir." Kaylee wasn't planning on arguing with him. That would only delay his departure. "I'll do it this morning."

"Good. If things escalate, I want you to promise that you'll give me a call." He was holding out a card he'd pulled from his pocket. "You can call me on my cell day or night."

She took it from him but frowned. "If you're in Florida what would you be able to do?"

"Advise you at the very least. Are you going to promise me?"

He was being so stubborn she really didn't have much choice. She nodded in agreement and set the card on the countertop. It wasn't like she was ever going to need it in reality.

"I guess I'll say goodbye then. It was very nice meeting you, Kaylee."

He walked toward the front door and she followed right behind. It was sweet of him to lie like that. She was sure it hadn't been nice meeting her and then having to babysit to make sure she didn't die in a pool of her own vomit.

"It was nice meeting you too. Have a safe trip and enjoy your vacation. Thank you for everything."

Dear God, he was so slow in leaving. Couldn't he let her wallow in mortification privately?

He finally strode down the driveway to where his huge truck was parked. Waving, he slid into the driver's seat, started the engine, and pulled out of her cul-de-sac. She watched him leave until he was out of sight and then closed and locked the door behind her. Resting against it, she groaned and scraped her fingers through her partially dry hair.

"That was the most embarrassing thing to happen to me in years. Thank God he's gone."

"So everything is fine with Kaylee." Reed lifted the soda can from the cup holder and took a long drink. He was cruising down I-57 toward Kentucky and talking to Logan. "I turned her house into a fortress—well, a fortress for what can be done in an afternoon and made her promise to report the emails to the police. They were nasty but nothing personal. I gave her my cell number as well if the situation should get worse."

"Ava's talking to Kaylee right now as a matter of fact. I'm sure she's saying the exact same thing. I can't tell you how much I appreciate this. Hopefully Ava can relax a little bit now. Her blood pressure has been too high and all she's been talking about is Kaylee. I've been trying to distract her with deciding on nursery decorations and names."

Somehow Reed doubted that Ava was going to forget about the whole situation, and even if she did she might well just find something else to obsess about. His own sisters loved to talk about birth scare stories when they'd been pregnant.

"She can set her mind to rest about this," Reed assured him. "From what Kaylee said she gets email like this fairly often. She ignores them and they go away."

"Smart," Logan chuckled. "Kaylee's a bright girl and if she isn't worried then I'm sure everything is okay." Logan's voice dropped to a whisper. "Ava's just plain bored. She's gotten to the point she's been asking me to bring home case files so she can review them with me. No way am I letting my pregnant wife start looking at crime scenes. Hell, no."

"Isn't she working on a book?"

From what Reed had heard Ava was always working on a book.

"That's just it," Logan sighed. "Apparently Mark and Melissa aren't talking to her right now. She's difficult to live with when the muse isn't flowing."

There was a screeching sound in the background and Logan cursed in frustration. "What, honey? Can you hold on a minute, Reed? Ava's yelling something from the bedroom."

Logan must have put his hand over the microphone on his cell as Reed could only hear muffled voices.

"Reed? Are you still there?"

Logan sounded as if he were at the end of his rope. Reed wasn't too damn sure the man was going to make it until the birth of those twins.

"I'm here, buddy. What's going on?"

"Apparently Kaylee just told Ava that she received a letter again today. A real snail mail letter that said the usual crappy things but there was also a drawing of a red heart with a knife through it. Ava's about to blow a blood vessel."

"If she hasn't already called the police she should call them now. It looks like they know where she lives. This was the escalation I was worried about. He's starting to make it personal."

There was a small silence and then Logan sighed heavily into the phone.

"Listen, I hate to ask this but can you turn around and go back? Ava's terrified something is going to happen to Kaylee and she said that Kaylee is pretty frightened as well."

Son of a bitch.

"I'm already over an hour out of Champaign, Logan. Greg is expecting me at his place in Vero," Reed said desperately. He did not want to get involved in this. The police were perfectly capable of dealing with the situation. She didn't need a babysitter. Hell, she'd practically kicked him out of her front door this morning she was in such a hurry to see the backside of him, and Reed wasn't about to tell Logan about that kiss.

"I know you're supposed to be on vacation. But shit, I need you to go back, buddy. If anything happens to Ava I don't know what I'll do. She's worried about Kaylee, and honestly I can't say that I blame her. If this was happening to Ava I'd be going out of my fucking mind. It's not Kaylee's fault she doesn't have someone to look after her."

Aww fuck. The guilt card. Reed steeled himself to ignore it.

"I doubt Champaign's finest will be happy about me sticking my nose into their investigation. And to be honest, I'm not sure Kaylee would be happy about me hanging around either."

"You two didn't get on?" Logan asked. "Kaylee gets along with everyone. So do you, for that matter."

"We got along fine but she's pretty independent."

"Exactly. That's what Ava's afraid of. That Kaylee won't accept any help and something will happen to her. If I could do it myself I would, Reed. But I can't leave Ava."

Shit. Just...shit.

"Logan, I–" Reed broke off, not sure what to even say. He didn't want to get involved. If he went back it wasn't going to be just another case. He was going to have to *care* about what happened to her. On a personal basis. One on one.

"I know this isn't the vacation you pictured."

That was the truth.

"But I'm begging you, buddy, to go back and help Kaylee. Find this guy and get him out of her life. You're the only one I can ask—hell, the only one I'd trust with her life."

A sign for an exit a half-mile up the road flashed past. Reed knew he was beaten.

"I don't like the fact that this person knows where she lives either," Reed conceded. "I'll go. But it will take me a little while to circle back. She needs to call the police in the meantime. I'll get there as soon as I can."

"I knew you would. Thanks. Ava will sleep easier knowing you've moved in and are guarding Kaylee until this nut is found. So will I, honestly."

Logan sounded exultant and it took Reed a moment for the words to penetrate his brain.

"Move in? What do you mean 'move in'? I can't move in with Kaylee."

"How else can you make sure she's safe?" Logan scoffed. "Don't worry, Kaylee is an awesome cook. You'll probably gain five pounds by the time you catch the guy. Call me later after you see the letter. I can't wait to tell Ava that you're staying. Thanks again."

Just like that Logan was gone and Reed was left holding his cell phone. Swearing under his breath, he maneuvered the truck onto the off-ramp of the exit so he could turn around and head north. He needed to call Greg and tell him that he didn't know when the hell he'd get to Florida. Then he'd start trying to trace those emails, and at the same time try and keep things with Kaylee on a purely casual, friendly basis. If that was even possible.

But one thing was for sure, if someone was threatening Kaylee, Reed would find them and put a stop to it once and for all.

Chapter Five

Everything was going to hell in a hand basket.

The police had shown up and they were currently questioning Kaylee about the emails she'd received. While one was very friendly, his partner looked slightly judgmental. Apparently he equated erotic romance to straight-on porn. She wasn't in the mood to enlighten him. After receiving that letter she wasn't in a good mood at all.

"You don't know anyone who could have sent these letters?" the judgmental one asked again for about the sixth time.

"No," Kaylee answered firmly. "No one has ever said anything like that to me face to face."

She wasn't dumb enough to think that everyone loved her writing but she hoped no one wanted to hurt her over it. It was just a damn story, for heaven's sake. This wasn't world peace.

Her attention was pulled from the two officers when the front door swung open without so much as a knock or a ring of the doorbell. Reed Mitchell stood in her foyer. Heat flooded her cheeks as her behavior from the night before came rushing back. Why was he here? She'd watched him drive away almost three hours ago. Seeing him again was so humiliating.

"Reed? What are you doing here?"

"The door was half-open so I just came in," he said, not bothering to answer her question. He strode into the living room looking completely confident and totally the opposite of how she currently felt. The letter this morning had turned her well-ordered life on its ear.

"Of course you did. Did you forget something?" she asked again, although she had a sneaking suspicion as to why he was here.

Ava.

If only Kaylee hadn't been on the phone with her friend this morning when the mail had arrived. She'd been sifting through it as she chatted with Ava and hadn't been able to cover up her very real alarm at what she had received. Reed had warned her about escalation and this appeared to be a giant step up in intensity.

This person knew where she lived and that was frightening.

"No. I got a call from Logan. Where's the letter?"

One theory confirmed. Kaylee pointed to the table where it sat in a plastic bag the officers had brought. She'd known they would take it with them so she'd snapped a few photos of it with her cell before they'd arrived.

"It's right here. You didn't need to turn around and come back."

Reed looked at her for a minute and then turned to the two policemen and began firing off questions one after the other. By the time he was finished both cops looked like they'd rather be any place but right there talking to him. It was clear Sheriff Reed Mitchell knew proper procedure and he was making sure these men knew he'd be watching over their investigation.

Kaylee walked the men to their car and promised to let them know if she received any more communications. Reed stood next to her, tall and imposing as the officers drove away down the tree lined street. When they were out of sight she turned on him and scowled.

"You were rude. They were trying to help."

"Questioning their standard operating procedure is not being rude, it's being informed. If someone knowledgeable questioned me I wouldn't be insulted—hell, I'd be glad that someone had a clue as to what was going on." He walked over to his truck and pulled a bag from the back seat. "I'm starving. Do you want to go out for lunch or eat in?"

He brushed past her into the house and she followed on his heels with a growing sense of foreboding. Just what was that suitcase for? What in the hell had Logan and Ava said to him?

He was standing in the middle of her living room when she joined him inside. "I rarely even eat lunch but I guess we can go out. I need to stop at the grocery store anyway. Will you be here for dinner?"

His grin was too sexy and way too knowing. "Honey, I'm here for the duration. Until this harasser is caught I'm your house guest." He looked around the large room. "Will I be bunking on the couch again or do you have a guest room?"

All the air seemed to be sucked from Kaylee's lungs. "You can't stay here," she sputtered, her mind immediately rejecting the idea but her pulse picked up at the mere thought of a man this sexy sleeping just feet from her own bed. "Aren't you supposed to be heading for Florida?"

"I was, but now I'm here courtesy of Logan and Ava Wright. You are welcome."

"So you don't really want to be here," she replied tartly. "I can take care of myself, Reed. I don't need a babysitter. A rude one at that."

She'd gone too far. She could see that now. Reed's grin had disappeared and his soft hazel eyes had grown cold. He dropped his bag and stalked over to her until he was peering down from his six-foot plus height.

"You don't have any fucking idea what you need, Kaylee. Logan asked me to be here because Ava is worried about you. She thinks you won't be careful, that you'll do something stupid and get yourself hurt. At the moment I'd have to agree with her. You're being foolhardy because you're embarrassed about last night. Well, tough. I'm doing a friend a favor and staying here to *babysit* you. The least you could damn well do is be polite about it."

Kaylee swallowed hard and took a deep breath. The man was right. She was being a bitch and all because of her stupid antics last night. He was giving up his time off and she was acting like he was the criminal, not the letter-sender.

And she was scared.

"I'm sorry," she said softly. "I am embarrassed. You probably think I'm a slut or a drunk. Maybe both."

His expression softened and a ghost of a smile crossed his features. "I don't think either one of those things. I think we went out to dinner and you had a drink that made you tipsy, featherweight that you are. That lowered your inhibitions and let you drink more. That's it, honey. When was the last time you went out anyway?"

"A while ago," she admitted. "I work most of the time. In the evening I read or watch television. I guess I'm kind of an introvert."

"Me too," he agreed readily. "So let's put last night to rest shall we? You had a little too much to drink and we kissed. Period. End of story. Now back to my original question. Is there a guest room?"

Kaylee nodded and pointed to the stairs. "Second door on the right. The bathroom next door will be yours. I have my own."

"Sounds good, although I can sleep anywhere." Reed bounded up the stairs two at a time while Kaylee stood frozen to her spot on the floor. She was going to be sharing a home for the foreseeable future with the hottest man she'd ever met.

Eat? She was too damn nervous to eat. She might never eat or sleep again.

What in the hell had she done? No, what had Ava done?

Grabbing her purse from the foyer table, she found her cell and punched a few buttons. She knew Ava would have her own phone right next to her.

"Hey, girl. I didn't expect to hear from you again today. Did Reed make it back?"

Kaylee took a slow, calming breath. This wasn't anything to yell about but she'd been manipulated into a corner.

"He did and that's what I want to discuss with you. Why did you and Logan send him back? I'm perfectly capable of dealing with this on my own."

"You need someone to help you with this," Ava replied. "Reed knows how to catch criminals so he's the perfect person."

Kaylee's stomach churned at the thought of having Reed in her home day after day. He was too disturbing. Too handsome. Too…everything.

"I love you like a sister Ava, but it was presumptuous. You should have talked to me first. It's my life. Mine."

She heard Ava's swift intake of breath and instantly felt crappy for her harsh words. Ava was trying to help but she didn't know everything that had happened between Kaylee and Reed.

"You're right. It was presumptuous. And pushy. And bossy. And I don't regret a bit of it. I know you. I know how you are. You just want everything to be okay so you can have your quiet time to write. Well, this isn't going to just go away. It has to be dealt with, and dammit, I don't know anyone better to deal with it than Reed, except for Logan and he can't be there. So you're going to accept help, do you hear me? Your rigid independence is simply going to have to take a back seat. So get over it."

Unable to stay upset with her best friend, laughter bubbled from Kaylee's lips. "Get over it, huh? That's classy. Let's say that I can let someone help me, although I'm not admitting that I need help. What about Reed? He has places to go, people to see. How long is he supposed to hang out here and look for this person?"

"The man hasn't taken a vacation in over five years so he's got months of time saved up. The new mayor in his town made him take some of it. But if you feel guilty you can always show him around the area. Make sure he enjoys himself."

Kaylee was fighting a losing battle. Reed was here and currently unpacking in her spare room. Ava wasn't going to give in, and honestly that nasty letter had shaken Kaylee's sense of well-being. If Reed could help find the person who wrote it, wouldn't that be a good thing?

"I'm reserving judgment about whether this is a good idea, just so you know."

"I wouldn't expect anything else from you," Ava laughed. "So…what do you think of Reed? Hotter than sin, isn't he?"

Kaylee plopped down on the couch with a sigh. "I don't want to talk about this."

"That is so funny. I think I said the exact same thing when I first started spending time with Logan. But I do remember your advice. I distinctly remember you telling me to go for it."

"I don't think I said that," Kaylee said indignantly. "I probably just said something like have fun."

"You wanted me to take his picture with my cell and send it to you." Kaylee could hear the gales of laughter coming from Ava through the phone. "Reed is just as sexy but in a different way. He's so cool and emotionally contained."

"He makes me want to stomp on his foot to get a reaction." The words popped out of Kaylee's mouth before she could stop them.

"So he's getting to you? Have fun, but just remember it's only casual with him. Use him but don't fall in love. You're welcome."

"You think I should be thanking you for interfering in my life?" Kaylee huffed. "Are you actually encouraging me to sleep with Reed Mitchell?"

"Tell me you haven't already thought about it," Ava scoffed. "He's absolutely gorgeous and oozes sex. Something that you think about all day, every day. Maybe you'll get some new material for one of your books."

Kaylee wasn't going to mention the kiss from last night. It was definitely going into a story.

"Reed might be sex on a stick but that doesn't mean he's interested in me. I sure as hell am not going to throw myself at him."

Again. The first time had been too humiliating. What she could remember of it.

"Suit yourself." There was rustling in the background of the call. "Listen, I need to go. Presley is here and she's made me lunch. Call me later, okay?"

Kaylee hung up and stood to slip her phone back into her purse and almost choked on her spit. Reed was standing directly behind her, leaning on the banister. He looked calm, cool, and a trifle smug.

Asshole.

"How long have you been standing there?" Kaylee could feel heat suffusing her cheeks.

"A few minutes." He straightened and shrugged.

"It was a private call."

"Funny how I heard my name mentioned a few times, plus the phone was on speaker."

A dimple in his cheek appeared. It was official. He was laughing at her.

"I'll ask again. How long were you standing there?"

"Enough to hear that I better watch my feet. Are you ready to go to lunch?"

She was mortified. Again. He probably thought she wanted to go to bed with him—which she did—but she wasn't planning to do anything about it. If anything, she'd been planning to keep her distance.

"I need to change."

Brushing past him to climb the stairs, she halted when he put a hand on her shoulder. "Relax, Kaylee. You're wound tighter than an eight-day clock as my dad used to say."

"You're always relaxed, I suppose," she asked, not turning her head to look at him. "Must be nice to be you."

"You'll live longer," he offered. "Take life as it comes, honey. No one here is judging you."

Except for herself, and she was her toughest critic. Ruthless, in fact. A double-edged sword, it's what made her a success as a writer and a failure with people.

"Thanks for the advice. Give me ten minutes."

She hurried up the stairs and into her bedroom, closing the door behind her. Space. She needed a little bit of space and breathing room. When she was with Reed it was as if he was larger than life, filling any empty space around him. She needed to be alone simply to catch her breath.

Reed Mitchell made her breathless indeed.

Chapter Six

Kaylee was fixing dinner at the huge island in the middle of her kitchen when Reed came down the stairs. Dressed in blue jeans, a white blouse, and her long auburn hair tamed into a braid she looked much younger than he knew her age to be. After he'd unpacked and they'd had lunch, he'd spent the better part of the afternoon researching his hostess, wanting to know more about her. Knowing about her life might help him catch whoever was harassing her. But she hadn't made it easy.

Kaylee Blue wasn't her real name.

He shouldn't have been surprised. Writers often used pen names but for some reason he hadn't thought she had. She was so upfront and honest it had taken him by surprise.

"What's for dinner, Miss Carter? It is Caroline Carter, isn't it?"

She looked up from where she was shaping some dough and wrinkled her nose. "I wondered what you were doing up there while I was writing. We've been busy, haven't we? I would have told you anything you wanted to know if you'd just asked me."

That was probably true. Other than being embarrassed about the heat and awareness that simmered between them she was pretty much an open book.

"Why did you change it? Caroline Carter is a nice name. It has alliteration. Kind of trips off the tongue."

Kaylee smiled and slid the round piece of dough onto a pizza pan with a bunch of holes in it. "Because I wanted my privacy, although that is apparently shot all to hell if someone was able to send a letter to my home. I've been Kaylee for awhile now so I rarely even hear the name Caroline. Now the bank, the IRS, and the power company, they don't know who Kaylee is but they like her money."

"What do you want me to call you?"

"Writing Goddess? O Powerful One?" she teased as she smeared tomato sauce from a pan on the stove onto the dough. "Kaylee is fine. I answer to it and it makes things easier unless you're planning to bill me for your services. Then send that to Caroline. She handles the bills."

"You talk like she's a separate person." Reed straddled one of the stools at the island to watch her cook. Logan had said Kaylee knew her way around the kitchen.

"She is in a way. Just my old friends call me Caroline and I don't see them very often. They're all busy with families and jobs. Everyone else calls me Kaylee. What do you like on your pizza?"

She had bowls of toppings set out with pretty much anything a person could want on their pizza. Reed pointed to the sausage and mushrooms and his stomach growled in appreciation. He'd heard the bread machine going earlier this afternoon. She'd made the dough and sauce from scratch. This was going to taste delicious.

"And your family," said Reed as she sprinkled the sausage on the pie.

"My family?" Kaylee paused and frowned. "What do you mean?"

"Your family must call you Caroline, right?"

Her expression grew sad and she resumed topping the pizza. "I don't have any family. Not close. I lived with my mother and grandmother when I was growing up. Mother died several years back and Gram died nine months ago. I moved back here to deal with her property."

He'd known that from his computer work this afternoon but he'd managed to find her father and a few cousins on that side of the family.

"I'm sorry, that must have been tough for you. What about your dad?" His research hadn't told him much about Kaylee's childhood but he'd been able to trace her father's whereabouts after her parents' divorce. "Do you ever visit Atlanta to see him?"

Kaylee froze and her eyes looked suspiciously bright but her chin lifted as if to repudiate her own reaction. "I didn't even know he lived in Atlanta. After he lost his job when I was nine and we were about to get thrown out of our rented home, he left one morning to go to the store and never came back. We moved into my grandmother's house because my mother had no job and no place else to go. She never really recovered from what he did. For all I care he can burn in hell."

Her voice was shaking by the time she finished, turning back to sprinkle shredded cheese all over the pizza. He felt like ten kinds of shit for even bringing her dad up. It was a reminder that any information he found needed to be placed in context. If anyone researched his past they might get the wrong idea as well.

"I'm really sorry, honey," he said softly, capturing one of her hands in his. "I fucked up and never should have said anything."

Kaylee brushed at her damp cheek and smiled. She really was a very attractive woman, even when she cried. "You apologize really well. I'm sorry that it can still get to me. Every time I think I'm past this it finds me again."

"I'm sorry that happened to you."

"I'm not." Kaylee shook her head and picked up the pizza pan, sliding it in the oven. "Some lessons are hard to learn in life, but the sooner you learn them the better. It took my dad and David, but I did learn."

Reed frowned as she cleaned up the counter top. "What did you learn?"

Kaylee wiped up spots of sauce from the marble. "Men don't hang around when the chips are down. When things get difficult, men get gone. I've seen it twice up close and personal. They get you to depend on them and then when everything isn't rosy? They leave you to deal with things. Better to know up front that you're on your own."

From her unemotional tone it was clear she believed this with all her heart. It explained her almost militant independence.

"Kaylee some men do stay and stick it out. Look at Ava and Logan or my parents. Men don't always cut and run."

Although he'd seen plenty in his years of law enforcement. But a sweet young woman such as Kaylee didn't need to be as jaded and cynical as he was.

She shrugged and wiped her hands on a dish towel. "There are always exceptions. But what are the chances? Let's say I go all in with some guy, like I did with David. We set up house and I really think we're a team. We pool our money, we dream about the future. The whole nine yards. And then something bad or unexpected happens. Something that wasn't in the plan. Will he be there to see it through with me? Maybe yes, maybe no. Personally I don't like my odds."

Her father had a lot to answer for and so did this David guy. If he was around, Reed would cheerfully kick the man's ass for whatever he'd done. It probably hadn't seemed like a big deal to David but it had done terrible damage to Kaylee's psyche.

But then who was he to talk? He had his own issues, and he wasn't planning to change either. In fact, he'd better change the damn subject before she started asking him personal questions.

"So do you make everything from scratch? That pizza is starting to smell really good. I could eat a horse."

Kaylee giggled and pulled the fixings for a salad from the refrigerator. "We just had lunch six hours ago. I don't usually eat two big meals in a day."

"Logan said you're a great cook."

She turned a pretty pink and began chopping up greens. "Logan's only had a few things I've made but he was an appreciative audience. I swear those two live off pizza and cheese-cake."

"I promise I'll be just as grateful. I don't cook much for myself. This is a real treat."

Her face glowed with happiness and he felt something lurch in his chest. She was a nice woman, pretty and smart. The kind his mother would have told him was "a keeper."

But he didn't keep anyone anymore.

"Do you want any coffee?" Kaylee asked. They'd had dinner, talked about books, movies, and music, and generally got to know each other without getting too personal. She'd learned that Reed was indeed an introvert who enjoyed quiet evenings reading a variety of books. In fact, she'd given him one of hers and he said he was going to start it right away.

"No, thank you." Reed shook his head. "What do you normally do in the evenings? I don't want to get in your way. You know, just pretend I'm not here."

There was no way that was going to happen. Effortlessly and as if he didn't care one way or the other, he took over every room he was in. He'd be the perfect Dominant in her next book.

"If it's nice, I sit out on the back patio and read or write. It's covered and screened in, plus there's a heater for when it's chilly."

"That sounds great. As I said, if you need to work just ignore me."

She with her laptop and he with his book settled on the glider sofa with its overstuffed, bright red cushions. Snapping on the small lamp next to him, Reed stretched out his long legs to read while she turned on the propane heater. It glowed in the dim light and she instantly felt the heat begin to warm the chill that had descended quickly after sundown. It was late in October and winter was just around the corner.

Opening her laptop, she tried to concentrate on her work in progress but the presence of the man next to her made it almost impossible. She could feel his body heat and smell the clean scent of his skin. Her fingers itched to reach out and touch him, running her hands along the dips and planes of his muscles. She'd only had a glimpse of them yesterday but it had been enough to fire up her imagination for the last twenty-four hours.

"You're really good," Reed murmured, still intent on the pages of the paperback. "I mean really good, Kaylee."

She felt a flood of warmth invade her from head to toe. She was hard on herself at the best of times, and hearing praise from someone she liked and respected meant more than he could imagine.

"Thank you. I'm glad you like it. I was kind of afraid to give it to you if you want the truth."

They were speaking softly although there wasn't another living soul around, her neighbors inside to escape the dropping temperature. But wrapped in the gray darkness it seemed right and proper to keep their voices down.

"You have a gift of revealing a human's strengths and weaknesses with love and humor while at the same time keeping the tension between them high."

Tears pricked the back of her eyes. He got it. He really got what she was trying to do in her stories and her chest tightened at the overwhelming feeling of being understood. She had regular friends and writer friends and only a few ever really comprehended what she was trying to convey. Ava was one of them and now this man.

"Thank you," she said again, her voice thick. "You know, I didn't expect you to be a book kind of guy."

Luckily he didn't take offense at her awkwardly worded statement. Instead he tucked a piece of paper into the pages and placed the book on the side table.

"You thought I would be out shooting bears and playing rugby?"

His voice was tinged with amusement and she had to smile. That was exactly what she'd thought.

"Ava said you were an alpha, a man's man so I guess I pictured you differently." She hesitated, not sure how to put it into words. "More aggressive, I guess."

"More violent?" he queried. "A gun-toting cowboy cop with more brawn than brains?"

Scrunching up her face, she nodded. "It sounds really bad when you say it out loud, but yes, I think that's what I thought."

His warm chuckle made her want to move closer but she stayed pinned to her spot on the glider.

"I can be aggressive, Kaylee. When I need to be that way. I like to think things through before I do them. But I do carry a gun, go hunting, and drink beer in bars on occasion. I don't think any of those things make me an alpha male."

"They don't," she agreed. "You're very self-confident, assured, and calm. You're a born leader I would guess that people naturally follow."

"I'm also possessive and territorial. Just ask any of my deputies. It's hard for me to delegate which is one of the reasons I haven't taken any vacation time."

"What are the other reasons?"

He shrugged and stared at the sky visible through the screen. "Mostly I love what I do. It isn't what I planned when I was younger but it's what I was meant to do, even if it was by accident."

She wanted to know more about him but Ava had warned her he was a closed book. "What did you want to be?"

Kaylee didn't really expect him to answer but he didn't ignore her question.

"I planned on being a veterinarian. They're always needed on a ranch."

What the heck, she'd push her luck and ask him more.

"You grew up on a ranch? Was it fun?"

"Yes."

"Yes, you grew up on a ranch or yes it was fun?"

Reed turned so he was facing her. "Kaylee, I don't talk about myself much, especially the past. It's over and nothing can be done to change it, so I leave it back there. It's nothing personal."

She thought about his words for a moment. "Do you want to change it?"

Reed shook his head and leaned back on the cushion. "Nice try but I'm not biting. If you want to talk about the past we can discuss yours. Mine is off-limits."

She didn't have any secrets. Maybe if she opened up about her life he might open up—just a little—about his.

"Ask me anything you want. I've got nothing to hide."

His eyebrow lifted and a smile turned up the corners of his mouth. "Good to know. Why don't you tell me about this David? He seems like a good place to start."

Okay, maybe she had a few secrets. Or at least a couple of topics she didn't like to revisit. But not being honest with him wasn't going to give him the confidence to be honest with her. Time to pull up her big girl panties and face the past.

"I already told you most of it. David was a big mistake in my life. I dated him my senior year in college and when he got a job at a newspaper in Portland I moved with him. Things went downhill from there."

She paused thinking Reed might remark but he stayed silent, waiting for her to continue.

"I guess that once we were living together he decided that he needed to whip me into shape or something. He didn't like that I'm a night person and that I slept late in the morning. He didn't like that I didn't want to socialize every night of the week and preferred to stay at home. He especially didn't like that I was carrying what he considered to be excess weight. He was constantly harping at me about it. He once told me that I didn't 'present well' to his friends."

She congratulated herself at keeping the bitterness out of her voice. It was a long time ago and she'd moved beyond it, understanding that it had to do more with David than it did with her or anything she'd done.

"He sounds like a real asshole."

Kaylee giggled at Reed's caustic tone. "He was. But I was young and in love. I didn't see then that a man needs to love me for myself."

"So you dumped his ass," Reed stated.

If only she could say that.

"Actually, no. Not right away." She wrestled with how much to reveal but it couldn't hurt her anymore if she didn't let it. "It all sort of fell apart when I had trouble finding a job in journalism. I was waiting tables and pretty miserable about things. David was less than supportive. The only time I was happy was when I was writing."

She could feel Reed's body tense. "This guy doesn't sound like he has too many redeeming qualities. I can't imagine how you got mixed up with him."

She'd had time to look back on that. "He wasn't bad at the beginning. It was only when we moved in together that he changed. Believe me, I've been over and over this a million times. He started out a pretty nice guy. Anyway, I published my first book and the sales really tanked. I mean, I released it to crickets. David didn't have much patience for the entire endeavor and basically told me I'd wasted my time. I released my second book a few months later and that's when sales started to happen. But David resented that too. I really couldn't do anything right. I found him in bed with a friend not long after. As I told you before, I later learned they'd been sleeping together for months. That's when I dumped him."

"And you've never trusted a man since."

"I'm not sure I trusted them before. I think I was waiting for David to screw up. I always knew it was coming."

Reed sat up and looked down at her, his expression solemn. "Perhaps—and I'm just going out on a limb here—but maybe you've chosen men that you knew would let you down. Subconsciously you sought out males that would reaffirm your opinion."

He could see way too deeply inside her psyche. That same thought had been niggling at the back of her mind for a while now but she'd never given in to the actual words. Now they were out there and there was no taking them back.

"It's cold out here. We should go inside."

She moved to stand but Reed's hand gently wrapped around her arm, staying her on the couch. "I'm sorry, Kaylee. It's none of my business. Just forget I said anything. This David guy sounds like a jerk."

Reed's mere touch set off fireworks in her stomach and electrified her nerves. "You don't have anything to be sorry for. I told you a story and you were simply remarking on it."

Their gazes locked and she looked into his eyes for a long time. There was no sound but the rustle of the leaves and the thud of her heart. It roared in her ears but she knew he couldn't hear it. She didn't dream that he was as affected by this moment as she was. It had been so long since she'd been close to someone—physically or emotionally. It was crazy but she wanted to be close to Reed. She wanted to feel the electricity between them, the heat that they created simply by being close.

At some point she'd swayed closer to him, their lips close to one another. His pupils had dilated in the dim light and she reached and ran her hand up his chest and around his neck, his body hard and hot under her palm. She couldn't be certain but she thought she heard him swear under his breath before his lips took hers, not rough or harsh but gently and reverently.

The kiss wasn't too soft or too hard. His mouth was firm and warm and she opened eagerly to his questing tongue, letting him explore as waves of pleasure shook her to the core. Her fingers sunk into his dark hair and she kissed him back eagerly, her toes curling at his expertise.

When it was over he pulled away and shook his head, a wry smile on his lips. "That shouldn't have happened, honey."

Probably not but she wouldn't turn back the clock for anything.

"I'm not drunk, Reed. I'm a grown woman and we wanted to kiss. Don't worry, you don't have to marry me or anything."

He rubbed the back of his neck and chuckled. "I doubt I'd be any kind of a husband. It's just we have to live here together and I don't want to unnecessarily complicate things."

A kiss certainly didn't make things easier but it had been more than pleasant. She'd forgotten how much she liked to kiss if she were honest, and this man had some mad skills. There was something about him that drew her even though she knew it wasn't wise.

"I think I'll just say goodnight then." She stood and this time he didn't stop her. Tucking her laptop under her arm, she turned toward the French doors. "Will you lock up behind me and turn off the heater?"

"No problem. I'm going to read for a while longer. Good night, Kaylee."

"Night, Reed."

He picked up the book as she stepped inside and headed for the stairs. It had been quite a day and tomorrow promised to be just as eventful. But one thing was honest to God true.

She wanted to kiss Reed Mitchell again.

Chapter Seven

The next morning Kaylee was busy in the kitchen making something that smelled delicious while Reed was in her office tapping away at her laptop, trying to pinpoint the origin of the two emails. Sitting at the desk he had an excellent view of the quiet street she lived on. It looked like most of the neighbors were at home on a Saturday which Reed made a note of. Kaylee was most vulnerable when there were no people around.

Swearing at the keyboard, he was getting frustrated and cranky when cars began to pull into the drive and park along the street. He frowned as women and men, obviously familiar to one another, ambled up the driveway, laptops tucked under their arms along with large bowls and trays. Was Kaylee having a party in the middle of the day?

Pulling back the drapes to get a better look, Reed scowled at the gathering crowd on the front porch. He hadn't said anything to her yesterday but he wanted a list of people in her life so he could check them out. Most victims were familiar with their stalkers, although not necessarily friends. A casual acquaintance she'd only met once or twice could be sending those letters. That would be why they knew where she lived. The idea that this was someone far away that only knew her from her books seemed far-fetched to him, but then he didn't know any successful authors other than her and Ava.

He heard a few taps on the door to the office and she stuck her head in the room. "I forgot to tell you that my writing group is meeting here today. There's lunch out on the dining room table if you're hungry. It's buffet style. We'll try and keep it down."

Reed stood and held up his hand. "Wait, who are these people? What does your writing group do?"

Kaylee opened the door wider and stepped into the room. "I started a writer's group when I moved back. We meet every month and read what we've written and critique it. Sometimes we talk about an issue in publishing. It helps keep people motivated."

"How did you meet these people?" Reed could hear them moving around in the living room, glasses clinking and chattering voices.

"Friends of friends. Some live in the neighborhood."

He'd be checking each and every person in this group out, but first he wanted to meet them.

"Sounds good. I'll join you."

"What?" Pretty Kaylee looked gobsmacked by his declaration, her forehead wrinkled in worry. She was dressed in faded denim jeans and an oversized cream-colored sweater that hid all of her most beautiful assets. They really needed to have a discussion about her figure. Her lush body didn't need to be covered up but highlighted.

"I'll join the group if you don't mind," he repeated, enjoying how her green eyes fringed with dark lashes were wide with surprise.

"Uh, sure. We eat first so go ahead and fill your plate," she said over her shoulder as she headed back to the living room.

Reed chuckled softly to himself as he followed Kaylee down the hall. She was perplexed obviously and now wasn't the time to enlighten her about his suspicions. If these were her friends she was probably not going to like him doing background checks on them but he needed to do it. Her delicate sensibilities were going to have to suck it up, at least for this.

He filled his plate, trying to keep in the background as Kaylee laughed and talked to her guests. Despite his efforts he was garnering more than his share of attention until finally two women approached him, clearly curious as to who he was.

"Hi." The attractive middle-aged brunette held out her hand. "My name is Cheryl Hill and I write thrillers. This is Linda Thorp and she writes cozy mysteries." Cheryl elbowed the blonde. "You must be new to the group."

Reed shook both their hands and nodded. "I'm Reed, a friend of Kaylee's. I hope you don't mind me sitting in today. I'm very interested in the group."

It seemed wise to keep his answers simple and honest. He was interested in the group but not for the reasons these women assumed.

The brunette smiled coyly and held on to his hand a tad too long. "We love new members," she gushed. "Have you been writing long?"

"Just started, actually. This is all fascinating to me."

It wasn't a lie. Kaylee was fascinating. Everything he learned about her made him want to know more.

"I'd be happy to help you out. I'll give you my phone number and you can call if you have any questions. Day or night."

Reed could swear he saw Linda roll her eyes but it was quickly masked with a bland expression. He also wasn't in the habit of taking what was on offer simply because a woman was looking at him with interest. He was too finicky for that. Besides, despite it being a bad idea, Reed only had eyes for one woman at the moment.

And that woman was currently chatting with a man that stood way too close. His eyes were hot and hungry and his sweet hostess didn't have a clue that she was being devoured visually.

Without thinking about the reasons why or how rude he looked to Cheryl and Linda, Reed marched over to where Kaylee stood and planted himself right next to her. He didn't like the way the man looked at her and he sure as fuck didn't like the way he put his hand on her arm.

"Reed, I see you met Cheryl and Linda. Cheryl lives just a few blocks over." Kaylee didn't look upset that he'd interrupted, her face wreathed in smiles. "This is Brent Sharp. Brent, this is my friend Reed Mitchell."

Brent shook hands with Reed but didn't seem as happy to see him as Cheryl and Linda had. Reed was going to put this guy's name at the top of the list to check out.

"Are you joining our little group? Kaylee's done an amazing job of organizing us."

Reed crowded nearer to Kaylee, invading both her personal space and Brent's. She didn't seem to mind but Brent took a few steps back although he still had to look up as Reed was several inches taller. He wanted to see if the man was aggressive and so far Brent was easily intimidated.

To test him further Reed casually draped his arm over Kaylee's shoulders. The other man stiffened and his eyes narrowed, taking in every detail of the more than friendly scene. Reed grinned as Brent's cheeks turned a ruddy shade of red.

"I'm just a guest today but I am very interested to see what goes on," Reed replied.

"I should say hello to the others," Brent muttered and shuffled away. Reed watched him closely as he huddled with Cheryl and Linda, the three of them clearly talking about Reed, their gazes darting to him and then back.

He hissed as Kaylee's sharp elbow connected with his ribs. "Shit, that hurt. What was that for?"

Her lips were twisted as if she was trying not to laugh. "Why didn't you just pee on me to mark your territory? It would have been simpler. Did you have to intimidate poor Brent?"

Reed leaned down so only she could hear him. "Poor Brent? Poor Brent had his hands on you and I didn't like it. We don't know who your letter writer is, and until we do he needs to keep his distance."

Her eyebrows shot up in astonishment. "Brent is harmless and you don't get to decide who touches me and who doesn't."

Before he could bark back that he would do that very thing, another man in his mid-thirties sidled up and gave Kaylee a hug.

"Walt, we haven't seen you in a few months. I heard you had a nasty cold. I hope you're feeling better. I want you to meet someone. Walt, this is Reed Mitchell. Reed, this is Walter Cummings."

The man seemed affable enough, shaking his hand and smiling. He wasn't nearly as possessive of Kaylee as Brent had been. They chatted about natural remedies for the common cold and then speculated as to how snowy the winter was going to be.

"How long will you be here?" Walt asked, draining his wine glass. Reed wondered how many the man had drunk already. His nose and cheeks were a tell-tale red.

"I'm not sure," Reed admitted. "I'm keeping things open-ended."

"Nice area. Good people," Walt nodded. "Careful or you'll be like me. I came for a visit and ended up staying."

Reed didn't have a chance to ask what had attracted the man to Champaign-Urbana. Kaylee had stepped away and was loudly calling the meeting to order. Chairs were placed in the living room and everyone settled into a seat. Reed commandeered the chair next to Kaylee's and she shot him a mean-eyed look that made him have to muffle his laughter. It was hard to be afraid of a little thing about half his size.

Each person took turns reading a few thousand words and the group would comment briefly on whether they liked it or not, offering constructive criticism when appropriate. Everyone seemed to value what Kaylee said as she seemed to have the most experience publishing her work. Linda and Cheryl read interesting passages from their books but Reed wasn't particularly fond of Brent's. He was trying to write a military thriller but the guy hadn't done his homework.

"It's not a latrine, it's a head," Reed said when Brent finished reading. "If your character is in the Navy, it's a head. Also, no soldier would call a rifle a gun. He'd call it a rifle or weapon."

Brent flushed and shifted in his seat. "No one will know details like that. It's the story that counts."

"I know those things." Reed shrugged, only trying to help Brent out. "I assume you're trying to appeal to that type of audience. If a veteran reads your book, or even someone who just loves the genre, they're going to know all the little details that make it real."

"I don't think anyone will care," Brent argued, sneaking looks at Kaylee. "Were you in the Army? If so, that's why you think it's important."

"I was in the Navy. The Army is only one part of the military." God help Brent if he ever ran into a Marine. "I think it's important because realism makes a story better. It draws me in."

"Were you a Navy SEAL?" Cheryl asked, her eyes going wide and admiring. Reed nodded, hating to even talk about it. Civilians had a lot of fucked up ideas about the military in general and SEALs and Marines in particular. There were more SEALs in fiction than there actually were in real life.

Cheryl clasped her hands together with delight. "A real-live hero right here in our midst. This is so exciting." Linda and everyone else were nodding. All except for Brent, who was scowling and clearly not very damn happy. "Can you tell us some stories, Reed? I think we'd all love to hear them."

Reed doubted that very much. What he'd seen hadn't been pretty or made for television. It had been hard and dirty with vividly real blood, guts, and death. It wasn't romantic or heroic. Reed had been doing his fucking job.

"Sorry," Reed shook his head. "The government doesn't like us talking about our missions."

It was as good a reason as any and wouldn't scare the bejesus out of the civilians.

"Let's continue," Kaylee cut in. "Does anyone else have any comments for Brent?"

The group seemed to have lost its enthusiasm for discussing his work so they moved on. They were wrapping up at the end when Cheryl raised her hand.

"Kaylee, when is your new book coming out? I want to make sure I download it right away."

Kaylee's entire face lit up and she looked so damn beautiful it was like a punch to Reed's solar plexus, robbing him temporarily of oxygen. "On Tuesday. I'm so excited about this one. It's the last in the series so I'm sad to leave the world behind but looking forward to starting something new. It's actually out on pre-order."

The group moved slowly toward the door as if they didn't want to leave, but eventually one by one they got in their cars and left. Linda and Cheryl were the last, hanging around to help clean up the food. Cheryl pressed a slip of paper into the palm of his hand when it was time for her to go.

"Call me if you need help with your work in progress. Or if you need…anything."

There was promise in her words but Reed wasn't interested. She was the type of woman who wanted to possess him for no other reason than his looks. She didn't care if he was a good person or kicked puppies. It was all about the exterior packaging. That was something he'd never been able to understand. Eventually you had to get out of bed and talk to someone.

When the door was finally shut for the last time Kaylee leaned against it and heaved a big sigh.

"That was different."

"Different how?" Reed crossed his arms over his chest and grinned at her discomfiture. "Better or worse?"

"I have no idea," she declared, straightening up and heading for the kitchen where leftover cookies were piled on the island. "I'm not used to people coming into my home and propositioning my houseguest. Are you going to take Cheryl up on it?"

"No, Cheryl's not my type. Too obvious. I prefer to be the aggressor." Reed snatched up one of the snickerdoodles Kaylee had made this morning.

"I'm sure she'd let you if you were so inclined," she said but she wasn't looking him in the eye. "What you do is your own business. What should we have for dinner?"

She was gazing into the refrigerator as if it had the secrets to the universe. They both knew damn well that something was simmering between them but Reed didn't think it was a good idea to muck things up with emotions. Protecting her had to be his number one priority.

"We just had a huge lunch. Come talk to me. I need some information to help with my investigation."

She swung the door closed and sat on a stool while he took the one opposite. "Did you find out where the emails are coming from?"

"Not yet but I'm working on it. Whoever is doing this knows enough to cover their tracks. Right now I've traced the first email to a server in the Ukraine."

"I don't think I've sold any books there."

"That's not where the emails are coming from. That's just a stop along the way. I'll have the real origin by dinnertime. Now, let's talk about the people you come into contact with. The ones in the writing group, for example. In fact, let's make a list of everyone you see or talk to regularly."

Kaylee's mouth fell open in shock. "Are you kidding? Everyone? They're all suspects? My friends would never send me nasty letters and threaten me, Reed."

"Good, then it won't take long to clear them," he replied. He wasn't backing down an inch about this. "And yes, I am serious. I know you think this is a stranger but the statistics don't bear that out. Sixty-six percent of female stalking victims know their stalker. That means we need to look at everyone who might have access to you."

At first she looked like she wanted to argue but then the fight went out of her and she nodded. "Fine. If I don't cooperate you'll just call Logan who will tell Ava and then she'll call me, so let's get this over with." Kaylee stood and grabbed a spiral notebook and pen from next to the phone. Reed had noticed she had them all over the house, probably keeping them close in case she had ideas for a story. "Where do you want to start?"

"Let's start with Brent and your other writer friends since they're fresh in our minds," Reed said. "And I wouldn't have called Logan and Ava. You're a smart woman and you know deep down this needs to be done. Otherwise I'll be living in your guest room forever."

He tried to joke to lighten the tense atmosphere and a smile tugged at the corners of her mouth. "You're actually nice to have around. I really do feel safe now that you're here."

That's exactly how he intended to keep Kaylee. Safe and sound. Even from himself.

Chapter Eight

"Any help you can give me would be appreciated," Reed said to Jared Monroe, one of his best friends and also a fellow small town sheriff in Montana. Reed was back in Kaylee's office pounding away at her laptop. He was close to finding the origin of those two emails.

"I'll do what I can," Jared agreed. "Hell of a thing, having to deal with this on your vacation. Although you're probably just as happy. You don't relax well."

Reed laughed at his friend's understatement. It was well known that Reed was a workaholic.

"My buddy in Florida isn't too happy but this is alright. Kaylee's a good cook and we get along fine."

In fact, he enjoyed her company more than any woman he could remember. He'd never really been friends with a woman before, at least as an adult.

"I didn't really ask about her but I see where your mind is going. Is she cute?"

"Doesn't matter if she is or isn't. If I step out of line Logan will kick my ass."

Jared chuckled, clearly happy with the image Reed painted. "I think it would be a draw. Both of you are ornery as rattlesnakes and fight just as dirty. I wouldn't know which of you to put my money on, personally."

"I'll email the list over to you." Reed changed the subject, not wanting to continue discussing Kaylee or her attractiveness. He hadn't liked how jealous he'd felt earlier when she'd been talking to Brent. It was an alien emotion and it had taken him a few hours to even figure out what it was. He'd never felt it before and he didn't like it one bit. "Anything else going on there?"

"Nice and quiet. Just how Griffin likes it. Some network offered him and Jazz a load of money to televise their wedding but they put the kibosh on that."

As long as matrimony wasn't contagious, Reed was happy for Griffin. He and Jazz seemed like a good match. Griffin certainly seemed happier than ever.

"Griffin should have said yes and let them pay for the wedding," Reed joked, knowing that it wouldn't happen in a million years. Griffin hated attention of any kind.

"I need to get back to work. I'll keep in touch and call you right away if I find anything."

"I'll do the same. Take care."

Jared hung up and Reed tossed the cell down on the desk, a grin spreading across his face.

"I've got you, you little bastard. You thought you could hide from me but you're not as smart as you think you are."

A few more keystrokes and a location lit up clearly on the screen. The map was local and so was the address.

"Yes," Reed hissed. "You're under my thumb, you judgmental piece of shit."

Entering the address into the search engine, the name of the location popped up first in the results.

Son of a bitch.

The public library. A place where everyone was welcome to use the computers. His only hope was a camera or someone remembering their suspect at that particular moment. And Reed wasn't that lucky.

No, he'd have to do this the old-fashioned way. But one thing was now clear. His gut had been right. This stalker was someone who knew Kaylee.

Maybe it was the man who delivered her paper or the person who bagged her groceries. Or perhaps the guy who changed the oil in her car. Whoever it was, Reed guessed it was someone who appeared harmless. They might even blend into their surroundings. They were good at getting people to trust them.

Kaylee fidgeted in the kitchen chair and pushed the French toast around her plate. Last night Reed had given her laptop back after disclosing that the emails she'd received had been sent from the library. His theory that the person threatening her was someone she knew appeared to be plausible. She couldn't imagine who would want to do this and that bugged the hell out of her. Was she so trusting and gullible that she believed everyone to be good and nice?

"It may not be any of your friends."

Reed had finished his breakfast and was rinsing the plate in the sink. They'd only been living together for two days but she'd already found out he was very tidy and low maintenance.

"You think it is." She pushed the plate away in defeat, her appetite nonexistent. Reed sat back down and lifted her fork, cutting a small piece of toast before spearing it.

"No, I said that I thought it was someone you have contact with. You can be around people and not be friends with them. It may be someone you see every now and then but somehow in their mind they've twisted it into some sort of relationship." He lifted the fork to her lips. "You need to eat or you'll make yourself sick. You picked at dinner last night too."

"I don't think I need to worry about starving for a while." Kaylee patted her generous hips but Reed didn't laugh. Instead he scowled, his soft hazel eyes turning an icy green.

"There's nothing wrong with how you look, woman. Now eat your breakfast," he growled. His expression said he was completely serious and she opened her mouth and took the toast from the fork.

"Better." He held up the utensil so it was dangling from his fingers. "Now I want you to eat at least half of it. Damn if it isn't the best French toast I've ever had."

She chewed and swallowed, barely tasting the food before taking the fork from his hand. "You're bossy," she stated.

"I am. You'll learn to deal with me, I would imagine. My advice is to just do what I tell you to. It'll make your life easier."

Laughter bubbled up at his pronouncement. "I'm sure it would make your life easier but I'm not so sure about mine. You're lucky I like you, Reed Mitchell. I could make your life difficult if I chose to."

"I'm sure you could." He pushed his chair back and stood with a stretch. "I'm going to take a shower and then head for the library. I'm hoping they have surveillance cameras. We know the exact date and time the emails were sent."

"Won't the police be doing the very same thing?" she asked. She couldn't help but admire how good he looked in the morning even before his shower. His hair was slightly tousled and his chin had a dark shadow of whiskers that she yearned to rub against her palm.

"The police have dozens of cases and I only have this one so we won't be waiting for them. If they're anything like my town they're underfunded and understaffed. They work hard and they do the very best they can but we can give them a hand here."

"Then I'm going with you." Reed opened his mouth to object but she waved away whatever he was going to say. "You won't win this one so save your breath. I know the librarians and that might make things easier."

"Fine." He pointed to her plate. "Eat your breakfast and then you can go."

"I'll eat my breakfast but not because you told me to." She sounded like a stubborn toddler, but he was so incredibly high-handed this morning.

Reed laughed as he mounted the stairs. "Whatever works, Kaylee. Be ready to leave in fifteen minutes."

Arrogant, know-it-all, bossy, handsome, sweet, and incredibly sexy. Reed had her twisted around and tied up into knots.

And it had never been so much fun.

"Cameras?" the librarian asked, looking alarmed at Reed's question. "Yes, we do have cameras placed throughout the library. Why are you asking?"

Reed reined in his impatience knowing the woman's reticence was normal. This wasn't his own town where he was the law. He was a guest here and he needed to act accordingly. He was used to walking into a business and automatically having credibility. But before he could launch into an explanation Kaylee did it for him.

Sort of.

She left out a few things like the picture of the heart with a knife through it but the librarian seemed to get the idea.

"So basically I'd like to see the tape from those two dates and times. I might recognize someone. Can you do that for me, Teri?"

The woman chewed on her lip. Her gaze darting back and forth between Kaylee and Reed. This didn't look promising.

"I don't want to get in trouble. Wouldn't I be violating someone's right to privacy or something?"

Reed leaned forward, his hands on the counter. "There is no expectation of privacy in a public venue like the library."

Courts had various opinions about things like that, and if they were in Montana Reed would have had a search warrant just in case.

"I'm going to have to ask my boss. Wait here for a minute."

Teri disappeared behind a door and he took the opportunity to take a good look around the library. Large, open, and airy, the three-story structure seemed to have everything a bibliophile would want, even a coffee cafe on the first floor.

An older woman came out with Teri and joined them at the counter. "Hello, Kaylee. Teri tells me you have a problem."

Kaylee greeted the woman warmly and gave her a brief overview but Reed could tell that this had been a useless errand. The woman's expression told the story without her saying a word. She couldn't or wouldn't help them.

"So that's why we're here, Betty. We just want a look at the surveillance tapes."

"I wish I could help you but we only keep the digital recordings for five days, then the files are overwritten. Those days are gone."

He could feel Kaylee's disappointment as she exhaled slowly. "Well, thank you, Betty. I appreciate the help."

Reed murmured his thanks and stepped away from the counter, already thinking about the next step in the investigation.

Kaylee was still talking with Betty and Teri about books and their latest good reads. When she joined him she nodded toward the door.

"This was a bust. Are you ready to go?"

"In a minute. First I'd like to see the computer room where our friendly letter sender would have done this. Do you know where it is?"

"Of course. The adult computer room is on the second floor." Kaylee's head was tilted in question but Reed wasn't sure exactly what he thought he would find in that room. He simply needed to see it.

"Lead the way."

He followed her up the stairs and into the computer room that was—despite the hour of the day—filled with people. Ignoring the looks he was receiving, he walked the perimeter of the space, peering up at the cameras and getting an overall feel of the location.

"Let's go," he said when he was done. The trip hadn't been all that enlightening but it had underlined some of his initial thoughts about the case. They exited the library and climbed into Reed's truck.

"So?" she asked as he started up the engine. "Did anything jump out at you?"

"A few things. The first is that the place is crawling with cameras—interior and exterior. Look." He pointed to the cameras on the corners of the building. "Those cameras are going to get everyone that goes in or out. Also, the computer room was shaped in such a way there was no place to sit that was out of a camera angle."

"And?" she prompted. "I'm sure Ava would know what that means since she writes crime but I write romance. Emotions I know. How to commit a crime and not get caught? I'm clueless."

"Most people are. You don't find too many geniuses robbing banks and knocking over convenience stores. There are easier, less dangerous ways to make a living than being a crook." He turned on the leather seat so he was facing her. "What I saw was a place that the perpetrator couldn't hide. It could mean a couple of different things. One—that the person can blend in and not stand out. Chances are he wouldn't have wanted to ask for help so he may have used these computers in the past or at the very least frequented the library to see the routine. Or the guy doesn't give a shit about being caught. The camera is as clear as day in that room. Hell, maybe he got a thrill sending you those emails while Big Brother was watching."

"Eww." Kaylee wrinkled her nose and slumped down into her seat. "That's a disgusting thought. Which are you leaning?"

Reed always trusted his gut and often couldn't explain why he felt a certain way. He simply knew it was the right thing to do. "I think it's the former. If the person wanted to be caught I think they would have left more clues in the letters. No, this person doesn't want to be identified but they did feel very comfortable in that library."

"You're going to check out everyone in my writing group, aren't you?" she sighed.

"I am and the librarians too," he confirmed. "It's for your own protection. I wouldn't be doing my job if I just let this go."

"I know you're going to do it but I don't have to like it," she retorted. "I wish this whole thing were over."

Reed did as well. If he could find her stalker, then he could get back to his vacation although the desire to visit Florida had waned. Maybe he'd flip a coin and pick a direction to point the truck and see where he ended up. He'd certainly miss Kaylee's excellent cooking and her low-key company. She was pleasant to be around and incredibly smart. She challenged and fascinated him in a way he hadn't been in a long time. Maybe ever.

"I'll do everything in my power to end this as soon as possible," he vowed, putting the truck in reverse. "Do we need to stop anywhere on the way home?"

Kaylee gave him a sideways glance. "I promised Ava I would show you a good time since you are technically on vacation. I have an idea. I need to pick up a couple of pumpkins for Halloween. Will you help me pick them out? You can be the muscle and carry them too."

"At least I'm good for something," he laughed. "Point me in the right direction."

He should insist that they head back to the house so he could work on the background checks but the delighted look on Kaylee's face was too much to resist. He could make up the time later tonight and work while she slept. An hour or two of pumpkin hunting was just what she needed to get her mind off of all the crap she had to deal with.

Chapter Nine

"How about this one?" Reed was wearing a huge grin on his face as he pointed to the sadly misshapen pumpkin. "It's like the Charlie Brown tree. It needs a good home."

Kaylee had brought Reed to Curtis Orchard to pick out her pumpkins. It had a huge pumpkin patch for the season along with some amazing Honeycrisp apples. She'd pick up a dozen of those along with two or three pumpkins for carving.

A sunny but cool, crisp autumn day, it was perfect for doing almost anything outside. These were the hardest days to stay in and write knowing that soon the weather would be so bad she wouldn't want to be outdoors for several months.

What she hadn't expected was Reed's playfulness as they'd pulled the red Radio Flyer wagon through the vast field looking for the perfect gourd. For a man who was a workaholic, he was having a great deal of fun doing nothing with her.

"There isn't a decent side to carve." Kaylee shook her head and pointed to another a few feet away. "That one looks better."

Reed frowned and stepped two pumpkins over. "This one? It looks fine."

"No, not that one. That one. The tall, thin one."

Laughing, Reed threw up his hands. "If you tell me 'it's the orange one', I'm getting in my truck and driving away."

Kaylee slapped her hand over her mouth and burst into a fit of giggles. It was true there was nothing but a sea of orange surrounding them as far as the eye could see. She climbed over the wagon and indicated the correct pumpkin but once she got there she wasn't as enamored. Sighing, she wiped off her dusty hands on her jeans.

"Maybe you should wait in the cafe. This might take me awhile."

"You got me into this, now we're going to pick two of the best pumpkins in this patch. The kind The Great Pumpkin would love."

"That's two *Peanuts* references. You must like them." Kaylee leaned down and inspected a fat, round gourd and patted the bright orange skin. "This one. It's almost perfect."

Reed bent over and it into the wagon. "I guess I do. I always felt sorry for Charlie Brown when Lucy would pull the football away from him. That seemed kind of mean."

"She could be nice though. Remember how she got up in the middle of the night and brought Linus in from the cold pumpkin patch? That's a pretty good sister."

He nodded and pointed out another perfect-pumpkin contender. "I always liked Linus. He was smart about jumping into leaves and things like that."

Did Reed have to be this perfect?

"I have the Halloween special on DVD. Do you want to watch it tonight? I haven't seen it yet this year."

Reed stroked his chin as if he was considering her offer but he was also smiling. "I wouldn't mind. Have you seen *Young Frankenstein*? I like to watch that movie this time of year too."

Her eyes went wide and she squealed with happiness. "I love it. I have it as well. We could have a movie marathon. Do you like *Ghostbusters?* We can grill some steaks and I'll make a chocolate cake for dessert."

His chuckle was warm and throaty and it made a shiver run up her spine. "You make the cake and I'll grill the steaks. That's a man's job."

"I hope you are not serious," she mocked. "A woman can do anything a man does and just as well."

He stepped close so she had to look up at him. She could smell his clean scent mixed with the damp aroma of the earth. His dark hair had fallen down on his forehead. She had to resist the urge to reach up and sweep it off to the side.

"She can but she shouldn't have to. I'm happy to share in the chores and cooking while I'm staying with you."

"You're my guest," she protested. "I promised Ava that you would have some kind of vacation."

"I'm not the vacation type." Reed shrugged and pointed out another perfect pumpkin farther down the row. "I don't need entertaining, and you're not a B & B. I'm happy with a nice meal and a good book."

He liked to present himself as a simple man but Kaylee could tell there were depths he didn't reveal. He had the tall, dark, and mysterious thing down pat.

"We'll see—" she began but was interrupted by her ringtone—the University of Illinois fight song. Digging into her purse, she pulled out her phone and almost groaned at the name on the display. The timing sucked.

"Shit," she muttered under her breath. "Can you give me a minute?"

Kaylee pressed the accept button and took a deep breath. "Hi Brent, how are you today?"

"I'm fine, Kaylee. How are you? I had a great time at the writer's group yesterday."

"I'm fine. I had a good time too. It's always fun, isn't it?"

Her stomach tightened with tension as the realization of what was about to happen hit her. Brent was working up the courage here to ask her out. If she'd been paying attention these last few months instead of working on her latest book she might have been able to head this off at the pass without hurting a nice man.

Shit and double shit.

"It is." There was a pause and it sounded like he dropped the phone but then he was back. "Listen, I was wondering whether you might be free for dinner tonight?"

Kaylee looked up at Reed who was regarding her steadily, his expression blank. He could easily hear both sides of the conversation. If she was looking for a clue as to how he felt about another man calling her for a date she wouldn't find it there.

"Dinner? Tonight?" she parroted.

"If you're not busy. Maybe we could discuss this scene that's giving me so much trouble." Brent's words came out in a rush. "Unless you already have plans?"

Hell and damnation, she felt like she was stepping on a defenseless bug or kicking a puppy. "I'm afraid I already do have plans Brent, but thank you for asking. Maybe you could come over early before the next writer's group and we could work on that scene."

"Sure. I could do that. Well, I should have known better than to call for dinner just a few hours before. I know you're busy."

The enthusiasm had drained from his voice and Kaylee felt like a total bitch. Brent was a good guy, but he simply didn't make her hormones stand up and take notice. He would never be anything but a friend.

"I need to get back to work," Brent said. "I'll see you at the next meeting."

Just that quick he was gone. She stared at her phone for a few seconds wondering if there was another way she could have handled that, a less hurtful way, before stowing it in her purse. Reed had already turned back to their task and was hunting through the pumpkins again.

"This one looks good," Reed observed, lifting up the massive gourd for her inspection.

"It's fine." Kaylee wasn't interested in pumpkins anymore. Shit, this was why she didn't date often. She had no flipping idea what she was doing. "Dammit, I feel like the Wicked Witch of the West."

Reed set the pumpkin into the wagon and wiped his hands on his jeans. "Your friend Brent is a grown man, honey. And grown men know they are taking a chance when they ask a woman out on a date. Sometimes you get turned down. He'll be okay, I promise you."

"How would you know? I bet you've never been turned down in your life."

She couldn't imagine the woman that would say no to Reed.

Reed lifted up the handle on the Radio Flyer and they both started walking back to the cashier.

"I'll have you know that Allison Avery broke my heart. I asked her to be my girlfriend and she turned me down flat."

Allison Avery needed her head examined. "Was this recently?"

"I was thirteen and passed her a note after history class. By gym I'd received a resounding no. Turns out she liked sensitive, poetry writing blonds."

"That was a long time ago." Kaylee laughed, liking the fact that he could be self-deprecating. "It hardly counts."

"It was at a very crucial time in my development. But I did learn something important from it."

"What was that?" she teased. "Teenage girls are fickle?"

Reed stopped in his tracks, his expression quite serious despite their levity. "I survived. I thought it was the worst thing in the world but it turns out it wasn't even close. The survival instinct is more powerful than you can possibly imagine."

That statement left Kaylee with only two questions.

What terrible thing had happened to him that made him close off his emotions? Was Reed Mitchell living or only surviving?

✧ ✧ ✧ ✧

Reed pounded on the laptop keyboard later that day but the results didn't change. Kaylee was not going to like this. Hopefully she wouldn't kill the messenger.

"Are you getting hungry for dinner?"

They were sitting in her kitchen, Reed on the laptop and Kaylee bustling around the kitchen. She opened the oven and the heavenly aroma of chocolate cake wafted around him, his stomach growling in approval.

"I can always eat so, whenever you get hungry let me know and I'll put the steaks on the grill."

They were currently marinating in the refrigerator along with some diced potatoes mixed with garlic and shallots and then wrapped in foil. The chocolate cake was going to be the perfect end to a great meal.

"I love a man with an appetite. You've been tapping away for at least three hours and your shoulders have to be killing you. I have a heating pad you can use if you like."

Reed had noticed the little nagging aches and pains she had from being bent over a keyboard so much. She was constantly rubbing at her neck and shoulders and rotating her wrists, saying they felt stiff. What she needed was a relaxing massage.

Reed swallowed hard as the image of Kaylee barely clad, her skin shiny from oil, floated through his mind. Damn, he needed to focus. It was almost as if he was torturing himself on purpose. After spending the last few days with this woman he found himself wanting more. More time, more intimacy. Neither was a very good idea.

"Reed?" Kaylee prompted, giving him a strange look. "Did you hear me?"

"I did. I'm okay though. I've been working on these background checks."

"By the tone of your voice you've found something. Few people live perfect lives, you know."

God knows I haven't.

"Your friend, Brent? The one you felt so sorry for this morning? He sure hasn't."

Kaylee stopped wiping her hands on a dishtowel. "Brent? What could he have done?"

"How long have you known him anyway?" Kaylee talked about how she couldn't trust men but outside of relationships she was too trusting by far. Reed shuddered at the things he'd found out about the people that had been in her home just yesterday.

"I met him a few months ago through Linda and Cheryl. He does website design and development. He freelances."

"So he might know how to spoof an email server in the Ukraine or Hong Kong." Reed didn't make it sound like a question because it wasn't.

"He might," Kaylee said defensively. "Is that all you've got because that's pretty flimsy evidence."

"Did you know that he was recently a resident of the Vandalia Correctional Center? It's a minimum security prison in southern Illinois."

"I know where Vandalia is," she said sharply, her lips pressed into a line. Reed could tell she was trying to keep herself from asking what he'd been in for. Finally she groaned and tossed down the dishtowel in disgust. "Just tell me already. What did he do?"

"He was selling drugs at his last place of employment."

Letting the words sink in, Reed watched a parade of emotions flit across her expressive features. First there was clear denial, then anger—probably at not knowing, but acceptance won the day. Damn, she was a sweet woman. The urge to confess his own sins and receive her tender absolution was strong and unexpected but he ruthlessly pushed it away. The time for mercy had long passed.

"That doesn't mean he's a stalker."

"You're right," he agreed, not wanting to argue with her when they had a pleasant evening planned. "It doesn't mean a thing except that he's someone to keep an eye on."

"Anything else? Anyone else?" she asked reluctantly, her usual smile wiped from her face.

"Yes." Reed handed her a stack of papers he'd printed up earlier. "A few of your writer friends like to drink and party. A couple have records for theft which might be a reason not to have these little get-togethers at your home any longer. I'm still working on the rest of the list we made yesterday."

Kaylee scanned the pages, her complexion paler than before. Reed felt crappy having to do this to her but right now she had to be aware of everyone she came into contact with.

"I hate this," she said, her voice choked and her eyes bright with tears. "Dammit, these people are my friends. I doubt my life could stand up to this kind of scrutiny. I wonder what people would think about me?"

Kaylee had been the first person he'd checked out and she was clean as a whistle other than a few points on her driver's license for speeding. "They'd think you were a good person. All these people are probably good, honey. I've seen some of the best people make a mistake and get themselves into a bad situation. It doesn't make them evil, it just makes them human."

"Then why are we doing this?"

"Because some asshole has forced us to," he answered heavily, not any more thrilled about the task than she was. "When this is all over we'll have a burning ceremony and send those papers up in flames."

"Promise?" Her expression was hopeful and this was something he could give assurance on.

"Cross my heart. Now how about those steaks? I'll heat up the grill."

Kaylee nodded and Reed headed to the back yard. He needed to talk to Jared and see if he'd found anything, but most of all he needed for this guy to make another move, to reveal more about himself. It was the only way Reed would be able to find this person and stop them. He could investigate everyone around Kaylee and he could stay here and protect her, but the ball wasn't in his court. It was a waiting game and Reed hated games.

Chapter Ten

R eed hadn't mentioned any more about her friends, background checks, or her stalker so the evening had turned out quite pleasant. They had eaten dinner and were now ensconced on the couch watching *Young Frankenstein,* having already finished the Peanuts special. Kaylee had her head on Reed's shoulder and his arm was on the back of the cushion but his fingers were playing idly in her hair. It was a cozy, domestic scene, but despite the veneer of serenity her heart was thumping and her breath was shallow. She wanted this man badly.

Breathing in his heavenly male scent, she snuggled closer into the heat of his body, loving how his muscular frame wrapped snuggly around her. Watching television had never been this exciting before.

"Are you cold?" His voice was low and close to her ear. He pulled the cotton throw more closely around her, tucking it under her feet.

"Not now," she whispered, loathe to break the companionable silence between them. She felt warm and protected here in his arms, never wanting it to end. Of course it would but she was determined to make the most of the present and let the future take care of itself. She was almost asleep when the living room was suddenly flooded with light. She heard the splintering of breaking glass and the roar of an engine along with squealing tires.

She sat up, almost falling off the couch as Reed leapt to his feet. Standing up to see what had happened behind them, she was instead pushed back down onto the sofa with a strong hand on her shoulder.

"Stay," he commanded before striding toward the front of the house where her dining room table sat overlooking the front yard. Peeking over the back cushions, her heart pounded in her chest as she crouched down waiting for word from Reed. He'd flipped on all the exterior lights and she could hear him walking around the perimeter of the house.

Shards of broken glass lay on the oak top of her dining table and on the floor as well. A cold breeze was wafting through the damaged window and she pulled the throw closer around her body. No glass company was going to come out this time of night. They'd have to nail some boards over the opening until tomorrow.

When he came back into the house his expression had turned grim and his jaw was tight. He assessed the damage to the window and then frowned, leaning over to pick up something from the floor.

He held up the brick wrapped with paper and heavy twine. The word "Slut" was scrawled across the side. "More escalation. Hopefully we got the asshole on camera."

She'd forgotten about the cameras he'd set up. The rush of light must have been the motion-sensor lamps he'd placed around the house. Her heart was still racing but she took a few deep breaths to calm herself down. She trusted Reed to take care of this. Being alone and independent wasn't looking all that attractive right about now. It felt good to have someone to lean on, someone who knew about these things.

She watched as he dug into his laptop bag he'd stowed in the foyer, pulling out rubber gloves wrapped in plastic. He tugged them on before using a pocket knife to slice through the twine and unwrapping the heavy brick.

"Does it say anything?" she asked, not really wanting to know but needing to at the same time.

He didn't answer her right away, instead studying the thick cream colored paper. It looked like something that her butcher would wrap around steaks.

"It says 'your turn' and has another drawing."

If Reed's thunderous expression was anything to go by, it wasn't something she wanted to see. But she was a grown woman and she needed to face this head on. She walked to his side and steeled herself.

"Show me."

Reed sighed and angled the paper toward her. Acid rose in her throat and her stomach churned at the sickness displayed. The words had been cut letter by letter from magazines. She'd always thought that was something they only did in movies. But that wasn't the worst of it. The sender had hand-drawn another picture—as crudely rendered as the last. This one featured a figure that she supposed to be herself lying in a coffin with a rose on her chest while mourners gathered around.

It was sick. And twisted. And it terrified her. Why did someone want to do this to her? What had she done?

Reed set the brick on the table and pulled her into his arms. Rubbing her back, he let her draw strength from his nearness.

"You okay, honey? This guy is just trying to get you rattled. Don't let him get inside your head."

"He's succeeding. That last letter was bad enough but now this? It scares me, Reed."

There, she'd said it. She'd been trying to play this entire situation and all the letters off as if it were no big deal. But now that she knew he had her address everything had changed. First a violent drawing and now a brick with another creepy picture through her front window? She could only shudder at what might be next.

"I'm not going to let anything happen to you, honey. Anybody trying to get to you is going to have to go through me."

Reed held her for a long time until she stopped shaking and her pulse was back to normal. Pulling reluctantly away, she grimaced at the drapes blowing in the breeze. "I guess we should cover that up."

"First we need to call the police and make sure they have a report of the incident. I also want a look at the tape before they get here. Do you have anything in the garage to put over the window?"

"There's some plywood out there from when they fixed the roof but I'm not sure how much."

"If there's not enough I saw some cardboard in your office. We'll make do."

Reed picked up his cell from the end table and she padded into the kitchen to put on a pot of coffee. The police would probably appreciate a cup and she had a feeling it might be a long night. The last thing she could imagine doing was sleeping. Her life had slowly morphed into a nightmare. The only good thing was that Reed was still here.

Reed flexed his shoulders tiredly and rubbed the back of his neck. He'd been looking at this footage from the security cameras over and over, zooming in, and slowing it down but nothing worked. He couldn't make out the figure who had thrown the brick into Kaylee's home.

His head still buzzing with anger, he'd talked to the police showing them what had been done. They'd taken down the details but without any proof their hands were pretty well tied. Reed had hoped to be able to provide them with evidence in the form of pictures from the security camera but that hadn't helped much. They'd only learned that the stalker was probably about five-seven based on the height of the surrounding trees and bushes. The perpetrator was also smart enough to dress in an oversized overcoat that dwarfed their frame, heavy boots, a large brimmed hat that covered their features, and even gloves on their hands.

Kaylee's stalker could be that Brent guy. It could even be the waitress that had served them at lunch today. Reed growled in frustration and re-started the footage.

"Reed? It's almost one in the morning."

Kaylee's soft voice pulled him from his black thoughts and he turned to see her standing tentatively at the door of her own office. Dressed in red and green plaid flannel pajama bottoms and a red t-shirt, she looked delightfully soft and warm. His heart tripped and his chest felt tight. Kaylee Blue was dangerous to the life he'd built.

All he wanted to do was protect her and make all her demons go away. He didn't like the look of fear on her face that she was still wearing even hours later. It was hard for her to trust someone to take care of her, to depend on someone besides herself. It felt good that she'd allowed him to do exactly that tonight. She'd be back to her stubborn self tomorrow of course, but he'd enjoy the peace now.

"I know, honey. I'm looking at what we got from the cameras again. I thought you were in bed."

"I couldn't sleep." She came up behind him and began to massage the knotted muscles of his shoulders and the base of his skull. He groaned in relief and let his head fall forward. "There's nothing more you can do tonight. You need to sleep too."

"I keep thinking there's something I'm missing. It's like this guy knew he was being taped."

"I doubt that. No one knows you put those cameras out there. They're well hidden. They probably just didn't want to be recognized and the fact that we can't tell who they are on film is a bonus. Were you able to see the car we heard?"

"No, but I'll talk to the neighbors tomorrow and see if they saw anything. One of them might have heard the squealing tires and looked out their window. I'll also change the angle of one of the cameras to capture a view of the street." He wrapped his arm around her middle and gave her an encouraging smile. "You should go to bed. I'm just going to stay up a few more minutes and see if I can enhance this picture any more than I already have."

He felt a shudder go through her body and her teeth sunk into her full lower lip. "I don't want to be by myself." Her fingers clutched his shoulders tightly. "Will you sleep with me? Just sleep."

Kaylee's words came out quickly but he could tell she was still scared. "I'm not propositioning you or anything. I just don't think I can sleep alone tonight."

A few days ago Reed wouldn't have known how much that confession must have cost her but he knew now. He closed the laptop and stood, determined to make her feel safe again.

"Of course I'll sleep with you. Let me change and brush my teeth. I'll come to you, okay?"

"Okay—you won't be long?"

Reed hated to hear the fear in her voice. "Five minutes."

She smiled her thanks and retreated from the room. Reed rubbed his temples knowing the next several hours weren't going to be easy. She needed him to hold and comfort her, nothing more.

It was going to be a long night.

Chapter Eleven

"**D**id they see anything?" asked Kaylee the next day when Reed stepped in the back door. He'd been talking to neighbors since early this morning trying to catch them before they left for work or school. Neither one of them had slept very well last night but she had finally dozed off about four in the morning and had woken with his arms wrapped tightly around her. She'd never felt so safe and secure in her entire life.

She'd lain there quietly, not wanting to move so she wouldn't wake him up. He had dark smudges under his eyes and she'd had a feeling he'd stayed awake much longer than she had. She'd had the luxury of watching him sleep, but even in rest his features looked tortured and frustrated. She'd wanted to run her fingers over the lines in his forehead, soothing away his worries.

"One neighbor heard the tires and the engine and looked out of his window. He saw a four-door sedan that he thought might be a Camry or an Accord. Or maybe a Malibu. It was too dark so he can't be sure."

Reed poured himself a cup of coffee and leaned against the counter, clearly frustrated by the lack of witnesses.

"At least we now know it was a sedan," she said in a hopeful tone. "It was more than we knew yesterday."

"What amazes me is the complete lack of curiosity of the average American. Pretty much they all heard the car but only one guy even looked out of his window. What is the world coming to when no one gives a shit what goes on in their own damn neighborhood?"

"I don't know what happens in Montana but cars race up and down the street fairly often. The Miller family down the block has a teenage son and he just got a truck. Add in his friends that come visit and this street is their personal racetrack." She stood and headed for the stove. "Sit down and let me make you some breakfast. How about eggs and bacon? Or would you rather have French toast again?"

Reed sat heavily in a chair and scraped his fingers through his hair. "I'll eat anything you make." His gaze swept over her, taking in every detail. "You look better this morning. Less...tense."

"I got a few hours of sleep. More than you did, I'd wager." She cracked a few eggs into a bowl and added milk before beating them with a fork. "Actually, now that I'm over the shock of a heavy object flying through a window and into my home along with a grisly note and picture, I'm mad. Mad that someone is doing this to me. I don't deserve this."

"No, you don't. As for being angry, that's probably not a bad emotion to have. Being cowed and retreating is not a good way to live. We'll only catch this guy if we're aggressive in looking for him."

"I'm ready to do what needs to be done." She poured the eggs into the frying pan and sprinkled shredded cheese on top along with salt and pepper. "So what's next?"

Kaylee dropped two slices of bread into the toaster as Reed re-filled his cup. "I need to talk to Jared and see if he's made any progress with the background checks. Then we'll cross-reference the names on the list with DMV records and see who drives a four-door sedan and is around five-seven, give or take a few inches on either side. Narrowing our list of suspects is key."

She flipped the scrambled eggs onto the plate, adding the bacon she'd cooked earlier and the two slices of toast. "Brent drives a four-door Camry. He's also the right height."

She hated to think he had done this. He seemed like a nice man, quiet and unassuming.

"He's suspect number one on my list," Reed agreed. "But I've learned not to focus in on just one person to the exclusion of others. I try to keep an open mind even when it's not easy. He did ask you out on a date for last night and you did turn him down. He might think that's a good enough reason to take out a window and scare you."

She slid the plate in front of him and thought back to the men she'd dated in the past. "I've never inspired a passion strong enough in a man that he committed a crime when I said no. Other women might get reactions like that but not me."

"I think we've had this discussion before. You've been dating the wrong men. But this isn't about passion, this is about obsession. Whoever is doing this is obsessed with you."

"Why?" Kaylee fell into the chair opposite him at a loss as to why this was happening. "What about me makes them do this?"

"In my experience with stalkers, or harassers for want of a better term, is that the victim has something that the other person wants. Fame, money, admiration, even another human being."

"This person thinks I write trash," she reminded him.

"They want to make you feel badly about what you do. They may even actually believe you write trash but I think the real thing is they don't like that you have some fame and money from it. That's what really bothers them."

"They're jealous? Of me? Ask a hundred people randomly and not one of them is going to know who the heck I am, Reed."

Make that a million people. Her books were well-known in a small circle of readers but she wasn't Nora Roberts. Kaylee made a nice living off of her books but she wasn't considered a big name in publishing.

"Brent would love to have your writing career I bet. That may be why he's asking you out. If he can't do it on his own he wants to somehow be a part of it. Or maybe he simply asked you out yesterday because he felt threatened by my presence and thought he'd better make his move."

Her head hurt from lack of sleep and trying to figure this out.

"I just want to go back to when my life was boring and all I did was write."

Reed stood and rinsed off his plate before loading it into the dishwasher. "I'll try and stay out of your way today while you work. Do you have a deadline or something?"

"No, I started a new work in progress a few weeks ago but I have a new book coming out—" Kaylee broke off and slapped her forehead with the palm of her hand. "God, this is what happens when I don't get enough sleep. Shit, I can't believe it completely slipped my mind."

"What slipped your mind?"

"I have a book releasing tomorrow. I need to send out my newsletter and do some social media stuff. Damn."

She'd let this whole stalker thing completely disrupt her routine. She needed to get her head on straight and get back to work.

"Then I'll definitely stay out of your way. In fact, why don't we go out to dinner tonight? We can celebrate your new book and you don't have to cook."

"I don't mind cooking," she argued but the thought was tempting. She hadn't exactly had her nose to the grindstone since Reed had arrived. She needed a good long day of productivity.

"I know you don't but this way it's one less thing to do. How about it?"

"We could do that," she capitulated. "There's some great pizza in this town. Is that okay?"

"That sounds fine but I'd be happy to take you some place fancy."

She simply wasn't a get-dressed up and go out to eat kind of person. It was a big deal when she got out of her pajamas and put on a bra. She'd worn regular clothes more in the last three days than she had in the last three weeks combined.

"What are you in the mood for? I know a few good steakhouses."

"Whatever you want. Your wish is my command." His smile was designed to charm and it did exactly that. He was flying right over all the defenses she'd built up as if they were nothing. She was beginning to depend on Reed Mitchell.

"Please tell me that you've found something. Anything." Out on the back patio, Reed was talking to Jared while Kaylee worked in the office. "I'm hitting roadblocks everywhere I turn here. He's escalating, I can feel it. His first contacts were remote, almost impersonal. Then he sends a more threatening type of letter to her home. He was letting her know he could get to her if he wanted to. Now he's damaged her property and threatened her again. He could have hurt her if she'd been sitting in front of that window."

"It does sound like it," Jared replied. "But here's the thing. He didn't injure her. Does she sit at that table very often?"

"I've never seen her sit there. We eat at the island or in the living room. I doubt she sits there when she eats alone."

"I bet your stalker knew that too. He's probably watching her. That may be why he's escalating. Your presence has shaken him up."

"Yeah, I've been thinking about that. It's a funny coincidence that things started heating up when I got here. I'll be honest—I don't like these cat and mouse games. I much prefer when the enemy comes straight after me in a fair fight. This one's acting like a big pussy with all this creepy shit."

"He's fucking with her head, just toying with her. I doubt he intended to hurt her last night."

"He wanted to scare her," Reed stated, still pissed that this asshole was jerking them around. "Shit, he succeeded. She didn't want to be by herself, and we sure as hell didn't get much sleep. I think she dozed off about three and I fell asleep about five."

"It sounds like you and Kaylee are getting rather close."

Fuck Jared. Reed knew when he was being baited and he was too tired and irritable to appreciate it at the moment.

"I'm not in the mood to play games with you. Say whatever it is you want to say, dammit."

"Fine, I'll say it. Are you sleeping with her?"

"No," Reed answered shortly. "I am not. At least in the sense you mean. She was scared and didn't want to sleep alone. Nothing happened."

"When was the last time you slept in the same bed with a woman out of the goodness of your heart? It sounds like you have feelings for her. Do you?"

That was the fucking million-dollar question. Reed hadn't felt this vulnerable about a female in about fifteen years. That little factoid wasn't improving his mood any more than the lack of sleep.

"She's an easy woman to like," Reed finally said. "I'm not falling in love with her if that's where you're going with this. But I do want to protect her."

"It's nice to see you give a shit about anything other than work." Reed searched for amusement in Jared's words but there was none.

"This is work," Reed said abruptly. "I want to find this guy because it's the right thing to do. Then I'll finish my vacation and head back home."

"You know, nothing bad would happen if you let someone into your life, man. I don't know what's happened to–"

"Let's change the subject," Reed interjected. He loved Jared like a brother but digging up long-buried ghosts wasn't on the agenda today. "Did you find anything or not?"

At first Reed thought Jared wasn't going to drop the subject but then he finally answered. "I did find a few things as a matter of fact. Out of the writing group, Linda had a juvenile record. She stole beer from a liquor store when she was seventeen. Hell, probably did it on a dare or some shit like that. Been clean ever since. Then this Cheryl doesn't have a record but her personal life is interesting. She's been married four times. She's not even forty yet. Four times. And with each successive husband she gets better at taking them for their money. She's got quite a tidy sum in the bank."

"What about Walter?"

Reed had gotten a hinky vibe from the man that day and hadn't been able to shake it since. If Brent wasn't their guy, the next on his list was Walter.

"Now this Walter Cummings is interesting and do you know why? He exists but he doesn't exist. I see he was born in Kankakee, which is north of Champaign. He graduated from high school and he has a checking account with a balance of two hundred and six dollars. He doesn't own any property or have any credit cards. He's not even registered to vote. From what I can see he has no visible means of support. Is he handsome enough to get women to pay his bills?"

Reed sighed in frustration. "I don't think I'm a good one to ask. Damn, I need to talk to him. He's still on my list along with Brent."

"What did you find out about him?"

"He's got a record. Selling drugs. He did some time in a minimum security prison here in Illinois. Other than that he seems pretty ne'er do well. He's gone from job to job, apartment to apartment with no real direction in his life. From what I can see he has less than five hundred bucks to his name and no real assets."

"Doesn't make him a criminal though," Jared said doubtfully. "Did you find anything else? You said you were going to check out Kaylee herself and see if there was something in her past that was coming back to haunt her. What about this David she used to live with? Do you think he could be doing this?"

Reed flipped open the file folder on the desk that contained everything he'd found out about his hostess. He already knew he had more information about her life than she did. She hadn't known about her father. Would she want to hear that her ex-boyfriend was now single? Did she still have feelings for him despite her statements that he was an asshole?

"Kaylee lived a quiet life in East Central Illinois. She was in the drama club in high school and got good grades at the University of Illinois. There's no report of run-ins with campus police or anything. Even in Portland she didn't even get a parking ticket. From what I can see she was a model citizen. If she garnered someone's attention she certainly wasn't trying. As for David Benton, he's newly single in the last six months but he still lives in Portland. I've pretty much eliminated everyone Kaylee knows from Portland or social media. I think this guy is local."

"So what's the next step? What can we do?"

Jared Monroe was just one of seven other small town sheriffs that Reed met and worked with on a regular basis. They were always there for one another and it made keeping the peace much easier.

"I'm waiting on fingerprint results from the cops. They have the two letters and drawings. Also I've scanned the hand-drawn pictures into the computer and I have a program running in the background scouring the Internet for anything that looks even remotely close. I also have a program running that's cross-referencing DMV records with the list of names. I'm looking for those that have a four-door sedan registered to them. And this morning I put up more cameras to capture different angles and put sensors on the every door and window. A good stiff breeze would set this place off now."

"You're a busy man. Sounds like she's safe as long as she stays in the house," Jared chuckled.

"Wish me luck with that," Reed groaned. "This woman is stubborn as a mule. If she wants to leave the house, believe me she will."

"She sounds like your perfect match. Seriously though, is there anything we can help you with?"

Reed stroked his chin. "I can't think of anything right now but I'll definitely call you if anything comes up. Right now I'm trying to be as proactive as I can in a reactive situation."

"I don't envy you," Jared agreed. "But it sounds like you have things in hand. You'll get this guy. He'll slip up and you'll catch him. It's only a matter of time."

Reed could only hope that was the case. He ended the call but before he could set the phone down on the table next to him it was ringing again.

"Hey Logan, what's up? I just got off the phone with Jared."

"Then my timing is impeccable. I was calling to see how everything is going but also wondering about Kaylee. Ava has been trying to get her on the phone for the last hour or so and there's been no answer. She was worried. Since I was going to call you anyway I offered to see if she's okay. Did she write all night and need a nap? Ava does that all the time."

"Actually Kaylee is writing now so I bet she turned off her phone. If it's okay I'll have her call Ava when she takes a break."

"Sounds good. Is everything going well there? Any more communication from the stalker?"

The last thing Reed wanted to do was upset Ava and by extension Logan. They were both worried about Kaylee and for good reason, but Reed wasn't the type to keep something like this from his friend. Without any drama or emotion he recited what had happened and the steps he'd taken to mitigate any risk. He tried to make it sound like business as usual in Kaylee's home.

"Shit, is she okay?" Logan asked when Reed was done. "Is she scared?"

Relating truthful facts to Logan were one thing; characterizing Kaylee's fear was something else. There was nothing to be gained by describing how shaken up she had been last night and even today. That would only worry Ava more.

"She's hanging tough. She told me this morning that she's mad this is happening to her and I think that's a healthy response."

"That sounds like something my Ava would say," Logan laughed heartily. "I feel better knowing you're there and protecting her. I know I've said thank you before but I'll say it again. I appreciate what you're doing."

Reed had stopped doing this for Logan and Ava at some point last night. Now he was doing it for Kaylee and himself. Something had happened to him as he'd held her in his arms, listening to her even breathing and feeling the steady thrum of her heartbeat. She'd felt small, vulnerable, and scared. He'd vowed to protect her with his life. Nothing and no one would hurt her. He'd made mistakes in the past but this time he would do things right.

"I'm happy to help, Logan. Nothing is going to happen to Kaylee."

Chapter Twelve

*R*od's hand slipped beneath the hem of her skirt, sliding up her thigh and leaving a trail of heat in his wake. Tamsyn shivered as he traced patterns on her skin before his fingers delved under the elastic of her panties. She was hot and wet for him and he groaned his approval against her neck and whispered that she was beautiful and sexy.

Whew.

Kaylee pushed her chair away from the desk and took a deep, calming breath, fanning her warm face. Writing a sex scene was always difficult but today seemed extra challenging. It might have something to do with what had happened last night and to her life in general. She had someone who was threatening her and they had no idea who they were or why they were doing this.

But that wasn't the real reason she was having problems.

This was entirely Reed Mitchell's fault. Every time she tried to imagine her characters Rod and Tamsyn making love her brain completely twisted things and suddenly she had pictures of Reed and herself naked and entwined on her king-sized bed doing incredibly naughty things to one another. The whole endeavor had her hot, bothered, and wanting to do something about it. It had been many months since she'd had sex, and she was sure that sex with Reed would be like nothing she'd had before.

If she were brutally honest with herself she hadn't had much luck with making love. It was one of the reasons she'd chosen erotic romance when she'd started writing. If she couldn't reach those passionate heights she'd read about—and she sure as heck didn't with David—then writing about them was the next best thing. Most of the time she took care of business herself with a variable speed Hitachi vibrator that had been worth every penny of its expensive price tag.

She needed a break and a cool drink. Heading into the kitchen she spied Reed on the back patio talking on the phone. She must have caught his eye because he nodded and ended the call, setting his laptop on the side table and joining her in the kitchen.

"Taking a break?" he asked with a smile. "That was Logan on the phone. Ava's been trying to call you this morning and was worried. I told them you were writing but I would pass on the message."

When she really needed to get something done Kaylee shut off her cell and the Internet and today was no exception. In three hours she'd managed to get four thousand new words on her work in progress.

"Just a little break. I was thirsty. I'll call Ava in a while. She must be bored." Kaylee kept her eyes averted as she popped open a can of soda and poured it into a glass. "Would you like one?"

"I'm good." Reed looked at her, his brows pulled down into a frown. "Are you running a fever? Your face is all red."

More heat flooded her cheeks. Fuck a mallard. She hadn't expected him to notice her aroused state but then this was a man who noticed everything.

"I'm fine," she denied. "It was just warm in the office. Maybe I'll turn down the heat."

He didn't take his gaze away, simply crossing his muscular arms over his chest and regarding her with steady interest. Eventually a smile spread across his face and those to-die-for dimples made an appearance.

"You were working on a sex scene, weren't you? I've never read anything as hot as what you write, honey. Damn, those scenes in that book were smokin'. I would imagine this happens to you all the time."

If there had been any justice or fairness in the world a gigantic hole would have opened up in the floor below and swallowed her whole. She was mortified, and he didn't even know that he'd been the star in her fantasies.

"It was just warm in there. I'm going to turn the heat down." She whirled around so he wouldn't see her flaming face but his large hand closed over her upper arm. He was gentle but firm and she pressed her fingers over her eyes, unwilling to see him laughing at her humiliation.

"Kaylee, honey?" Reed's voice was soft and there was no mirth in his tone. "Look at me, sweetheart. I'm sorry if I've upset you. I didn't mean to hurt your feelings."

Slowly she took her hands away and looked up at all six feet plus of him. This simply wasn't fair. She wanted him so badly and here he was calm, cool, and collected. Ava had warned Kaylee that Reed didn't care if a woman was panting after him, but the reality of it royally pissed her off. Anger churned in her stomach and indignation loosened her tongue.

"This is all your fault."

Reed's eyebrows shot up in surprise. "My fault? How is this my fault? I haven't touched the thermostat, and if I did I wouldn't keep it so warm in the house to begin with."

Kaylee jerked her arm away and began to pace up and down the kitchen, her gut tight. She was mad and fearful all at the same time. Mad that he didn't feel the electricity and heat between them as she did. Fear that now that she'd opened her big mouth she'd ruined the easy friendship they'd built the last few days.

Too late now.

"I was fine before you came here. Okay, maybe sometimes I was a little lonely but I like being by myself most of the time. And as for sex, I'd gotten used to the fact that it wasn't worth worrying about. Everything was good." She halted and spun around so she was facing him. "Then you came along with your muscles and your dimples, and the lock of hair that falls over your forehead. And you had to be so damn nice and funny. Intelligent and dammit, you read my book and got what I was trying to do. I was doomed."

Kaylee took a few deep breaths and swallowed the lump that had taken up residence in her throat. "That's why this is all your fault. When I write those scenes now I see you and me."

There it was. The miserable truth laid bare for him to ridicule. She had no more secrets from him, nothing to hide behind. Stripped of any dignity, she stared at her sock covered feet and waited for his inevitable derision.

"Then I think we should go upstairs."

His deep voice had reached her ears but her brain was having a hard time unscrambling his words.

"What did you say?" She finally looked up and sucked in a breath at what she saw. There was passion in his expression, the irises of his eyes almost golden.

"I said..." Reed took a few steps closer so she had to tip her head back to look at his face. Heat emanated from his body and she placed her hands on his chest to feel the burn against her palms. "That we should go upstairs. I can think of a few things we can do that you probably haven't written about yet."

Anger and shame turned to joy and instead of her stomach twisting in her abdomen it felt like a thousand butterflies being set free. Her tongue snaked out to wet her dry lips and his gaze instantly zeroed in on her action.

"What about Logan and your friendship?"

A corner of his mouth tipped up. "I'll handle things with him. Besides, I think Ava is on our side."

Kaylee remembered he had overheard her phone conversation when Ava had told her to go for it with Reed. Just not to expect any future from him.

Still needing reassurance that this wasn't a dream, her fingers dug into the soft cotton of his t-shirt where she could feel the firm muscles underneath.

"Are you sure?" The words came out barely audible and he bent his head closer to pick them up. His fingers captured her chin and his thumb caressed her lips, sending tingles directly to her toes and making her weak at the knees.

"Honey, if I were any more sure my hard cock would punch a hole clean through this zipper. I've wanted you since the day I met you."

It sounded like the sweetest poetry Kaylee had ever heard. This time her legs really did give out but it didn't matter as Reed swept her up into his arms and headed straight for the stairs.

Today she would be with him and not think about tomorrow.

Reed simply could not deny himself this gorgeous woman any longer. He'd deal with Logan, or Ava would at any rate. Kaylee knew there was no future with a man like him and she said she was fine with it. He could only hope that was true because stopping now was unthinkable.

He laid her on the bed and came down on top of her, his lips going directly to that sensitive spot on her neck where it met her shoulder. Her skin smelled fresh and dewy like after a spring shower in Montana. She moaned as his teeth nipped at the creamy flesh and wriggled underneath him. His teeth snapped together and he held back a groan of pain as her hips brushed against his already aching cock. He needed to take a breather and slow down. Already hotter than a firecracker and ready to blow, he wanted this first time to be more than a quick fuck. Even though this wasn't about forever, she meant more than that.

Biting gently into the lobe of her ear, he immediately soothed the hurt with his tongue even as her frantic fingers were sliding under his t-shirt in an effort to strip it from his body. His hands covered hers to still them and he pulled away slightly to look into her eyes.

"Easy, honey. Let's slow this down a little. We've got nowhere we need to be so let's take our time."

To his amusement, her mouth fell open and she pushed at his chest with her palms. "Slow down? Do you have any idea what I've been doing today? I've been writing sex for the last three hours. Three hours, Reed. Three hours of imagining the two of us doing some of the most debauched things I've ever written about. I need you now. You can take your damn time later."

She was muttering under her breath even as she continued to wrestle with his shirt. He had to stifle his laughter and delight at her urgent words. He loved that she wanted him and made no bones about it. Giving her whatever she needed was number one on his list. Her demand was a godsend as his balls were already pulled up in readiness. Going slow would have been pure torture for them both.

"You want a quickie, honey? I can do that. But we'll go slow next time."

Kaylee finally managed to pull his shirt over his head. "Whatever."

His jeans were next and his jaw tightened in pleasure-like agony as her small hands popped open the button and pulled the zipper tab. His own hands joined hers, shoving the heavy material down and off his legs along with his white cotton socks and flannel boxers. His cock slapped against the skin of his stomach and this time he did groan out loud as she encircled him, her thumb tracing the slit where a drop of pre-cum glistened.

Her gaze never leaving him, she raised her thumb to her mouth and sucked the moisture from the skin.

Seductress.

She'd pay at some point for teasing him. His pulse drummed and the pressure in his lower back built as he plucked at the tiny pearl buttons on the front of her sweater before tossing it on the floor. Her generously round breasts were contained in a simple satin and lace bra but he could clearly see the dark outline of her nipples. He reached behind her and squeezed the hooks together and then yanked the offending garment out of the way.

Fucking gorgeous.

Pale pink tips on ivory skin that shimmered in the sunlight streaming through the window. Already hard and pointed, he bent his head to one, pulling it into his mouth and worrying the edges with his teeth. Her fingers dug into his scalp and she ground her groin against his insistently. He released one with a pop only to take the other between his lips and roll it with his tongue.

"Yes," she hissed under her breath.

Trailing kisses down her belly, he slipped the button of her jeans through the hole and drew the zipper down before skating them down her legs and off. Wearing only a pair of tiny white panties, her skin was flushed and her hair tumbled around her face. Reed was looking forward to tangling his fingers in its silkiness while he fucked her hard and fast.

"Tell me what you want, Kaylee."

"You," she sighed. "I want you."

"You've got me, honey," he assured her. "But tell me want you really want. What you need. I'll give it to you, I promise. I'm a man that likes to hear a woman speak explicitly about her desires."

The fact was dirty talk turned him on. Considering Kaylee liked words, he had a feeling she might be the same. He liked sexy, raunchy things. Dirty talk, lingerie, toys, spankings, and bondage just to name a few.

After reading some of the scenes Kaylee had dreamed up out of her imagination, he may have found his perfect match.

Her lips trembled as if she couldn't find the words or maybe was too shy to articulate them. He waited patiently knowing that there was something inside of her that needed to be set free other than in between the pages of a book.

"I want you to fuck me."

Reed wanted to do that more than he wanted to breathe, but he needed to know more.

"Tell me how you want me to fuck you. Hard? Soft? Fast? Slow? Do you want me to suck on your pretty nipples while I do it? Kiss you? Smack your ass? Tell me everything you want, baby, and I'll make sure you get it."

He held his breath, praying and hoping that this woman could find the strength and trust to set herself free.

Chapter Thirteen

The words hung on the tip of Kaylee's tongue.

She desperately wanted to express all the things she'd longed for but fear of being judged for her desires kept her silent. But Reed wasn't like any of her other lovers. Patient and cool, he simply hovered on top of her and waited, obviously not making another move until she spoke.

Shaking inside and her heart racing, she opened her mouth determined to vanquish the demons that had held her prisoner for so long. No man had ever been able to satisfy her because she'd never told anyone what she needed.

His expression was soft and encouraging, the warmth of his gaze giving her daring. This would either be the smartest thing she'd ever done or the stupidest. Closing her eyes, she mentally jumped off the cliff.

"I want you to fuck me hard and fast with your big cock. Make me come. But first I want you in my mouth. I want to run my tongue all over and suck on the head until you can't take it anymore."

Not a flicker of distaste crossed his features. He simply nodded as if she'd asked him to change the television channel.

"I like the sound of all of that, baby. Anything else you want?"

Ignoring the lump of relief in her throat, she shook her head. "That will be a good start."

If he was truly willing and open to it, there were so many fantasies she'd written about that she'd love to see come to life. This was only the first.

"You want my cock, honey? Come get it."

Kaylee sat up while Reed knelt on the mattress, his guiding hand on the back of her head. Extending her tongue, she flicked it around the head before laving the hard shaft all the way to the root then back up. Her hand wrapped around him, so thick her fingers didn't meet, and she pumped up and down while her mouth engulfed the head.

Reed's fingers tightened in her hair but only to push it out of the way so he could watch her ministrations. His hot gaze followed her every move until she'd sent him close to the edge. His jaw tight, he cursed and dragged himself away, reaching for his jeans that she'd tossed away so carelessly in her haste.

"That sweet little mouth of yours is dangerous. Just a little bit more of that tongue and you would have gotten a surprise. But now it's time to shuck those panties and get down to business. I believe you had some specific criteria as to how you wanted to be fucked and it's going to be my pleasure to deliver."

"I wouldn't have minded," Kaylee said bravely as he tore open a condom packet with his teeth and rolled it on. She'd never swallowed before but she had a feeling she'd be experiencing many firsts with Reed.

"Maybe yes, maybe no, but I don't want anything to ruin this for us. Now about those panties..."

She burst into giggles as he dove for the skimpy fabric, yanking them down her legs even as his lips were kissing the sensitive skin of her inner thighs, revving up her arousal even more. His large hands pushed her legs apart and he situated his wide shoulders in between them, a finger lazily trailing down her abdomen toward her drenched pussy.

Lifting her hips for more contact, she mewled in frustration when his strong hands pinned her legs out and wide, her cunt on brazen display. She felt a deep flush of embarrassment as Reed simply looked at her all laid out for him. Finally that finger that had been tickling her stomach and ribs dragged through her wet folds gathering the gushing cream.

"Such a pretty pink pussy, all nice and wet for me. You turned me on earlier when you put your thumb in your mouth with my cum on it. Does it do the same thing for you?"

It did. He lifted his thick digit to his lips and sucked off the honey before delving inside her pussy again and repeating, a look of satisfaction on his face. Her heart was beating loudly in her ears and she had to concentrate on her breathing so she wouldn't hyperventilate. It was hot to watch him savor her taste.

"I need more."

She half screamed when he put his hot mouth on her, licking and probing with his pointed tongue but not touching the one place she desperately needed him to. He had her pinned to the bed and she could do nothing but give herself over to the rush of pleasure and arousal. Her climax hovered just out of her reach, shining there like an oasis, but she relaxed her body and let Reed take control believing he would give her everything she craved.

He didn't disappoint her, closing his mouth over her clit and gently sucking. This time she did scream his name as her orgasm slammed into her with all the force of a freight train. Stars and fireworks burst behind her eyelids and the pleasure tumbled through her more powerful than anything she'd ever experienced. By the time she opened her eyes again her breathing was ragged and her pulse erratic.

She wanted to speak, to say something about how momentous it had been but there was no opportunity. Reed's hands were on her hips and his cock was pushing at her entrance. She splayed her legs out farther and tilted her pelvis to take him more easily as her long-unused muscles resisted his intrusion. Her fingers dug into his buttocks and she sucked in a breath even as he paused.

"Easy, honey. You can take me. Relax and let me in."

"It's been awhile," she said breathlessly, a fluttering already starting in her abdomen. "Just thrust hard."

She could feel rather than hear his chuckle against her neck. "No way. We'll get there."

They did and getting there was half the fun. Each advance drove him deeper and rubbed those little sensitive spots inside of her that she'd heard and read about but no one had ever seemed to find before. When he was in to the hilt, she groaned at the delicious feeling of fullness and the tingles that were compelling her to move underneath him.

Digging her heels into the mattress, she swayed her hips and was rewarded with a half-strangled sound that seem to be dragged from Reed's lungs. His hands clamped onto her thighs and he wrapped her legs around his waist.

"Naughty girl," he said with a chuckle. "I may have to spank you later for that."

The mere thought of Reed's hand coming down on her ass had her pussy tightening on his cock. He captured her lips in a searing kiss, their tongues battling for supremacy.

"I can feel how much you like the idea of my heating up your bottom. We'll have to try that. Now I believe you wanted to be fucked hard and fast. Let's get that done because your hot cunt feels too amazing to hold back anymore."

Words couldn't express how good it felt to please him. Luckily there was no time for talking as he pulled out almost all the way before slamming back into her hard and fast. He rode her in the rough way she'd always dreamed of but at the same time she knew he was aware of his own strength. He held his weight on his elbows as his fingers plucked at her nipples.

Their bodies were burnished with sweat and Kaylee teetered close to the edge of the precipice. The room tilted and whirled and she clung to Reed as if he were an anchor in a dangerous storm.

"Come for me, honey. Come with me."

Reed's deep voice was rough in her ear but it pushed her over as he thrust one last time, his eyes closed in ecstasy. Her own orgasm ripped through her but she kept her gaze on Reed as he found his own completion. His cock seemed to swell inside of her and she watched as the mask he wore each and every day was torn from his features. For a brief moment, he looked vulnerable and young and she cherished the fact that she'd been able to see it, that she'd brought him to that state if for only seconds. She deliberately didn't wonder whether other women had seen it. Right now he was hers alone.

Kaylee dragged oxygen into her starved lungs as they both returned to earth. Her fingers glided down his muscled back, loving the feeling of his hot skin so different from her own. She mewled in protest when he pulled away from her arms but he simply chuckled and kissed her briefly on the lips.

"I'll be right back. Don't go anywhere."

As if she could move. If she tried to stand she was sure she'd find her legs had turned to jelly and besides, there wasn't anywhere she wanted to be other than right here, right now. Reed was a fantasy come true.

He padded back from the bathroom and pulled the covers up on the bed so they could slide in together. She pillowed her head on his shoulder, not saying anything, just enjoying the closeness. His fingers were caressing her arm and playing with a few stray strands of hair and she placed her hand on his chest so she could feel the steady beat of his heart.

"That was pretty fantastic."

For a writer, that was a lame attempt to describe what had happened between them. At the moment she didn't have the words to express how good it was and how he had made her feel.

"I don't have any complaints. Did my penchant for dirty talk bother you?"

He looked slightly abashed but she placed her hand on his jaw and shook her head. "Not in the least. I thought it was hot, to be honest. What else do you like?"

It was a bold question but he was a man straight from the pages of one of her books. Was he like the men in her stories in more way than just looks?

"If you must know, I like a lot of the things you've written about or at least what I've read. You know, spankings and bondage. Toys. I think the scenes you write are very sensual and erotic. Do you try everything before you write it?"

The question was so absurd she couldn't control the laughter that bubbled through her. "Hardly. It's always funny to me that people think that I've done everything I've written about. No one thinks thriller writers have killed someone or stolen government secrets."

"So they're not your fantasies?"

He actually sounded a little disappointed.

"Some of them are. Some of them are my characters' fantasies. But yes, I think most of them are pretty damn hot." Kaylee stared down at the comforter. "I wouldn't mind living out some of them, if that's where your mind was heading."

Reed tugged on her hair so she was gazing up at him. A grin a mile wide, he looked like a sinful little boy. "That's exactly where I was going. Pick out some fantasies and let's get to work on them."

Old habits die hard. Despite the freedom she felt with Reed and the trust she had, the fear of being judged was strong.

"You won't think I'm a...freak?" she asked carefully, watching his expression for any distaste or aversion.

Reed's arms tightened around her and he dropped a kiss on her nose. "If you're a freak then I'm one too. A big one. Let's be freaky together."

Other than terminal embarrassment, she couldn't think of one reason to say no. And she'd never actually heard of anyone dying from awkwardness.

"I could get some of my books and show you a few of my favorite scenes," she offered, still unsure whether his enthusiasm was genuine. She shouldn't have worried because his smile grew even wider.

"Grab those books, honey, and let's get reading."

Even reading with Reed was fun. Was there no end to his perfection?

Chapter Fourteen

Reed was about to poke his own eye out due to boredom. He was currently sitting at a table with two women, both of whom he'd met in this bar and had cornered him to the point that they'd invited themselves to sit with him. They were both decent-looking but had an annoying habit of yammering on and on about themselves, rarely taking a breath. It appeared they were competing with each other to be the woman he took home tonight.

The door to the dark bar opened and a luscious curvy woman with long auburn hair walked into the bar and paused briefly to take a look around. Dressed in a cream-colored knitted dress that hugged the generous contours of her body and a pair of brown suede boots, she was the only thing Reed could see in the entire bar. Even the constant chatter from the two women couldn't pull at his attention when such a perfect specimen was before his eyes. He also knew how smart and funny she was too.

The woman was Kaylee.

And this little scene was one of her very own from a book she'd written a few years ago. Reed was planning on enjoying every minute of this. Since their relationship had taken an intimate turn yesterday, they'd played at several different fantasies but this was the first they'd taken out of the house and into public.

Kaylee's shoulders went back and she marched up to his table, determination in every line of her body.

"My friends made a bet with me that I couldn't get the best-looking man here to kiss me," she declared loudly enough for the people close by to hear. Despite knowing that he was a sure thing, Kaylee appeared to be nervous. Her lips were trembling and her hand fluttered uselessly until it rested at the base of her throat.

Reed grinned as the women sitting on either side of him stiffened in shock. "What do you get if you lose the bet?"

"Mortified, first off. Then I have to let them fix me up on some blind dates. That means more mortification."

"And if you win?" he asked lazily, taking a long draw from his bottle of beer. He was trying to give the impression that he wasn't eager to kiss her and was simply thinking about the possibility.

"I get a kiss from you and they lay off my love life. What do you say?" she asked boldly. "I just popped a breath mint."

"What do I win if I help you with this bet? What's in it for me? And don't say a kiss, honey, because I'm a grown man. A kiss isn't the biggest attraction for me these days."

"What do you want?" Kaylee's tone was playful and cheeky and damn if Reed couldn't wait to do all the things the characters in her book had done. Naughty sexy stuff that had his cock already hard but luckily covered by the table.

The women were watching the back and forth between himself and Kaylee as if it were a tennis match. The ball was firmly in his court.

"You," he stated bluntly. "In my bed. Doing anything I want. That's the deal. No negotiations, just a simple yes or no."

The two women sucked in their breath and swung their gaze back to Kaylee who was looking at him with a smug smile.

"Deal. Now do I get that kiss?"

"Yes, ma'am."

He stood from the chair and walked around to where she stood at the front of the table. Not wasting any time he pulled her into his arms, his hand snaking into her thick hair and anchoring her head exactly where he wanted it. He bent his head and captured her lips in a passionate kiss, bending her backward over his arm.

He couldn't be sure but it appeared the two women were swooning by the time he lifted his head. Even his pretty Kaylee had pink cheeks and swollen lips. Yes, he was going to make good use of that mouth the minute he got her home.

Letting her stand on her own two feet, he reluctantly let her loose, unwilling to go any further with an audience. Roleplaying was fun but he was in the mood for something far more primitive and base.

"You get what you wanted?" he asked.

"Yes," she nodded. "Now it's your turn. Where do you want me do this?"

A quick glance in the direction of their onlookers and the women's eyes were as round as saucers. "We can go back to my place but we have to go now."

"Just let me tell my friends. Should we exchange names?"

Reed smirked as he put his hand under her elbow and led her to the door. "No, it's hotter if we don't."

He could hear a few patrons choking on their beverages as he led her outside. When they were standing by his truck he pulled her in for a long hot kiss.

"That definitely got my motor running, honey," he said when he lifted his head. "Let's get you home and naked."

"But don't tell me your name. It's hotter that way," Kaylee giggled as he helped her into the truck. This woman had redefined hot and sexy and he couldn't wait for more.

Kaylee was sitting on the back patio typing away at her laptop when Reed stuck his head around the doorway.

"Miss Blue, will you step into my office, please?"

Her heart leapt in her chest as she gathered up her notepad and pen and followed him to her office. She tugged at the tight skirt she was wearing as it slid up her thighs when she sat down, showing a generous amount of leg in addition to the stockings she was wearing underneath.

"We need to talk about your job performance, Miss Blue. I'm sorry to say it has been less than desirable lately. What do you have to say for yourself?"

She loved the stern tone of his voice and it sent shivers through her body and cream leaking from her pussy. His expression matched his tone as well, hard and unyielding. He'd missed his calling. He should have been an actor.

"I'm very sorry, Mr. Mitchell that you're unhappy with my work. I'm trying very hard to please you."

She used her best innocent, breathless voice. She was playing the role of a dedicated secretary who had very good reasons for her work being sub-standard, one of them that her roommate had turned up dead. However, Kaylee was already planning for this conversation to go in another purely physical fun and games direction.

"You've been late three days this week, in addition to several errors in your work. If you don't want this job I'm sure there are people who would be grateful for it."

"I had a really good reason for that," she explained but a wave of his hand cut her off.

"I am not interested in excuses, only results. What do you think I should do? Do you think you should be fired?"

"No, I think you should punish me."

Shock and desire had lit up his eyes briefly at her statement but he covered it and moved along smoothly despite the fact that she'd changed the scene. He seemed to consider her words, weighing their authenticity.

"If you were me, how would I punish you?"

"I think a good hard spanking would teach me a lesson, Mr. Mitchell."

Reed stroked his chin, his hand trying to hide his obvious grin. "I think you are correct, Miss Blue. Once disciplined, you'll think twice about showing up late in the future. Take off your skirt and shirt and drape yourself across my lap."

The real scene in the book hadn't gone in this direction but Kaylee was feeling adventurous today. They'd already played a few scenes out but they always seemed to end up the same way—with a nice vigorous fucking.

Kaylee slid the zipper down on her skirt and let it fall into a pool around her ankles before plucking open the buttons down the front of her silk blouse and at the cuffs. It too joined her skirt and she stood before him in an outfit she'd purchased long ago but had never worn. She'd ordered it to be able to see how stockings worked for a scene but now she was actually going to experience it.

His heated gaze took in the sight of her near naked body and she wanted to shield herself with her hands. Instead she forced herself to stand there so he could look his fill. In the lacy black bra and thong paired with fishnet stockings, she looked every inch the wanton.

"Is this what you wear to the office, Miss Blue? I see this spanking is long overdue."

Kaylee had to bite her lip to keep from laughing even as she arranged herself over his muscular thighs. When he placed his large hand on her bare posterior suddenly things weren't funny in the least. He was going to actually spank her bottom and the thought both filled her with excitement and trepidation.

He ran his finger under the string of her thong and into the folds of her pussy. "Wet. Even your thighs are shiny with honey. I think you want this very much. Were you late on purpose? I wouldn't put it past you."

She didn't answer his question because he never gave her the chance. His palm came down on her ass hard, the impact making her jump in surprise and pain. He did the same three more times and she was just about to call a halt when the heat from her bottom traveled to her pussy and clit. She'd written about this phenomenon but had never experienced it herself. Damned if it wasn't true.

She needed more.

Wriggling her ass, she braced herself more firmly on her palms as his hand came down again and again. Sometimes softly, almost teasing, and sometimes sharply enough to make her suck in a breath and flinch. Her ass cheeks had taken on a heated glow and she rubbed her clit against the rough denim of his jeans in an attempt to push herself over.

Reed chuckled, clearly amused by her predicament and lifted her off his lap, bending her over the desk. She heard the sound of his zipper and the crinkle of plastic and she shifted on her feet impatiently, needing what he was about to give.

His hand caressed her backside and his fingers curled around the fabric of her soaked thong. "This is in my way, Miss Blue. New rule in the office. No more panties."

The sound of ripping material took her breath away and Reed dropped the scraps of her undies on the floor. Gripping her hips, he thrust in hard with no preliminaries. She cried out at the sensation of being completely filled by him as her fingers gripped the edge of the desk. He was already fucking her fast and rough, giving it to her just as she had asked him for when they'd discussed this particular fantasy. Of course she hadn't told him about the spanking part but he'd already said that he enjoyed doing it.

"Yes, yes," she chanted in rhythm to his cock pounding in and out of her pussy. Arousal curled tightly in her belly, building with each stroke. She rested her head on the cool wood of her desk and closed her eyes, letting everything drift away but where their two bodies were joined. She gave herself permission to simply feel, switching off her mind and letting each stroke send her closer and closer to release.

His warm breath was right next to her ear. "Now, baby."

His rough fingers reached under her and gave her clit just the contact it needed. She screamed his name as she climaxed, white starbursts exploding behind her eyes. Wave after wave shook her world while her pussy tightened as Reed's own orgasm roared through him. He groaned deeply, his hands flexing on her hips. When it was over he covered her body protectively with his to keep the chill away until he lifted her into his arms and headed for the bathroom shower.

"Another fantasy off the list, Miss Blue." His voice was teasing and he was wearing a satisfied grin. "I can't wait to see what's next."

Kaylee wrapped her arms around his neck with a sigh. "Only about a hundred or so to go. Maybe we should pace ourselves."

Reed set her down on the cold tile of the bathroom. "A plan is always good. But right now we need a shower and some food. Then we'll regroup and pick something else on the list."

She simply couldn't decide which one to do next.

"Reed? Have you ever had sex in the shower?"

Chapter Fifteen

"Tell me again why we have to go to this party?" Reed asked patiently as they exited his truck and walked up the sidewalk to Linda's home. It was a crisp autumn evening and Kaylee pulled her wool cape more tightly around her shoulders. The street was lined with cars and they had been forced to park quite far away.

"Because Linda is my friend, first of all. Second, it's kind of a fun theme for Halloween, don't you think? She writes mysteries so she's having a murder mystery party. I think it's cute. She's gone all out for this even having the theater group she works with act out the parts. Where's your sense of adventure?" Kaylee teased. "Are you afraid I'll solve the mystery before you?"

"Halloween isn't until tomorrow," Reed reminded her. "And I can think of a few fun things for us to do instead of being here with a bunch of people."

Kaylee slid her arm around Reed's waist and pressed her head to his chest in a hug. "We can do both, I promise. Be good guests for Linda, and then go home and do things that will end up on the pages of one of my books."

In the last week they'd made good progress on the list of fantasies. It had been some comfort as the investigation into her stalker was going nowhere fast. The police had told them there were no fingerprints on the letters or envelopes but they'd sent DNA from the adhesive to the lab, but that could take weeks for results. As for cross-referencing Kaylee's friends and their vehicle types, it turned out about half the people she knew drove four-door sedans so that hadn't been much help. Brent was still a suspect in Reed's eyes but nothing had happened since the brick through the window. It made her wonder if Reed's mere presence had scared the person away.

"I still don't know how to feel about that. I've never been a character in a book before."

What Reed didn't understand is that men like him were being written about every day by authors in her genre. He was every hero she'd ever had all wrapped up in one delectable package.

"You'd make a great hero," Kaylee sighed. "So perfect."

Reed stopped abruptly and turned so he was looking down at her. "Don't say that. Don't even think it. I'm not perfect. Not even close."

A few times this week she'd thought he was about to say something about his past, but then…nothing. But the more time she spent with him the more she could see that something painful had happened and it affected him to this day. They would be having fun together—reading, cooking, watching movies—and it was as if he suddenly remembered he wasn't supposed to be happy. His expression would cloud over until she said something but he never revealed anything. If he would only talk about it Kaylee was sure he'd feel better.

"You can tell me about it. I won't tell anyone else if that's what you're worried about. I just want to take away the burden you're carrying around. You deserve to be happy, Reed."

His lips curled and there was a coldness in his eyes that matched the wintery weather. "Drop it, Kaylee. Just don't put me on any pedestal. I sure as hell don't want to be there."

She nodded, not trusting her voice. It was becoming more difficult as each day passed to pretend that she wasn't getting emotionally involved. Reed was the man she'd dreamed about but never hoped to find. Honest, hard-working, protective to a fault, he was the epitome of the alpha male. He was also gentle, cerebral, with a goofy sense of humor that never failed to make her smile and laugh. He was a good man, full stop. How was she supposed to hold out against an assault like that? She was exhausted from trying.

They walked the rest of the way in silence and Reed pressed the doorbell of the large Victorian house. Linda had recently completed renovations on the home and the outside looked freshly painted in light blue with white trim. The heavy wooden door swung open and Linda was standing there with a welcoming smile. She'd gone all out for the party and was wearing a scarlet cocktail dress and heels. It was a far cry from her usual sweater sets and slacks.

"Come in. Come in. Make yourself at home. We're almost ready to start."

"You look amazing," Kaylee said. "I feel underdressed."

Kaylee had dressed more for comfort and warmth although she'd left her usual jeans at home. Tonight she'd chosen an antique blue jersey dress that went down to her ankles paired with boots.

The party looked to be in full swing as they stepped in and Linda stowed their coats in a room off to the side. There were probably about thirty people total standing and chatting in the living and dining areas. A long table that would easily seat ten or twelve was the centerpiece of the evening. Decorated with jack-o-lanterns and orange and black tulle ribbon, it was weighed down with food for every taste including some delicious-looking desserts.

"Thank you. I love dressing up. Let's get you something to drink. I know Kaylee wants wine, but how about you, Reed?"

"Beer," he responded as Linda fluttered back to the kitchen, smiling gaily the entire way. She looked to be excited about having her mystery acted out this evening.

"I didn't know you drank wine." Reed's gaze scanned the room as usual. Used to his overprotective nature now, Kaylee didn't automatically freak when he checked every place they walked into for threats. When she'd asked him about it he said it was the cop in him.

"I don't very often," she sighed. "I don't know why Linda thinks I do. Maybe she's mixed me up with someone else. I'll thank her nicely and then go get a soda or something."

Reed's eyebrow lifted. "Not a Cosmo? How disappointing."

"I don't need the false courage now. I have you wrapped around my little finger and begging for more."

If only that were the case but she could still dream.

"I don't know if I'd use the word 'begging'," Reed laughed and placed his arm around her shoulders. "But I will say I'm enthusiastic."

They both were. After that first night together she'd barely been able to walk the next day. Not that she was complaining.

"Here you go," Linda sang with a bright smile. "One beer and one red wine. Enjoy! Now Kaylee, remember not to leave without getting a copy of my new book. I signed it just for you. Excuse me while I talk to the actors. It's almost time."

She was gone in a flurry and that gave Kaylee a chance to study the room of partiers. As a writer, people-watching was one of her favorite things to do and tonight was no exception.

"Brent's here," Reed intoned. "Is the entire writing group attending?"

"They're all invited but I don't know if they're all coming." Kaylee raised the glass but wrinkled her nose at the dark ruby contents. "If it was white I could have sipped at it. Red gives me a headache."

"It's the sulfites. Let's get you something else."

Reed preceded her to the kitchen and she placed her glass on the counter while he fixed her a soda from the vast choices on the table. There were several varieties of soda, wine, and even flavored water and tea.

"Here you go. Root beer."

Kaylee took a drink and smiled. "Thank you. You take good care of me."

"I aim to please."

He did that in spades.

Walt strolled into the kitchen and nodded to Reed while he gave her a hug. "Kaylee, it's good to see you. I wasn't sure if you were coming tonight."

"I wasn't sure you were coming either. Have you ever been to a party like this before?"

Walt's gaze was roaming the room but he nodded absently, his attention resting on her discarded glass. "Linda has these parties about once a year although this is the first Halloween themed. Is this your drink?"

"Yes and no. Linda poured me a glass of wine but I don't really drink red. I was just wondering what I should do with it. I hate to see it wasted."

Walt's eyes lit up. "No sense letting a perfectly good red go to waste. I'll take it off your hands."

Kaylee had noticed that Walt was fond of both grain and grape but she couldn't think of one good reason he shouldn't have the wine. He was a grown man after all and no one would be getting behind the wheel for hours.

"Of course, please take it. I swear I didn't drink out of the glass or anything."

He took it from her hands and studied the delicate crystal. "I knew that already. You're wearing a very distinctive red lip gloss and there's none on the rim." He raised the glass in salute, took a sip and grimaced, then dumped the contents into the sink. "Disgustingly sweet. If you'll excuse me, I need to talk to Brent."

"Don't tell me...he writes mysteries," Reed said as Walt pulled Brent onto the patio for what looked like a serious discussion. "And from what I've seen, very little alcohol is wasted around your friend Walt."

"He does write mysteries, and yes, he does drink but he never seems to get falling down drunk so I guess he can handle it." Kaylee rolled her eyes. "Unlike me. One drink and I'm under the table."

Reed tapped her on the nose and gave her his best smile complete with dimples. "I'm very fond of you tipsy. I have good memories of that first evening."

She shuddered and placed her hands over her face. "I have humiliating ones, thank you very much."

He tugged her hands away and made her look up at him. "I wanted you that night so—"

Whatever Reed had been about to say was drowned out by shouting in the living room. They both hurried to see what was going on and came to a halt near the fireplace and about five feet from the two men who were yelling at one another. One shoved the other in the shoulder and then that man shoved him right back. Reed moved to separate them but she caught his arm.

"I think this is the floorshow," she whispered. "Look at Linda's face. She's smiling."

Linda was indeed beaming as she stood next to Cheryl and Brent. It looked like Cheryl had also brought her latest boyfriend as well, her arm hooked cozily through his. An older gentleman, he appeared to be enjoying the show while Brent looked uncomfortable watching the two men skirmish with their booming voices and dramatic acting. Their argument had managed to silence the crowd of partiers and the actors clearly relished being the center of attention as they argued about one owing the other money.

"It's a mystery party, right?" Reed's voice was low so no one else would hear. "One of these guys is going down."

A third character, this time a female, intervened and the two men went their separate ways into the crowd while two more actresses sauntered into the middle of the room talking about the men.

"This must be the clues part," Kaylee said although her mind was honestly elsewhere. It was the first time she'd been in a room with all her friends since Reed had investigated them. It was strange to know all the personal details of someone's life. Details her friends thought were safely tucked away where no one would find them.

Just because they had a skeleton or two in their closet didn't make them a stalker. But it didn't make them innocent either. Was one of her friends really trying to scare her? And if so, which one and why?

Chapter Sixteen

The party seemed to drag on forever. More actors joined the two actresses and a few of them spoke in scathing terms about the original two men. Reed hooked his arm through hers and pulled her off to the side as the "play" continued to add conflicts and motive between the characters. It wasn't a surprise when one of the two original men staggered into the room holding his chest where a large crimson stain was blooming on his white shirt.

The dying man made quite a show of fading away, enough to earn some titters from the audience as he sank to the floor in a climactic heap. One of the actors approached the "dead" man and pulled his jacket away from his body.

"Shot," he pronounced. "Looks like a twenty-two caliber through and through."

"He can tell just from looking at the body?" Reed asked cynically. "If he can do that I ought to hire him. He didn't even take off the guy's shirt to see the bullet hole in the back."

"Shhhhhh," Kaylee warned. "It's just for fun."

"Not for the guy who was shot. Now he has to lie there all night while the rest of us find his killer."

Reed made a good point. The poor man's job was to lie there motionless while the party went on around him. What if he had to use the bathroom?

The actors were busy pointing fingers at each other and dropping clues. Kaylee was only half listening when a tap on her shoulder caught her attention.

"I thought that was you." Cheryl gave Kaylee a hug and Reed a thorough perusal despite having her own date. Reed did look handsome as hell in dark blue denims, an oatmeal-colored sweater with a white collared shirt underneath, and his favorite cowboy boots. She'd convinced him to leave the cowboy hat at home although secretly she thought he looked pretty hot in it. "Have you figured out who it is yet?"

"Not yet." Kaylee shook her head, noticing that Cheryl's date was now deep in conversation with Brent. "Honestly I haven't been paying enough attention. There are too many suspects to keep straight."

"It is easier when you only have one or two." Cheryl's attention swiveled back to Reed, her finger rubbing the rim of her glass in a seductive manner. "How are you enjoying our little city? Are you thinking you might stay?"

"Your little city is actually much larger than where I'm from. We have less than ten thousand in my town."

Reed hadn't answered her question about staying which wasn't a surprise. Cheryl, on the other hand, wasn't about to give up.

"There's so much to love about this area. Great sports teams, good restaurants, and a well educated and diverse population. Doesn't that tempt you?"

Kaylee could feel the tension radiating off of Reed. He hated to be questioned but any onlooker wouldn't be able to tell. His expression was perfectly bland. "Montana is home."

A simple statement that said so much and Cheryl seemed to get the message, turning her attention back to Kaylee.

"How did release day go on Tuesday? I bought your book of course. You must be making bank on this one."

Kaylee hated talking about sales and numbers. She loved talking books but the business side was better left to herself. She was a Midwestern girl, born and raised. Her mother and grandmother had told her that talking money was bad manners, and bragging about yourself was even worse.

"It went well. I was happy with the launch."

Brent and Walt walked up and joined them, the latter looking red in the face. Cheryl's date had moved on to chatting with other guests.

"I was just asking Kaylee about her book release. Have you seen its rankings?"

Both men nodded vigorously and Walt downed the last of his wine. White this time.

"It was in the top one hundred, wasn't it?" Brent asked. "How many a day is that?"

"Do you think you'll make New York Times?" Walt asked, scanning the room for something, perhaps another drink. "I want to do that someday. Just once so I can say I did."

"Do you think you will?" Cheryl persisted. None of them had let her get a word in edgewise, their questions coming one after the other in rapid succession. It didn't matter though as Kaylee didn't have any plans to answer their questions. As a rule she didn't ponder making bestseller lists as that was something she couldn't predict or control. The only thing she could concentrate on was to write the very best book she possibly could and hope for the best.

"I'm very pleased with the book launch. So far the reviews are positive," she replied, the words deliberately neutral. "But it's back to the grindstone. You're only as good as your last release."

"You're such a workaholic," Cheryl laughed. "If my books sold the way yours do, I would take a month off and visit Fiji or cruise around the world."

The secret was it didn't feel like work to Kaylee. Even when she planned to take vacations she couldn't seem to stop writing. She and Reed had that in common—they loved their work.

"Who's taking a cruise?" Linda popped her head into the conversation. "I've always wanted to do that."

"Linda," Reed interrupted, his voice deep enough to capture everyone's attention. "I can tell you've done major renovations to your home and I'm very impressed. Would you mind showing me around?"

It was the perfect thing to ask as Linda was a proud home-owner and she and her husband had done quite a bit of the work themselves. And it served the double purpose of stopping the sales talk cold.

Thank you, Reed.

Their hostess was delighted to show them all the little touch-es they'd added in the home including cedar closets and bamboo flooring. By the time they returned to the main party, the actors were accusing one another of being the murderer. Again. It was becoming rather tiresome and it looked like many of the guests shared the opinion. Most were simply ignoring the play being performed in their midst.

"I'll be right back," Kaylee told Reed and headed for the nearest bathroom, leaving him to the tender mercies of Cheryl, Brent, and Walt.

A true introvert, Kaylee was exhausted from being in a room full of people, even people she adored. She needed a few moments to herself to catch her breath. Locking the door behind her, she touched up her lipstick and ran a comb through her unruly hair.

Pulling open the door, she was surprised to see Brent waiting on the other side. Assuming he wanted the bathroom, she smiled and tried to side-step him but he held out his arm so she couldn't pass.

"Can we talk for a minute?"

"Um, sure." Kaylee stepped into the hallway as another guest needed the restroom. "What do you want to talk about?"

Brent shifted on his feet, his eyes looking down to the floor. "That guy you're with…Reed? Are you serious about him?"

It was a good question but far too personal for them to be talking about. Brent was a good friend but he wasn't a close friend like Ava. She wasn't going to discuss this with him.

"That's really none of your business," she said firmly. "Is that all you wanted to talk about? If so, we should go downstairs."

"Wait." Brent's hand, surprisingly strong, grasped her arm and kept her from leaving. She winced at his tight grip. "Listen, that guy is no good for you. I can tell."

She stared down at where he held her and then looked up into his eyes. "Let me go."

"He's—"

"Let me go." This time she said it louder and there was no doubt she meant it. Her heart was beating fast in her chest and for the first time she wondered if Brent might actually be someone who wanted to see her harmed. He'd never been this intense before.

"Dammit, Kaylee—"

Another hand dropped onto Brent's arm and she looked up in relief to see Reed. Brent's grip loosened and then fell away and Reed stepped in front of Kaylee, an impenetrable wall of man and muscle.

"When a lady asks you to unhand her, you should do exactly that."

If Kaylee had been Brent she would have been shaking in her shoes. She could feel the tightly coiled tension in his body as if he were only waiting for Brent to give him a reason.

"I just wanted to talk to her." Brent's tone was defensive and almost child-like as if he'd been denied dessert.

"Fine. You can talk to me and I'll pass on a message."

Kaylee couldn't see Brent from her vantage point but she could hear him snort and then stomp down the stairs out of the corner of her eye.

"That guy has a real attitude problem." Reed turned so she wasn't looking at his broad back anymore. "What do you think of your friend now? Not so harmless, is he?"

"Not so harmless," she conceded. "It doesn't prove anything though."

"It doesn't disprove anything either. Did he tell you what he wanted?"

Kaylee rubbed her aching arm. "He wanted to talk about you. He thinks you're no good for me."

"I've never presented myself as anything different but he's not any better." Reed's expression was cold and remote. "If he fucking hurt you…"

"I'm fine," she assured him. "Can we go home? I don't think I really care anymore who shot that guy."

"I was ready to go the minute we got here. Let me get the car and I'll pick you up in front of the house."

"I'm perfectly capable of walking. You worry too much."

"It's fucking cold outside. Can't you just do as you're told once in your life? Do you always have to be so damn independent?" The words had come out as a snarl and Kaylee's indrawn breath must have tipped Reed off that he'd stepped over a line. "Sorry. I just don't like it when men manhandle a woman. In my town I wouldn't need to kick anyone's ass because there would be a bunch of good ol' boy cowboys who would do it before I even got there."

Poor Reed. He didn't like caring about anything and here he was…caring about what happened to her. He was trying to play it off as business, but as pissed off as he was she guessed there was a little something personal there as well. It made her feel a little better about things. She was getting to him too. Not as much as he'd gotten to her, but she'd shaken his world.

"We don't kick a lot of asses around here," she replied, keeping her tone calm and even. "But thank you, I appreciate your thoughtfulness."

They descended the stairs and sought out Linda who didn't seem all that upset that Kaylee had a nasty headache. Apparently Brent had stomped out of the house moments ago with the excuse of having to get up early and work the next day.

"I'm just sorry you aren't here to see the killer unmasked," Linda said, clasping her hands with glee. "It's the best part of the evening."

"I'm almost positive the murderer is the dead man's secretary," Reed answered, his attention already on the front door.

Linda's mouth went slack and her eyes widened. "That's right. How did you know?"

"While everyone had opportunity, only one character had one of three major motives—money, love, or power. The secretary. But really I just followed my gut."

Reed had to be an excellent policeman from the look of things. Kaylee hadn't a clue who did it from what she'd seen acted out.

They retrieved their coats and Reed leaned down for a too quick kiss.

"Will you please wait inside? I'll circle the block and bring the car around."

"The fresh air will do me good. I'll walk with you." He started to protest but she laid her hand on his arm in a soothing manner. "It's not far and I want to go home. If I stay here any longer someone is going to try and entangle me in a conversation that I can't get away from. Okay?"

His lips twisted and she knew that she'd won. "Fine, but I don't like it."

"So noted. Let's get out of here."

They walked down the driveway and across the street, the neighborhood quiet and deserted now that darkness had descended. Reed's arm was wrapped around her protectively trying to fend off the whipping wind that was making a mockery of the barrette that held her thick hair back.

They were almost to the car when the clip flew from her hair, then landed and skittered on the road. Muttering a few four-letter words, she turned from the warmth of Reed's body and instinctively scrambled to retrieve it, but the inky blackness of the night wasn't cooperating.

"Kaylee, forget about it. You'll never find–"

It came out of nowhere.

The brighter than usual headlights blinded her for a moment as she knelt in the middle of the street. The engine roared as the driver accelerated, tires squealing loudly in her ears. Like a deer she froze, too terrified to move out of the way. Her heart stopped beating and time seemed to slow down as the car barreled toward her relentlessly, inevitably. She put up her hands to cover her eyes but something solid and unyielding hit her from the side instead and she sailed through the air before landing on something hard as the car flew by, her fall broken by Reed's own body.

She shook her head, trying to make some sense of what had happened. "Are you okay?"

Reed was rubbing the back of his head and groaning as he sat up but he appeared to have no major injuries. "I'm going to be bruised like a son of a gun but other than that I'm fine. What about you?"

Her heart was beating again although at a much faster clip than normal. She had to suck in air to her aching lungs as she may have also forgot to breathe when that vehicle had been bearing down on her.

"I'm good. Thanks to you. I froze." She pressed a shaking hand against her forehead. "I didn't know whether I should move right or left and in the end my legs weren't listening anyway."

She sat up and swept Reed's hair away from a cut above his eye. "You might need some stitches."

He brushed her hand away and stood with a groan. She tried to grab his arm so he would stay put, but he easily shook her off so he could look up and down the street.

"The bastard got away," he growled. "Son of a fucking bitch."

Reaching down, he easily lifted her to her feet but he held her until she was steady enough on her legs not to crumple in a heap on the pavement. The reality of what had just happened was becoming more real with each passing moment.

Someone had tried to run her down.

She couldn't seem to stop shaking. She had to lock her knees in place and wrap her arms around her torso to comfort herself.

"Maybe it was an accident?" Her tone was hopeful but his expression was anything but. His grim features told the story, truth and all.

"He was accelerating, not hitting his brakes. He also had his brights on so we would have trouble seeing."

Leaning against the mailbox, Kaylee tried to calm her breathing and heart rate but fear had crawled inside of her and wasn't going to surrender easily.

"Now he wants me dead? Who would do this to me?"

She didn't even want to say the word. Scaring her was one thing, killing her was something else entirely. Reed pulled her into his arms so she could lay her head on his chest, his hand smoothing her hair.

"I don't know for sure honey, but Brent left right before us. I think it's time someone had a chat with him."

Chapter Seventeen

Reed wanted to punch something, maybe put a hole in the wall or door. And then do it again and again. Anything to take his attention away from the pain in his heart.

He *cared* about Kaylee.

What a clusterfuck. This wasn't simply business, this was damn personal. If anything happened to her the perpetrator was going to wish he'd never been born. Reed had let one woman down in his past but he sure as hell wasn't going to let Kaylee down. He'd protect her with his life.

"Why don't you soak in the tub and relax a little," he offered, needing some space to deal with the events of the evening. Still filled with the horror of watching that car speeding toward her, he couldn't seem to turn off the images that kept playing over and over in front of his eyes.

"Will you join me?" Not surprisingly, she'd been clingy since he'd knocked her out of the path of the vehicle. She'd also stayed by his side when they'd talked to the police in Linda's kitchen. She'd come to depend on him which was another thing that was all fucked up. He needed to find this asshole and then get the hell out of here. Things could only get worse between him and Kaylee. If he cared, then dammit, she probably did too. He sure as shit didn't want to hurt anyone but nothing about his life was going to change. Not even for her.

Of course talking to the police in Linda's home meant that the secret was out about Kaylee's stalker. Guests had come streaming out of the front door when the red and blue lights of the police cruiser pulled up in front. Linda had insisted they come back inside where a woman who said she was a nurse had cleaned up his cut and applied a few butterfly bandages. She'd warned him it was going to scar but he didn't give a shit about it. The fact that Kaylee was alive was the only important thing.

"In a few. Go on upstairs."

She walked up the stairs reluctantly, clearly not happy but he needed to get his head on straight. If he went up there right now, he'd say or do something stupid that would only serve to make the situation worse.

Pulling his cell from his pocket, he pushed a few buttons and then stepped out on the back patio to make his call in private. The cold air was biting but it helped to focus his mind on something other than Kaylee trapped in the headlights of an oncoming vehicle.

"Tanner Marks."

"Hey, it's Reed. You got a minute?"

Sheriff Tanner Marks was the most senior of all the lawmen that Reed met with on a monthly basis. Not old enough to be a father figure but he had a few more years under his belt plus some adversity that had toughened him up. When anyone had a serious problem, they usually ended up talking it over with Tanner.

"Sure. I'm on duty but it's a quiet night. What's up?"

Tanner knew nobody would be calling him this late just to chat but nothing in his voice gave him away.

"A couple of things really. First, I'm going to have to call Logan tomorrow morning and tell him that there was an attempt on Kaylee's life tonight."

Reed assumed Tanner knew all about Kaylee and her stalker as the men gossiped worse than the women sometimes. Besides, Tanner was Logan's best friend so it was certain he had discussed Kaylee's problem.

"Is she okay?" Tanner asked sharply. "Are you injured?"

"Other than a cut on my head and some nasty bruises, I'm fine. Kaylee's okay too. A car tried to run her down tonight but I pushed her out of the way."

Tanner whistled at the news. "More escalation. Logan told me you were in Illinois dealing with a stalker. Did you catch him?"

"No, he was gone before we scraped ourselves off the pavement. No cameras as it's a residential neighborhood. But I did get a decent look at the car. A late model four-door sedan, dark color just like what was seen speeding on Kaylee's street after the brick landed in her house. Asshole had on his brights so I couldn't get a look at the front license plate."

"I can tell Logan for you if you like," Tanner offered. "But I hope he keeps this from Ava. Her blood pressure is already in dangerous territory from what I've heard. They're threatening to put her in the hospital."

"I'm sorry to hear that she's not any better but that's not what I'm calling about, actually. I'll call Logan tomorrow and tell him myself."

Reed could practically hear the wheels turning in Tanner's head. "I'm listening."

"It's about a woman."

"It always is but you've never been one to care. What's different now?"

"She's different." Reed was beginning to wish he'd never made this call. He didn't want to hear what Tanner was going to tell him but it was too damn late now. "She makes me…happy."

"Well, damn her all to hell," his friend chuckled. "How dare she?"

"Fuck you, asshole. I don't like this at all. I don't want to care about what happens to her. I don't want this to be personal."

"Then leave. Pack your shit and hit the road. I'm sure the police can protect her or she could hire security. This isn't on you. It's not your problem."

The thought of leaving was more nightmarish than staying but only by a small margin.

"Logan and Ava made it my problem," Reed argued. "They asked me for a favor."

"Logan is desperate to keep Ava happy and calm so they won't put her in a hospital sixty miles from Corville. He'd promise her puppies on every holiday from here to eternity if it meant keeping her safe. As long as Kaylee is protected does it really matter who is keeping her that way? If Jared had been on vacation instead of you, he'd be in the hot seat right now."

For some reason, the idea of Kaylee and Jared spending time together pissed Reed off.

"You're doing that reverse psychology Jedi mind-shit, aren't you? We both know I can't leave."

"We both know you don't want to," Tanner retorted. "I know you and you can't delegate a damn thing so how are you going to let someone else protect a woman you care about? And yes, I used the c-word. You care. Get over it. It had to happen eventually. Personally I was hoping you'd work up to it. Maybe start with a plant and then get a goldfish but I guess a woman is good too."

If Tanner only knew that Reed had once cared very much. More than cared. And he'd failed miserably at it.

"You're not helping," Reed groused. "I called you for advice."

"I've given you some advice but you don't like it. I can't help that. What I'm trying to say to you is that you do indeed have a choice. You don't have to stay there. I can call in a few favors and have a private security team there by eight tomorrow morning. Just say the word and I'll make the calls."

Reed didn't know what to say to the very clear-cut choice Tanner had given him. His brain was telling him to get away from Kaylee and this situation as quickly as possible but his instincts and emotions had other ideas.

"I'm staying," Reed finally said. "I want to see this through."

"And Kaylee? Does she *care* about you?"

Reed knew she did. She didn't try and hide her emotions from him although if she had a shred of self-preservation she would. When she looked at him he could see the respect and admiration in her eyes. It was a heady feeling to have someone look at him like that. Had he forgotten what it was like or maybe this was the first time? It had been so long he couldn't remember.

"Yes, and that's a problem too. I should set things back on a more business-like level."

Except he didn't want to. The thought of never kissing or making love to Kaylee again made his chest squeeze painfully.

"It would probably be best," Tanner agreed. "Don't be angling for a woman's love and respect if you don't intend to return it. That's not what men—good men—do."

There was a warning tone in Tanner's voice and Reed knew his friend meant well. It wouldn't be easy to put distance between himself and Kaylee but he needed to do it. When all this was over and her stalker was found, Reed wouldn't be hanging around, sending flowers, or even keeping contact. He'd move on with his life. Alone.

"I hear what you're saying. It's going to hurt her though."

"Better now than later, I would imagine. Unless you're thinking that this *caring* thing might turn into something more? Something with a future?"

"No way," Reed answered grimly. "She's a sweet woman but that's not in the cards. I've already told her that."

"Sounds like you have a plan. Find the asshole that's making her life a misery and then get the hell out of there. For her sake if nothing else. I'll be honest with you, Reed, there's nothing better than the love of a good woman but you're in no condition to be the man in anyone's life. You're not in the headspace to do it. Your past owns you lock, stock, and barrel. I've never pried and I'm not going to do it now. But until you make peace with whatever demon rides your ass you don't have any business inflicting yourself on some unsuspecting female."

Reed rubbed his temples and stifled a groan at Tanner's plain speech. "You're right, of course. I'd fuck up her life."

"I'm sorry I had to be so blunt."

"No, it was a good reminder. I'd make her miserable. I'm not planning on changing. This is who and what I am."

"You're a damn good cop. Go find the guy and finish your vacation. Sit on a beach. Fish or something. By the time you get back to Montana you'll have forgotten all about this."

Reed could only hope that was true.

✧ ✧ ✧ ✧

Reed wasn't joining Kaylee in the bathtub or even coming upstairs. Stepping into a pair of flannel pajama pants and a t-shirt, she ran a comb through her damp hair and padded down stairs in her bare feet. Reed wasn't in the living room or kitchen so she traveled to the office at the end of the hall and peeked around the corner.

The room was dark except for the desk lamp and he had spread all the reports and evidence on the desktop. It looked like he was settled in for the night with a bottle of water and a few cookies at his elbow.

"Hey, it's late. Are you coming to bed?"

Since the first time they'd made love, Reed had slept in Kaylee's bed. He still kept his clothes and belongings in the spare room, but when the lights went out they were together.

He twisted in the chair so he was facing her. "I want to go over all of this again, see if there's something I've missed. You go on up. I'll be there in a few minutes."

He was putting distance between them. She'd felt it earlier after the car had tried to run her down but she'd hoped it had been a figment of her imagination. But it was real. This was the beginning of the end.

"I'll stay up and help you. Two sets of eyes are better than one," she offered, knowing he was going to turn her down. He was looking for a way out. The going had gotten tough—and dangerous—and she was more trouble than he'd bargained for. So now he was going to leave.

The pain of betrayal was unbearable, almost sending her to her knees with its all mighty strength. How ironic that her stalker had sent a picture of a knife plunged into a heart but it was Reed that had actually done the deed. Hot tears pricked the back of her eyes and her stomach twisted into angry knots.

She'd believed in him. Trusted him.

Now he was setting the stage for his escape. By tomorrow morning he'd probably have a call from a buddy or maybe from work saying he was needed back at home.

She ought to make it easy for him but something inside of her rebelled at the thought. No, she'd make him do this all on his own. She wanted him to own up to what he was and what he was doing. She'd spent her life making things too easy for the men she cared about. It stopped today.

"I've got this," he said just as she had predicted. "Get some sleep. You've got to be exhausted after tonight. We'll talk in the morning."

He had to be tired as well but he showed no signs of moving from the desk. She could already hear the words he was going to say when they spoke again. He'd tell her she was great and that it had been fun, but he needed to go home. He'd check on her of course...

Except that he wouldn't. She would never see or hear from him again.

"I am tired." She congratulated herself on how normal she sounded instead of a voice that was thick with tears. This night stood in such stark contrast to when the brick had come through her window and he'd held her all night long in comfort. "Good night."

"Night, honey."

She quickly pulled the door shut and jogged down the hall and up the stairs until she was safely in her room behind a closed door. Pressing a hand over her mouth, salty tears began to run down her face and her body shook with sobs as she sank down on the bed. She'd let Reed Mitchell in and managed to get herself hurt all over again. Only this time it was worse.

She'd let herself depend on someone for the first time in years. She'd been taken in by a handsome face and gorgeous body, forgetting everything she'd learned the hard way. She couldn't afford to forget ever again.

Chapter Eighteen

Reed wasn't very proud of himself. After Kaylee had gone to bed, he'd remembered how scared she'd been the night the brick had broken her window. After what had happened at the party she had to be even more terrified now. Whether he liked it or not, she needed comfort and care from him. He'd set aside the evidence and joined her upstairs in the bedroom.

She'd already fallen asleep, but her features weren't relaxed and serene. Her cheeks were shiny with leftover tears and her forehead was scrunched as if she was concentrating even while she dreamed. Reed didn't know if she was crying because someone tried to kill her or because he was a giant asshole. Either way she deserved better. He'd crawled into bed and cuddled close to her already warm body. If she woke in the night or had a nightmare, he'd be there for her.

But she hadn't woken until morning. He'd closed his eyes and feigned sleep as she'd carefully slid out of bed trying not to disturb him. It had honestly seemed easier to let her sneak away from the bed than to deal with all the tension between them. It couldn't be ignored forever but this morning he'd take the reprieve with relief.

"Coffee?" Reed held up a mug when Kaylee entered the kitchen. She'd taken a shower and her long auburn hair was wild around her shoulders, a stark contrast to her pale features. She was studiously avoiding looking in his direction but she nodded as she took in the French toast in the frying pan.

Adding sugar and cream to her coffee, she sat down at the table, her fingers wrapped around the mug. The tightness in his chest was back as he gazed at her dejected form. Her shoulders were hunched and even her lips drooped. He hated to see her like this, scared and morose. He loved it when she smiled and laughed, her sunny nature filling every nook and cranny of this home with her happiness.

"What now?" Her voice sounded distant even though she was only a few feet away. "What do I do now?"

Reed's eyes narrowed at her seemingly innocent question. But Kaylee was a writer and she knew words had meaning. And her words had formed the question of what *she* was to do, not what *they* should do.

Like a freight train slamming into a car on the tracks, he realized he'd made a huge mistake. With her background she'd be looking for any sign of a man leaving, running away when things got tough. She'd taken his pulling away last night not as him dialing down how personal this had become but that he didn't want to be here at all.

She thought he was leaving.

"We," he emphasized the word deliberately and her bent head shot up, "go back to the beginning. Review everything. Then we start asking questions. Lots of them."

She still didn't look at him. "What kind of questions?"

"We need to talk to Linda and find out whom she can account for at the party at the time that car came after you. If she's not one hundred percent sure a guest was within sight we need to talk to them."

"And Brent?"

"We already know that he left early so we definitely need to talk to him."

Kaylee's stormy green eyes, almost gray at the moment, finally looked into his own. "But we can take Linda off the suspect list? We know she was in the house."

"As far as I'm concerned Linda is off the list," he conceded.

"Good. The toast is burning."

Reed let go a string of expletives but managed to save breakfast from disaster. He slid the toast onto two plates and put one down in front of her along with a fork.

"Why don't you just yell at me, honey, and we can move on with our day."

"Why would I yell at you?" she sniffed disdainfully. "Have you done something that I should be angry about?"

"Yes," he answered calmly. Kaylee needed to blow her top and get all that rage out. "We both know why so let's get it over with. We have work to do today."

She smacked her fork down on the table. "Fine. If you want to leave, Reed, then just fucking leave. I don't need a damn babysitter."

He regarded her steadily knowing they both had issues in their life that had scarred them. The least he could do was not make hers worse.

"I'm not going anywhere. I never planned to leave. I should have realized that when I pulled away last night that you would think that though. I'm sorry that I hurt you that way."

She really was beautiful when she was angry. Her formerly pale cheeks were bright pink and sparks practically flew from her eyes. "You were a jerk last night. I needed you. I was scared—I mean, I am scared. Dammit, Reed. I'm so angry with you."

His Kaylee wasn't a screamer when she was mad. If anything her voice had gone softer and softer until the last words had come out as a whisper.

"I was a jerk and I'm sorry." He tried to put as much sincerity in his tone as possible. "I'm in deep here, honey, and I'm not too proud to admit that it makes me edgy. I thought that pulling away from the personal side of our relationship would be a good idea. But I never intended to leave you. I'm here until we catch this son of a bitch. I wish you could trust me."

"I wish I could too," Kaylee said sadly. "But maybe it's best if I don't, especially since you don't want there to be anything personal between us. You want it to be strictly business?"

What he wanted and what he needed were two different things, but Tanner had made a good point last night when they'd spoken.

"It's not fair to you, Kaylee. My friend Tanner said it's wrong to angle for a woman's love if I don't intend to return it. And I simply cannot return it. I am not capable of love. He said my past owns me and he's probably right. I can't even begin to plan a future with someone when all I do is look over my shoulder. The present is all I have."

Her lips trembling, she brushed a few stray tears from her cheeks. He'd made her cry. Again. Just more evidence that he was bad for her.

"Then we're just friends. No benefits." Kaylee looked sad and he cursed the day he'd ever come into her life. She would have been better off never meeting him. "But I wish you could talk about it. It might help."

Reed couldn't picture any scenario where talking about what had happened would help.

"Talking about it won't change it. I wish I could be someone different for you. I wish I really was like the men in your books, but I'm just not hero material. I'm so sorry."

Kaylee picked up her fork and smiled a little too forcefully. "I'm sorry too. I told you at the beginning that I wouldn't hold you to some commitment and I meant it. I think we could have fun while you're here but I see that you've made up your mind. We'll keep things friendly and casual from now on."

She'd given him exactly what he wanted so why did he feel like shit? When he finally did leave she'd be well rid of him. She'd placed him on some sort of pedestal and everyone knew there was only one direction to go from there.

Down.

Kaylee had thought Reed might argue about her accompanying him to speak to Linda but he didn't bat an eye. Instead he'd simply stated that he didn't intend for her to be unprotected until this guy was caught which had been disheartening news. Being with Reed twenty-four-seven wasn't going to be easy. He wanted them to return to being friends but she craved the intimacy they'd found together. It wasn't just the sex, although that was beyond awesome; it was how close she felt to him before, during and after. She'd never felt that close to anyone in her life.

But she wouldn't push the issue. She could see that caring about her was frightening the living shit out of him and that thought alone made her smile. It gave her a tiny bit of hope that he might eventually change his mind. She wasn't looking for marriage and kids but she genuinely liked Reed. They could have something…special. She wouldn't ask him for more than he could give.

"Won't the police have talked to Linda already?" Kaylee asked as Reed parked his truck in Linda's driveway.

"They have and I'm sure they've talked to other people as well. But we're not privy to those conversations. I'm not a cop here and I'm trying to respect what they're doing. They seem sincere in their efforts and they've done all they could really. But I haven't done all I can. I have this one case to work on while they have dozens, if not hundreds. I want to talk to people myself and make my own conclusions."

"Then let's do this." Kaylee hopped out of the truck but not before seeing Reed wince as he did the same. He was hurting whether he wanted to admit it or not. No lightweight, she'd landed right on top of him last night. "Did you take anything for that?"

He lifted one shoulder carelessly. "I'm only bruised. I've had far worse."

"You're more stubborn than I am," she said, brushing past him to ring the doorbell. If he wanted to fucking suffer she'd be happy to let him.

Linda opened the door with a smile that didn't quite reach her eyes. Kaylee had called her before they'd shown up and there had been little enthusiasm in Linda's voice for this visit.

"Come in. I was just sitting down to have some coffee. Would you like a cup?" Linda asked as they followed her into the living room.

"None for me, thank you," Reed declined and sat down. Kaylee shook her head as well, simply wanting to get to whatever they were there for.

All three settled in and Linda lifted the cup to her lips. "How are you feeling, Kaylee? Did you see the doctor this morning?"

"I'm fine. It's Reed that took most of the impact when he pushed me out of the way. No doctor needed."

Linda's gaze swung to Reed and he smiled charmingly. "No doctor needed for me either." He leaned forward, his elbows on his knees. "Thank you for talking to us. I have some questions that I'd like to ask about last night."

Linda placed her cup on the end table and smoothed a few imaginary wrinkles in her slacks. "I already told the police everything I know. I'm not sure how I can help you."

"You never know what can be important. Sometimes it's the smallest detail. Can you remember who was in the room with you last night after Kaylee and I walked outside?"

Her brows pinched together in thought, Linda shook her head. "I can't remember everyone. I'd had a few glasses of wine."

Reed pulled a tiny notebook and stubby pencil from his shirt pocket under his sweater. "Whatever you can remember will be great. Only the ones you know for sure."

Linda reeled off several names and then shrugged. "That's all I can remember. There could have been others in the kitchen or even the bathrooms."

"But Brent left before we did?"

Linda nodded, her color high. It didn't take a genius to figure out that Brent would be a suspect in this case. The police knew about the words that had been exchanged between Reed and Brent.

"Did he ever come back to the party?"

"Not that I know of."

"What about Walt? You didn't see him when Kaylee and I were outside?"

"No, but he was around shortly after. I don't think there's any way he could have done this. I saw you both come back into the house and Walt was there too."

Reed scratched more on the notepad but the doorbell interrupted any more questions. Linda hopped up from the couch and looked out the front window.

"That's Cheryl. I talked to her this morning and told her you both were stopping by. She was worried about you so she asked if she could join us. I hope that's okay."

It had to be because Linda was opening the door whether they liked it or not. Cheryl's appearance did seem to put Linda more at ease as she poured another cup of coffee for her friend and refilled her own.

"I was so concerned about you," Cheryl said with a shudder. "I didn't sleep a wink last night."

"I didn't either," Linda declared. "What has the world come to? It's not safe to leave your house anymore."

Separately, Cheryl and Linda each a flair for the dramatic but together? They were a couple of Barrymores. Kaylee highly doubted either woman had lost much if any sleep.

"We're both fine," Kaylee assured them. "I don't think you have anything to worry about."

"But what about you? Some terrible person is trying to hurt you because they don't like your books. It's a horrible thing." Cheryl's cup clattered on the coffee table as she sat it down with too much force. "When you can't even write what you love the world has gone too far."

"Cheryl, where were you when Kaylee and I were outside?" Reed queried.

"Upstairs in the restroom. I came down when I heard all the racket."

"Linda, do you remember Cheryl coming downstairs?"

The two women quickly glanced at one another and Linda nodded vigorously. "Yes, she and Walt joined me downstairs at about the same time."

Reed scratched more notes. "Cheryl, did you see anyone else upstairs?"

"Hmmmmm." Cheryl tapped her chin. "I saw Walt and one of the actresses from the play. The one who played the waitress."

"What would they have been doing upstairs?" Kaylee asked. "Did they know each other?"

Dear Lord, had Walt been taking a woman to a...bedroom? *Ewww.*

"I can answer that," Linda interrupted. "Walt had a tad too much to drink last night and spilled some wine on his shirt. Alice was taking him upstairs to help him clean up. I gave her a bottle of club soda from the bar."

"And I think he got her phone number by the end of the evening." Cheryl wore a suggestive smile.

I guess there's a lid for every pot.

Reed asked a few more questions while Kaylee sat back and watched the reactions of the two women. Linda did appear more confident with Cheryl by her side but all Cheryl seemed to be thinking about was Reed. She'd turned on the charm every time she answered one of his questions.

Got jealousy?

"I just have one more question and it's for both of you. Have you ever heard anyone in your writer's group or friends that resent Kaylee's success? Anyone who has spoken ill of her?"

Kaylee sure as hell wanted the answer to this one. Were there people out there that talked badly behind her back? Everyone wasn't her friend but she didn't normally spend time counting her enemies.

Both women looked uncomfortable, fidgeting on the couch and glancing at each other instead of at Kaylee and Reed.

That's my answer. A resounding yes.

Finally Cheryl nodded. "I don't think he really means it. He's simply frustrated about his own career. He's just blowing off steam and Kaylee is the natural choice since she's the most successful of all of us. Plus she writes romance and it's very common for men to denigrate the genre."

"Who is he?" Reed's pencil was poised to take down the name. "Is it Brent?"

Linda's brows shot up in surprise. "Brent? No, he never has a bad word to say about anyone. Cheryl was talking about Walt."

Reed nodded and tucked away the notebook and pencil. "Thank you for being so honest. I'd like to talk to Walt so we can mark him off the list of suspects. I'm sure it's just as you say, he was blowing off steam. Do you know where I can find him?"

"He would be at his home," Cheryl shrugged. "He lives out in the country on some sort of a farm. I think he manages it for a friend."

"Do you know where exactly?"

Cheryl shook her head but Linda nodded.

"I was there once. I can draw you a map."

Linda stood and walked over to a desk on the far wall and retrieved a piece of paper and a pen from the drawer. "I don't know street names. I only know landmarks."

"That's fine. I can usually find my way around." Reed also stood to look over her shoulder as she marked the roads and intersections. He folded the map and shoved it in his hip pocket when she was done. "Thank you again. You've been a big help."

Kaylee and Reed said their goodbyes and climbed back into the truck.

"This cop stuff sucks. I hate putting my friends through this."

Reed kept his attention on the road. "One of your friends is a wolf in sheep's clothing, honey, and doesn't deserve your loyalty."

"In the meantime I may lose all of them, good or bad."

She couldn't keep the bitterness out of her tone. She was so tired of all this shit.

"Someone is trying to kill you. If they can't understand why we need to ask a few questions then they're not really your friends."

If she couldn't trust her friends, and she couldn't trust Reed…who the hell could she trust?

Kaylee rapped on the front door of Brent's apartment off of Springfield Avenue. It was one of those generic complexes where all the buildings look the same, the only difference was some overlooked the parking lot and some the pool at the center. Champaign-Urbana was a college town and this community appeared to be filled with students if the Fighting Illini banners and bumper stickers were anything to go by in addition to the piles of beer cans out by the front steps from what must have been a hell of a party last night.

"I don't think he's home," she sighed in frustration. She wanted all this done and over with. "Maybe we can come back by after we talk to Walt."

Reed knocked loudly on the door. "Sharp? Are you in there? We need to talk to you."

His deep voice boomed in the quiet hallway and she cringed when the door across the hall opened and a young man, perhaps in his mid-twenties, stuck his head out.

"Can you keep it down out here? I'm trying to sleep. Brent's not here, bro. He's out of town or something."

"Out of town?" Reed asked sharply. "I just saw him last night. When did he leave?"

The young man shrugged. "I dunno. He came home last night and then came back out with a suitcase and drove off. We were all outside but I don't remember what time it was. Maybe midnight?"

Reed put his arm around Kaylee and urged her toward the exit. "Thanks. Sorry I disturbed you."

She slid into the passenger seat next to Reed and rubbed her throbbing temples with her fingers. "This looks bad, doesn't it?"

"It doesn't look good," he agreed. "Could be perfectly innocent, could be something to worry about. Did Brent mention a trip to you?"

"No," she said wearily. "Nothing."

"It doesn't mean he's the guy. It just means he did something suspicious."

"I thought he was your prime suspect." Had Reed changed his mind? Kaylee was glad she wasn't a cop because all this mystery gave her a headache.

"He is, but as I said I don't want to look at him to the exclusion of everyone else. That's why we're going to talk to Walt."

"Ah yes, Walt. Someone I thought was my friend but says crappy things behind my back."

She'd thought she was over caring what others thought about her work but apparently not.

"You're a good writer, honey. You know it and I know it. It doesn't matter what anyone else thinks."

It mattered if they wanted her dead over it

Chapter Nineteen

Reed had never seen Kaylee looking so bleak. Finding out that someone she called a friend was saying nasty things behind her back had to be devastating to a woman as sensitive as she was. Finding out your other so-called friends had been covering it up hadn't helped either. He was starting to really dislike everyone around her. No wonder she had trust issues.

"I think you turn right here." Kaylee was pointing to the map but Reed was looking at the road, not that there were any cars around. In a way this area reminded him of Montana in how the houses had miles between them and privacy from your neighbors.

He turned the truck onto a long dirt lane that led to an old farmhouse surrounded by a few trees. Mostly it was prairie country here. Driving, one could see for miles in any direction the land was so flat. It wasn't something he was used to but it had a beauty all its own.

The home looked like it had seen better days with a sagging front porch and peeling paint. A couple of old cars were parked in the yard along with a rusted tractor. There was an old red barn to the back of the property along with cows, chickens, and horses.

Reed honked the horn before climbing out of the vehicle, wanting to be sure he gave ample notice to Walt. If there was one thing Reed had learned as a lawman was to never surprise a homeowner that had the potential to be well-armed.

The screen door swung open and Walt stepped out on the wooden porch but didn't appear to have anything in his hands.

Reed hopped out of the truck and held out his hand in friendship hoping it would indicate that he wasn't a threat. If Walt was Kaylee's stalker they could be walking into a dangerous situation.

So far no one today had noticed his shoulder holster under his leather jacket. He was completely legal and had a permit but Kaylee didn't look like the gun type so he hadn't made a big deal about it.

The man squinted at him and loped down the steps to shake Reed's hand.

"I wondered when you'd come here. You want to ask me some questions, don't you?"

"I do. Can we come in? It's pretty cold out here."

Walt jerked his head toward the door and Reed pressed the button on the key fob unlocking the truck. Kaylee climbed down from the vehicle and joined them as they walked back into the house. They all settled into chairs at Walt's kitchen table—Kaylee and Reed across from each other and Walt at the end.

The inside of the home was also shabby and run down except for a large desk in the corner of what was probably the dining room. A laptop computer with a large flat-screen monitor sat on the desk along with stacks of paper and books. There were several photos on the wall, some black and white along with knickknacks from various tourist locations. Reed could see a miniature St. Louis Arch and the side of something that looked like Mt. Rushmore.

He turned his attention back to Walt who didn't look half bad after drinking so much the night before. There was no alcohol on his breath nor did Reed see any in the cabinets or open shelves. Like the other times he'd seen Walt, the man was well groomed wearing blue jeans and a green sweater. His brown wavy hair was combed neatly and his face had been shaved recently.

"I didn't do it," Walt stated flatly. "I won't let the law railroad me for something I didn't do."

"I'm not the law here," Reed said using a soothing tone he'd perfected over the years. He'd try the "let's be friends" angle and see if he could get the man talking. "I'm only trying to protect Kaylee from someone that wants to hurt her."

"I don't want to hurt her," Walt swore and shook his head. "I like her." Walt looked at Kaylee beseechingly. "I do like you."

"We've heard that you've said some things, Walt." Reed held up his hands when Walt wanted to answer. "Now I know you didn't mean them. Hell, everyone gets frustrated sometimes. You work your ass off and no one appreciates it. I know how that feels. I know what it's like to be ignored."

"I write every day but no one reads anything," Walt grumbled. "Am I that bad? Am I? People say its good but no one buys it. Sometimes I wonder why I bother."

"You are good, Walt. Very good." Kaylee's tone was urgent and encouraging but Walt shook his head in repudiation.

"I don't think so. It's easy for you. Everything is easy for you. That's what I was complaining about to Linda and Cheryl. I suppose they're the ones that told you? Those two busybodies should mind their own business."

Reed didn't intend to answer the question. Instead he turned the conversation. "Do you know anyone that would want to hurt Kaylee enough to try and hit her with a car?"

"Everyone likes Kaylee." Walt shook his head again. "Everyone. She'll help anyone that asks and never acts impatient."

That sounded like his sweet woman but somebody was holding a grudge bad enough to want her dead.

"Someone wants to hurt her, Walt. I need to know who that person is."

Walt jumped up from the table and began to pace the small kitchen. "It's not me. I was in the house when that car tried to hit you, Kaylee. I swear on my momma's Bible."

"I believe you. I know you wouldn't do anything like this." Kaylee moved to stand but Reed shook his head silently. He needed to keep control of the questioning.

Reed's right hand hovered under his jacket in case Walt didn't like this next question. "One more question, Walt. When I checked you out I got some weird information. It seems you were born and then school. That's it. No job. No credit cards. A couple of hundred bucks in the bank. It's like you barely exist. I've never seen anything like it."

Walt's face turned bright red. "I'm not sure what you mean. Obviously I exist. You must have gotten it wrong. Although I'm not sure that I like the thought of you digging into my life. What did you do it for?"

Jared Monroe was so fucking perfect he drove everyone around him crazy. There was no way he'd screwed up Walt's background check but Reed had a few ideas about that too.

"To make sure that no one in Kaylee's life had a violent past they were hiding."

Walt looked affronted at the suggestion. "I'm not violent. Hell, no."

"It's just strange that I can't find anything about you after high school." Reed looked around the house that didn't fit with this man's personality at all. "Do you own this home or are you renting?"

"That's a personal question." Walt's jaw tightened. "Do you own your own home?"

Reed nodded and sat back in his chair trying to appear as cool and relaxed as possible. "Yes, I do. It's a fixer-upper just like this place but I'm working on it little by little. Do you have any projects going here? Are you restoring the muscle cars out front? I just finished laying tile in the second bathroom."

Walt shook his head and averted his gaze. "I'm not very handy," he mumbled. "I take care of the property for a friend. Is there anything else you want to ask me? I need to get back to work."

"No, that's about it. If you think of anything that might help us, give me a call." Reed placed a business card on the table and held out his hand to Kaylee who hadn't said much while they were there. Reed wanted to kiss her full on the lips. She'd obviously felt his unspoken signals to let him handle this. It wasn't in her nature to stay silent so he needed to remember to thank her when they got out of here.

They walked back to the truck and bade a sullen Walt good-bye.

"You did good, honey. Thank you for not interfering. I know it's rough on you thinking that a friend might be the one doing this."

Kaylee stared out of the window as he turned onto the main road and headed back to town. "I didn't say much because I didn't know what to say. How do you ask someone if they want you dead?"

Good question. He had to give credit where it was due. Kaylee Blue had a spine made of solid steel. She could have been in hysterics but she'd taken all this shit like a trooper. Maybe he could try and get her mind off of things if only for an hour or two.

"I'm starving. How about we stop somewhere and eat?"

"The Courier Cafe in Urbana is good. They have a large menu and make everything fresh."

He would have eaten a greasy burger but fresh sounded even better.

"I'll drive. You navigate."

As soon as he'd eaten, Reed would do some more checking on Walt. Reed's gut was telling him the man wasn't their guy but it was also telling him that he couldn't leave any stone unturned when Kaylee's life was on the line.

It was Halloween night and someone still wanted to hurt or kill her. That was scary enough but he had nothing to go on to find the stalker. Every path led him down a dead end or worse, sent him back to the beginning. How could he possibly keep her safe if he didn't know where the threat was coming from?

Chapter Twenty

Kaylee dug the boxes of Halloween candy out of the cabinet along with an oversized glass bowl. It was one of her favorite days of the year and she needed to get ready for the trick-or-treaters. There were tons of kids in the neighborhood so she'd bought quite a bit of candy in anticipation. If none of them showed up she could have herself a pity party for one and overdose on chocolate.

Feeling sorry for herself was stupid but she couldn't help the sadness in her heart at how she and Reed had crashed and burned in less than a week. She hadn't asked him for much…wait…that wasn't exactly true. She'd asked him to talk about his past which he'd been adamantly against, but she hadn't asked for a commitment. Reed wasn't giving those away.

She was dumping chocolate bars into a large bowl when he joined her in the kitchen.

"Full-size bars? Isn't that unusual? I thought people gave away those smaller treats."

Kaylee laughed and added another box of candy bars to the bowl. "It is unusual but I have fond memories of dressing up for trick or treat and then the surprise of going to a house where they gave out full-size bars. The news would spread among all my friends and then everyone wanted to go to that house. It was such an unexpected thing and I thought it was so cool. I just want to kind of carry on that tradition."

"And you want to be that house this year?" Reed asked. "The cool house."

She wished he wouldn't look at her like that. As if he liked her. Or cared. She already knew that even if he did, he didn't want to.

"Just passing on that feeling to a new generation. What about you? Do you have a great Halloween memory?"

Reed opened the refrigerator and pulled out a soda. "Not really. We lived on a ranch way out in the middle of nowhere. I didn't go trick or treating and no one came to our house either. Later in my teens we might go out and soap some windows or TP a house. Raise some general hell but nothing dangerous."

"That's too bad. Halloween is the best holiday."

"The best?" he teased. "How is it the best?"

She'd had to answer this question more than once so she was prepared. "It's all about candy and having fun. You don't have to buy and wrap presents, you're not obligated to visit family that might drive you crazy, and no one thinks it's strange if you don't celebrate it. It's dressing up, candy, and maybe a little scare. All good," she pronounced.

"I see you've given this some thought. Do you dress up?"

"I have in the past if there was a party or something. This year I'm going as a busy writer in a witch's hat." Kaylee pointed to the black hat sitting by the door. "There, the candy's ready. Now we need to carve the jack o' lanterns. My carving set is in the basement though along with a few decorations. I'll need to go get them."

"If you tell me where it is I'll get it. You don't need to be dragging things up and down the stairs."

Reed was doing that bossy thing again but this time she was happy to let him be the muscle. The Halloween box was heavy because she kept adding to it every year from the after holiday sales.

"It's a rectangle shaped clear plastic box with a white lid on the shelf in the corner. It's labeled Halloween. It should be right next to Thanksgiving and Christmas."

"Labeled, huh? Organized."

"I had to be when I moved."

Before long Reed was brandishing a carving knife and cutting the tops off of the pumpkins so she could scoop the guts out.

"I think you got the better job." Kaylee's arms were covered in goo up to her elbows. "How did that happen?"

"I'm simply doing the manly part and you're doing the womanly part," Reed grinned, his hazel eyes twinkling. "I don't see anything wrong with it."

He loved to say outrageous things simply to get her dander up. "It's not a good idea to say sexist crap when a female has a handful of pumpkin guts."

"If said female did what I think she might be contemplating, she'd find herself over my knee with a red bottom."

Instant lust ran through her at his teasing words. She'd allowed him to spank her during a boss and secretary fantasy and had found it more than pleasurable.

But this was a shitty thing to do on his part. Bringing up something that he had said couldn't happen again.

Asshole.

There was anger mixed with that lust. It made her want to do something, anything, that would break his cooler than cool facade. She wanted that mask he wore to crack and fall away so she could see the real Reed Mitchell.

Her fingers tightened around the wad of slippery, cold guts. Before she lost her courage she pulled out the ball, but instead of placing it on the newspaper she lobbed it in the air. It landed with a splat on the front of his shirt and he froze, his eyes widening in disbelief then narrowing dangerously.

Oh shit. What did I do?

Wet, orange strands and seeds clung to the cotton of Reed's t-shirt in a sort of abstract art blob. He slowly set down the large knife and scooped up the damp goo with his hand so it lay in his palm.

"I can't believe you did that."

Kaylee swallowed hard as her stomach tumbled in her abdomen. She wasn't afraid he would do her harm. No, Reed was far too protective for that. But he might just make good on that spanking threat and then leave her hanging without release.

That would be far crueler than what she'd done.

Reed finally looked up from his shirt and a slow grin spread across his face. "I'll give you a three second head start. One."

"Now, Reed–"

"Two," he intoned, that smile growing ever wider.

Move. Don't just stand here.

Kaylee lunged toward the stairs, climbing them as fast as her trembling legs would carry her. Adrenaline mixed with arousal made her pulse beat madly and she had to concentrate to keep from falling backwards on the steps.

"Three."

Her short legs were no match for his long ones. She'd barely made it to the top of the staircase when his muscled arm wrapped around her waist pulling her back against him. His own hard cock was pressed firmly against her bottom and it was some comfort to know he was as excited by their game as she was.

With a growl that set her on fire, he lifted her up and carried her into the bedroom.

"You are in so much trouble, honey." His voice rumbled in her ear but it didn't sound angry. It sounded like a promise.

Setting her feet on the floor, he trapped her against the wall with his big body. Not bothering to cover his laughter, he took his hand full of cold, slimy goo and rubbed it on her chest while she shrieked and tried to wriggle away. Giggling and screeching indignantly at the same time, she managed to bend her knees and duck under his arm, but even as she tried to crawl away his superior strength made catching her a cinch.

On all fours and helpless, he easily held her immobile with one arm while he spanked her denim-covered posterior with the other. She should have been angry but instead flames were licking along her veins and excitement made her face as red as her ass cheeks.

When he was done, her bottom was on fire and that heat had spread to all her intimate spots. Once he loosened his hold she rolled onto her back and pummeled his broad chest ineffectively with her fists. It only served to embolden him and he pinned her wrists over her head as he raked his gaze down her quivering body. There was no doubt she was aroused. Hard pointed nipples jutted out from her t-shirt, her breathing rising and falling rapidly. God help her, if he reached into her panties he'd find them soaked with honey.

"Reed," she whispered, an ache in her voice that only he could soothe.

His lips crashed down onto hers, not gentle or coaxing, but almost brutal in their intensity. This was not a tender kiss between lovers but a stamp of ownership from someone who had come to the end of his tether. The urgency between them was overwhelming in its strength and she couldn't deny the instinct to mate with this man—this good man—no matter what the future held for them. At this moment they were man and woman, not Reed and Kaylee.

It was that basic and simple. Later it would be complex and painful.

His tongue swept through her mouth and his large hand held her wrists above her head while the other insinuated itself under her shirt and bra. He pinched her nipples, somehow making them even harder than they already were and sending arrows of pleasure straight to her clit. Shoving the fabric up and out of the way, he moved his mouth from her lips to the aching tips of her breasts using his tongue and teeth to make her moan and writhe under his attentions.

Dominant and arrogant to the end, he smiled at her mindless submission to his skillful lovemaking. So fucking sure of himself, not a shred of self-doubt. She loved and hated that about him but it was part and parcel of who he was. If she wanted him she had to want all of him, not just the easy parts.

That was the coward's way and she was no fraidy-cat. A woman had to be brave and a little crazy to love a man like Reed Mitchell.

God, she loved him. She'd never tell him but she did. The thought didn't scare her but it did make her sad. This relationship was only going to end one way. Heartache and loneliness were in her future but she was determined to take everything she could get now.

Bucking under him, she ground her groin against his arm trying to get some friction to her poor clit. He chuckled and pinned her to the floor with his hips in no hurry to move further south from her breasts, content to feast on them until she was begging for mercy.

Then and only then did his lips wander down her belly to the waistband of her jeans. His sure fingers popped the button and pulled down the zipper before tugging at the fabric until they were out of the way. His splayed knees slid in between her thighs, pushing them far apart and up so her bottom was off the floor slightly. She closed her eyes knowing he could see every detail of her pussy, shiny with cream. For a moment shyness overcame her and she struggled against his iron grip but then he dragged his finger through the sensitive folds. She gasped as the sensation rocketed all the way to her toes.

He didn't say a word and she kept her eyelids tightly shut as he continued exploring her slit slowly and methodically as if he was trying to learn every intimate inch. She moaned as he pressed first one finger and then two inside and his thumb lightly brushed her clit.

"Please." Her voice was a wisp of sound but he wouldn't be hurried or pushed. He dragged his thumb back and forth over her swollen button over and over, but never enough to give her release. The tension in her lower abdomen built, taking her higher and higher until the pleasure was too great to bear. Pure bliss was all mixed up with pain as her pussy tightened on his fingers and her sore bottom brushed against the rug.

"Come for me, baby."

His thumb pressed on her clit and she exploded in a rush of white light. Waves crashed through her and she gave herself over gladly to the rush of pleasure that suffused her every pore. Through the haze of her orgasm she heard the rasp of a zipper and the crinkle of a condom. Before she could catch her breath Reed had thrust inside of her, his cock filling her pussy and making her toes curl with delight.

Their coming together was much like the kiss. Alpha to the core, Reed rode her hard and fast, dominating all of her senses.

The rough feel of his thighs against her own. The tang of salt on her tongue when she nipped at his shoulder. The panting of their breath as he powered into her again and again, sending her teetering near the precipice. She forced her eyes open so she could watch him as he fell over the edge with her, his face a mask of concentration.

At some point he'd let go of her wrists and her nails dug into his muscular arms as she wrapped her legs around his waist. Each stroke sent them higher until finally her climax erupted, shattering her into a million shimmering pieces that seemed to whirl around the room.

Reed groaned as his own orgasm took him, his teeth gritted and his eyes squeezed shut as if he wanted to block out the world at that moment. She wouldn't let him shut her out and kissed his neck and nibbled at his ear even as his body shuddered above her. When it was over, he rolled off and lay beside her, his breathing ragged as they both came back to earth.

Reality began to seep back into her brain and she blinked back a few tears she was determined not to let fall.

She would not cry over this man again.

She'd admitted she loved him but damn if that meant he could twist her life around and make her miserable. She'd wanted this as much as he had and being a crybaby about it wasn't going to make things better. Being brave was her only choice. Take what Reed could give her and not ask for more. He'd given her several warnings. Changing a man wasn't possible unless he wanted to change, and she'd never seen a man who wanted to change less than Reed.

He levered to his elbows and she could feel his gaze on her as if he was waiting for her to speak, or scream, or cry. She didn't do any of those things. With as much dignity as she could muster with a bare, pink ass and her shirt and bra shoved up to her armpits, she got to her feet and headed for the bathroom. She needed a shower and a few moments to get herself together before she could face him.

Would Reed pull away from her again? She'd put off finding out for just awhile longer.

Chapter Twenty-One

Reed had to tell Kaylee everything and he needed to do it tonight.

Since he had so spectacularly failed to keep his distance it was the only thing that would make any of this remotely right. She needed to understand why this was so hard for him. He wanted her, but he couldn't have her. Not forever.

He showered and changed in the other bathroom before going into the kitchen and finishing up the pumpkins. He'd heard the shower stop a while ago but he wouldn't blame her if she never came downstairs or spoke to him again. At this point she was probably just tired of all his damn issues.

"You didn't have to clean up." He turned to see her standing at the bottom of the stairs wearing a blue pair of sweatpants, a gray University of Illinois t-shirt, and bare feet.

"It's no big deal. Do we put these pumpkins on the porch?"

The tension between them was thick but he tried to act natural and at ease.

"We have to put the lights in them first. They're in the box."

She came over to the table and started rummaging through the box at the same time he reached in. Their hands brushed and she pulled back as if she'd been burned.

He quickly installed a light in each jack o' lantern and carried them out to the porch, letting her direct where they were to be placed. He could already see neighborhood kids in costume trick or treating, their sacks empty this early.

"What do we do now?" he asked. Trying to talk to her when they would be interrupted every few minutes by a ringing doorbell wasn't a good idea. He'd wait until later in the evening. He only hoped he had the courage to say all that needed to be said and then face whatever her reaction would be.

Would she think less of him? Would she be so disgusted she'd ask him to leave? He couldn't technically leave her without protection until her attacker was found.

She finished setting out the pumpkins just as a group of trick-or-treaters stomped up the steps. One was dressed as some kind of princess with a tiara, one was dressed as a cowboy, and the little one was dressed as a flower. Praising their costumes, Kaylee gave each one a candy bar, not dropping it into their bags but actually handing it to them.

The children's faces lit up.

She'd been absolutely right about the magic of a full-size candy bar. All three kids grinned, shoved the chocolate in their bags, and then ran back down the porch steps to excitedly tell their parents what they had received. She'd made their Halloween...all with a candy bar.

It was like that for the next two hours. Ghosts, zombies, vampires, fairies, and several Harry Potters all rang Kaylee's doorbell and yelled "Trick or Treat." She wore her witch's hat, chatted with the parents, and handed out candy to the children who all looked like they were hopped up on sugar. Those moms and dads weren't getting those kids to bed for hours.

At nine o'clock Kaylee turned off the porch light and locked the door. "Another Halloween has come and gone. I guess I can start my Christmas shopping."

It was time.

"Can you wait until tomorrow to do it? I'd like for us to talk, Kaylee."

She held the large candy bowl in front of her like a shield. "I don't think we have anything to talk about. Maybe we should just let things lie."

He'd been doing that for almost fifteen years and it hadn't been working all that well. Maybe it was time for a different tactic.

"I want to tell you," he said simply. "If you still want to hear it."

Her mouth fell open and her eyes went wide. She nodded and placed the bowl on the kitchen counter. "I do still want to hear about it. What changed your mind?"

"You," he answered immediately. "I need you to understand why this is so hard for me. Why I pulled away from you last night and today, and why there's no future with a man like me."

"Um, where do you want to do this?" She looked more nervous than he felt.

"Why don't I get us a couple of sodas and we can sit in the living room?"

He needed something to do with his hands so he wouldn't try and touch her. If he did he wouldn't make it through this story. He opened two root beers and they settled on the sofa. Kaylee hugged one of the oversized throw pillows and leaned back against the arm of the couch so she was facing him. She didn't say anything, simply letting him gather his thoughts and try and make some sense of them.

He might as well start at the very beginning.

"I met Julie when we were both twelve years old. She was the daughter of our ranch foreman. Dad had hired him away from a big spread in Wyoming and I remember the day our family met theirs. Sonny, her dad, had three sons and Julie so she was pretty tomboyish. We all hung out together, fishing, riding, getting in snowball fights. I'd like to say it was love at first sight but it wasn't. For either of us. We were buddies if anything. Julie was one of the guys."

"Julie. That's a pretty name," Kaylee said softly. "What did she look like?"

Reed smiled as images flashed through his mind. The prom. Their wedding. The day they'd gone swimming in the creek and Julie had been wearing that new red bikini. "She was tall. Hell, she had the longest damn legs and the longest hair. Long, straight dark hair and brown eyes. She could have been a model if she'd wanted to."

She'd never really had the chance to decide what she wanted to be when she grew up.

"After eighth grade, Julie went away to spend the summer with her grandparents in Florida. When she came back in August…" Reed whistled as he recalled how different she'd looked. "Let's just say she grew up. I guess I must have too because I noticed she was a girl and I was a boy. There was no chasing or game playing. We were just together from then on. A couple. I dated her all through high school and we both planned to attend Colorado State but her parents didn't want us to live together. My parents weren't too keen on the idea either."

Reed paused as he remembered arguing with his mom and dad. Even then he hadn't liked anyone telling him how to live his life.

"But you did anyway?" Kaylee prompted, pulling him out of the past.

He shook his head and smiled. Their solution to the problem hadn't been ingenious but it sure as hell got the job done. "We got married. We figured that married people lived together so our parents couldn't say anything. We drove to Seattle and got hitched in some wedding chapel two weeks after high school graduation."

Kaylee smiled and pushed a few stray hairs back, tucking them behind her ear. "How did Mom and Dad take it?"

"They were livid at first." Reed chuckled at how bullheaded he'd been back then. He had much more patience now but a teenage boy in love was entirely ruled by hormones and emotion. "But they got used to it. By the holidays it seemed like everyone had forgotten about it and we were happy. We were going to school and having fun just like every other young couple does."

Those halcyon days when you're too young and stupid to know it couldn't last. They'd thought those happy times would go on forever.

"It was the summer between our junior and senior year of college. We were having a rough time as Julie seemed to be irritable quite a bit, not feeling like herself. I wrote it off to my being so busy. I was working on the ranch and trying to save money for the school year and the work was from sunup to sundown." Reed took another drink of his soda, his mouth suddenly dry as memories of that day crowded in. "I got a call one day that Julie had been in a car accident and was in the hospital. Of course both families went, not just me and the doctor said she'd had a seizure while driving."

Reed could still see that doctor's face in his mind as if it happened minutes ago, not years. That doctor had known then how bad it was but hadn't wanted to say anything until he'd done more tests. But he'd known...and Reed had seen the painful knowledge in his eyes.

"Brain tumor." Reed hadn't uttered those words for fifteen years and his voice sounded shaky and rough saying them. "Inoperable. They gave her six months to a year."

He heard Kaylee suck in a breath. "Oh Reed. God, I'm so sorry. So very sorry."

"Thank you. It was hard news to hear. No more so of course than for Julie. She was so young."

"So were you," Kaylee said gently. "It couldn't have been easy for you either."

Had he ever been that young? He sure as shit didn't remember it anymore. That innocent feeling. It was strange knowing he'd once been that naïve, thinking the world was on his side, but he couldn't recall the actual way it felt. That was lost forever.

"I wasn't the one dying."

Although at times it had felt like it. Julie had been such an integral part of his life for so long he hadn't known how to function without her. After she'd gone, he joined the military and volunteered for every dangerous assignment he could. What he'd learned was that the will to survive, at least in him, was strong.

"You don't have to say anything else if you don't want to."

He didn't want to but he needed to. Kaylee deserved to understand that he was the one lacking, defective. She deserved better than a man who didn't know how to love the right way.

"The doctors sent us to a bigger hospital in Denver. They offered chemo and radiation to slow down the tumor growth and extend her life."

Reed remembered the look of horror that had crossed Julie's face when they had talked about shaving off her hair and the side effects from the chemo.

"Did those things help?"

"We'll never know." Reed shrugged, trying to shake away the images that had taken up residence in his mind. "Julie said she didn't want to extend her life but not have any quality to go with it. The doctors warned her the chemo would make her sick, and it wouldn't cure the cancer. In the end, she turned them down."

Reed had pleaded with her to do the treatments. He'd been selfish but he'd wanted more time with her, as much as he could get. He'd promised to be there for her every step of the way but she'd resisted pumping her body full of toxic chemicals. When Julie put her mind to something she could be very stubborn.

"So you went back home?"

"No, we stayed in Denver with the specialists. Her parents convinced her to stay there to manage the disease and her pain."

"I think I understand more now." Kaylee reached out and placed her hand over his. "You must have loved her very much. I can see why you wouldn't be able to love anyone else or make a life with someone."

He couldn't help himself letting his fingers tangle with hers, her touch warm and reassuring. "Honey, I don't deserve to have a life with anyone else. I don't know how to love. I failed Julie when she needed me most and I won't do that to another woman."

Her brow knitted and she leaned forward intently. "I can't imagine how you could fail anyone. I'm sure it was hard to watch her suffer and die. Were you not there when she passed on? Is that why you think you failed her? I'm sure Julie wouldn't want you to do this to yourself. She'd want you to forgive yourself."

Reed swallowed the lump that had formed in his throat and blinked back the moisture in his eyes. "Julie is the one that told me I'd failed her. Julie was the one that said I didn't love her enough. And I guess I didn't, if she believed that. I couldn't do what she needed me to do."

"I can't believe she said that," Kaylee denied, shaking her head and squeezing his hand reassuringly. "You could never fail anyone. What did she want you to do?"

He'd never told anyone his secret, not even his or Julie's family. No one.

"She wanted me to help her die. She begged me to end her life so she wouldn't have to linger and suffer. She told me that if I loved her I would get my gun and pull the trigger."

Chapter Twenty-Two

Kaylee recoiled in horror at Reed's bald statement. His words were bleak and filled with anguish. He'd been put in an impossible situation. Wanting the woman he loved to live and yet being asked to help her die. Kaylee had no idea what she'd do in the same situation.

"I'm sure she didn't mean that. She was probably just upset by her prognosis," she said desperately. Reed's eyes were shiny in the low light of the room, his features haggard as if he'd aged twenty years since this morning. The cool, suave cowboy cop she'd met a week ago was replaced by a man in an incredible amount of pain. He'd been hurting for so long he'd simply stopped trying to live. But he hadn't stopped the pain, he'd only masked it.

"She meant it," he replied grimly. "But there was no way I could shoot the woman I love in the head. No way. Then she suggested that I help her take a bunch of pain pills. She would go in her sleep supposedly. God help me, I just couldn't do it. I kept thinking there would be a miracle or something. Some procedure or drug that would save her and everything would go back to the way it was before. But it never happened, and I watched as she did suffer. In those last months she never let me forget that I'd let her down."

Reed may have been a married man but he'd also been a *young* man. Very young for those kind of adult responsibilities. Of course he'd been hoping for a miracle. If Kaylee had learned anything about Reed this week, she had seen how he valued life. He was willing to protect hers and he barely knew her. He protected his town and heck, had agreed to stay in her home so that Ava's blood pressure wouldn't go up.

He cared. Whether he liked it or not.

Kaylee took a few breaths to slow her pounding heart that ached in sympathy for what Reed had been through.

"Reed," she began carefully, "it wasn't fair of Julie to put all that on you. And it wasn't fair to blame you when you couldn't do it. Why didn't she ask anyone else?"

He reared back in surprise. "Anyone else? I was her husband."

"Yes, but it sounds like she had lots of people around to support her through this. What about her brothers? Or her parents? Or even her friends? Why did she lay all this on you?"

He seemed confused by her questions. "I was her husband," he repeated as if that explained it all. But it didn't.

"Did she ever try to do it herself?"

Reed frowned. "No, of course not."

"Do you think maybe…perhaps…she asked you *because* she knew you would say no? If she'd known you that long, she would know that you couldn't help her take her own life, Reed. Maybe there was a part of her that deep down wanted to live and hope for that miracle you talked about. Maybe that subconscious part of her knew you'd say no. I'm sure she was terrified of what the cancer was going to do to her and that despair made her just want to end everything. But she was young and in love. Surely she had some hope. Deep inside? If she really and truly wanted to die, I'm sure there were ways for her to do it. But she didn't."

"I—" Reed shook his head. "I don't understand what you're saying. Are you saying she wanted me to say no? That she really didn't want to die?"

"I don't know for sure," Kaylee said helplessly. She was a writer, not a psychologist, but she'd made a study of people's hopes, dreams, and motivations. "But isn't it worth thinking about? She was depending on you to make sense of something that was incomprehensible."

Too agitated to keep still, Reed levered from the couch and leaned against the fireplace mantle. "If she wanted me to say no, then why did she hate me for it? She said I didn't love her."

"Maybe she hated herself because she believed she lacked the courage to go through with it. I don't know why she said the things she did but I do know that you loved her. If you didn't you sure as hell wouldn't be ripping yourself up like this. You wouldn't have given up your entire life to her memory as if you don't have a right to be happy."

"I don't have a right to be happy. I ruined what was left of her life."

Dear God, he'd been torturing himself for so long. Logic and common sense had long fled and only pure emotion and regret were driving him.

"I don't believe that for a second. Knowing you, you stood by her every day that she had left. Didn't you, Reed?"

His forehead was resting on his arm and she couldn't see his face but she saw his head nod. "I stayed with her night and day. I quit school and tried to spend every moment I could with her, making things as good for her as I could." He paused. "She liked banana popsicles."

A good memory. That was a start. "Is that what you would bring her when she wasn't feeling good?"

He nodded again. "Popsicles helped her stomach. The pain medication they had her on was strong and she was sick to her stomach a lot. I would rub her forehead when she got bad headaches. She liked that."

"What else did you do to care for her?" Kaylee asked softly, afraid to break the spell. Reed was remembering how he'd cared—loved—Julie.

He straightened and moved to the front window, his shoulders stiff with tension. "I'd do silly stuff to try and make her laugh. You know, sing or tell bad jokes. I'd bring her books at first, but her headaches got too bad for her to be able to read so I would read to her, anything she wanted. Towards the end she couldn't do much for herself so I would help her in the bath, washing her hair and then combing it smooth. She wanted to look nice even when she was sick." He turned and two small silver streaks of tears ran down his cheeks. "I held her every night. She was the most scared then, always saying she was afraid she wouldn't wake up."

Kaylee's throat clogged with emotion and she had to blink to keep the tears from falling. How terrified Julie must have been. Sick and in pain. Dying young and leaving behind her husband and family. Her future. It was no wonder she had lashed out in anger and frustration.

But Kaylee wasn't convinced Julie had been mad at Reed.

Reed had simply been *there*. And if Julie knew she was loved unconditionally, lashing out at him would have been the safest thing to do.

"That sounds like the most wonderful kind of love to me. I would die a happy woman if someone loved me that much,"

Kaylee said simply. She meant every word. "Your Julie was a lucky woman to have you love her like that."

The pain and anguish in his expression was too much. He might not welcome her touch but she needed to hold him. She went to him and wrapped her arms tightly around his waist, so solid and strong.

"Julie's out of her pain, Reed. But you're not. Forgive yourself for whatever you think you've done wrong. I guarantee you Julie has. You don't have to carry this around with you anymore. *You loved her.* You are a man capable of loving deeply."

Her tone was fierce but she had to get through to him. If he was capable of hurting this badly for so long, he was capable of loving for a lifetime. He deserved to be loved more than anything even if it wasn't Kaylee he chose to do it with.

Because she loved him, his happiness was paramount. If she couldn't make him happy, she wanted him to find someone who could.

His long thick lashes were wet and his arms held her so tightly she could barely breathe. "I want to believe that. I really want to." He shook his head. "But I don't know how anymore. I've been this way for so long…I don't know if I can change or if I even want to."

She was asking him to give up a belief system that he'd carried around for more than a decade. The pain he felt every single day had become such a part of him he thought he'd miss it when it was gone. That pain had become a shield that kept the rest of the world out and made him feel safe. How could she make him see that he could fill himself with so much joy and love if he would only let go of the past?

"You have to want it. You have to want a future more than you want to hold on to the past."

The pain in her heart felt like it was ripping her in two. Despite all her protests and declarations to the contrary, she wanted a future with Reed Mitchell.

It was a future she wasn't going to have. He loved Julie. Maybe if he loved Kaylee too he might want to let go, but he didn't.

And just like Reed all those years ago, Kaylee would take whatever time he had to give her. She was greedy for every moment and every day. She'd make the most of this and build memories that would last her a lifetime. Because she had that same hope in her heart for a miracle. But in her case, she would hold on to the joy and not the disappointment and sadness.

"I don't know what I want," Reed said heavily. "Talking about this has been fucking exhausting. Now I know why I haven't done it before."

"You did good tonight. I'm proud of you."

"I thought you might hate me," he admitted, rubbing his chin on the top of her head. "I thought you might think I'd let her down."

"Never," she stated. "I'd never think that. Forgive yourself. No one is holding on to this but you."

"I am so fucked up, honey. So fucking damaged. I can't think why you've stood here tonight and listened to me."

She opened her mouth to tell him of her love but quickly snapped it shut and pressed her lips together tightly. Telling him would be about her needs, not his. He was clearly in no shape to deal with someone else's emotions and wants. He could barely deal with his own. She couldn't burden him like that, couldn't be that selfish.

"I think you are an amazing man," she said instead. "I think it's amazing how you've carried this all these years. There's a lot of strength inside of you."

"I don't feel that way. Shit, I don't know how I feel."

"Don't pressure yourself to feel anything for awhile," Kaylee offered. "Just…be. See how that feels."

"Just be, huh? That's a novel idea." His hand stroked her hair and she burrowed closer to him, rubbing her cheek on the cotton shirt covering his chest.

"It's been a long day. Maybe we should go to bed and get some sleep. That always makes me feel better. You don't have to decide the rest of your life tonight. In fact, I'd advise against it."

All she wanted to do was curl up next to him and hold him all night long to keep the demons away.

"That's the best idea I've heard all day." He tipped her chin up so she was looking into his eyes. "Thank you, honey."

"For what?" she said, cupping his face in her hands, his beard rough against her palms. "I didn't do anything."

"You believe in me. Even though I don't believe in myself."

She bit back the urge to tell him she would always believe in him, always love him. Instead she linked her arm in his and led him towards the stairs. Hopefully he could find some peace, not just tonight but forever.

Kaylee's lids fluttered open and her gaze took in the morning sun beginning to peep through the curtains. She was stretched out against the long length of Reed's body, her sleep as undisturbed as it could be under the circumstances. A few times last night she'd stirred, but he'd settled her into the crook of his arm and she'd fallen back to sleep feeling safe and warm in his arms.

His eyes were open and it looked as if he had been awake for awhile. "Morning."

"Good morning." She scraped her wild hair out of her face. "Did you sleep at all?"

"Some." He nodded. "Enough."

Lifting up on her elbow, she rested her chin on his chest. "Too much to think about? Did you come to any conclusions?"

Her fingers traced the ridges of his stomach idly. "Sure did. I decided about five this morning that I don't want to think about it for a little while. I'll worry about it tomorrow or maybe later today. I was thinking I'd try that 'just be' thing you were talking about."

He rolled her on her back, hovering above her. His face was covered with dark stubble and his hazel eyes were blurry from sleep or the lack of but at that moment he was the most beautiful man she'd ever seen.

That man proceeded to make love to her very softly, sweetly, and slowly as if she was the most precious thing on this earth. His lips were gentle on her own, coaxing and teasing a response before he nipped and licked a trail down her jaw and to her ear, giving it a bite and then soothing it with his tongue.

Her heart tripped in her chest and arousal began building in her abdomen as his mouth traveled down her neck and over her shoulder. Her body arched in invitation and he accepted it without a word. They'd said so many last night and there weren't any that were going to make this situation better. Kaylee would let her body do the talking for her this morning.

His tongue traced a damp line to her nipple and lapped at the tip, running circles around the areola before softly blowing on the hard bud. She moved restlessly under him but he was in no hurry, repeating the torture on the twin until she was gasping, her fingernails digging into the muscles of his shoulders.

Her eyes closed in ecstasy when his lips kissed a wet trail down her quivering belly. He pushed her thighs apart and bent his head, the tip of his tongue lashing at her clit over and over, her entire body tensing and on the edge. He gave her no mercy, teasing her, her fingers clutching the sheets for dear life as she moaned and panted her approval.

"Now, baby."

His mouth closed over the swollen bud and his teeth lightly scraped the sides. The pressure inside of her snapped, setting off an explosion of heat that consumed her entire being, flames dancing on her skin. He didn't allow her to bask in the afterglow of her release, instead pressing his cock to her pussy. Their gazes locked as he slowly entered her, savoring each sensation. They began to rock together, their breathing and heartbeats synchronized.

As if they were the only two people on earth, Reed powered into her sending her higher and farther than she'd ever been. This wasn't just sex or fun and games. This was something more. He might not love her, but he certainly cared for her. It showed in his every touch and caress.

"Come with me, Kaylee," he whispered in her ear.

His hand moved between them, his thumb brushing her sensitive clit. In seconds she was flying high with him, pleasure pouring through her veins like bubbling champagne. His own release hit him and his body went taut as he gulped in air. When it was over, he rested his forehead on hers, his lips teasing hers.

"That's a good way not to think too much."

She giggled, feeling the tickling rumble of his words in his chest. "Good morning, Reed."

"Good morning, Kaylee."

She didn't know what kind of day it was going to be. Had she broken through one barrier only to meet up with another? Just because he'd told her his story didn't mean that everything was going to be alright. In fact, things might be even worse than before.

One thing was for sure; this man had her love and she would do everything in her power to help him leave his past and the pain behind.

Chapter Twenty-Three

"How's that vacation going?" Jared Monroe asked, his voice sounding muffled on Reed's cell phone speaker. He couldn't be at the meeting with the other sheriffs in person today so calling in would have to do.

"It's been fine but frustrating. I'm at a dead end."

Reed set his coffee down on the side table, the liquid too hot to drink. He had settled on the back porch for his call while Kaylee worked in the office. He'd thought it might be weird or awkward this morning after what he'd told her, but as usual Kaylee showed a remarkable amount of sensitivity. She laughed and joked with him as she made breakfast, never bringing up what they'd talked about. Thankfully it was just like any other day.

Of course deep inside it wasn't and Reed knew that. He'd have to deal with all the emotions that had been uncovered last night. Even this morning he hadn't been able to keep his hands off of her, his need to be intimate with her, and only her, overwhelming.

"Maybe we can brainstorm some ideas today," Tanner offered. "Where are you in the investigation?"

"Stuck," Reed admitted grudgingly. "Brent is my number one suspect but Walt is a possibility too. I have zero evidence against either of them or anyone else for that matter."

Reed had tracked Brent's credit card and the guy was back in his hometown probably visiting his parents or old friends. If a guy was on the lam, heading straight to the bosom of his family would be a stupid thing to do.

"Seems like you have a lack of motive in general," Evan observed. "According to you, Kaylee is a sweet woman that no one would want to hurt. Except that someone does."

"That's exactly what she is," Reed replied sharply, not liking where Evan was going with this. "I checked her out myself."

"Now wait a minute," Evan said. "I wasn't implying what you think. I don't think your lady has some deep, dark secret in her past at all. What I'm saying is maybe we need to think outside the box on motive."

"Sorry," Reed grimaced, ignoring Evan's suggestion that Kaylee was Reed's "lady". "I guess I'm feeling the pressure. You think we need to look outside of love or greed?"

"There's a shit load of reasons for someone to want to hurt of kill someone." Seth must have been sitting right next to the phone as his voice came in loud and clear. "Jealousy, revenge, secrets, political, personal vendetta, or maybe the bastard is just a fucking loony toon."

"Even loony toons have a motive," Dare pointed out. "It's usually a stupid one but it's there."

"If it's this Brent guy, is it love or jealousy? Or both?" Griffin asked. "Is he so obsessed that he has to have her even in death or is he jealous of her success?"

Reed wasn't a fan of the way the word "death" was being thrown around so casually but since he had no intention of letting her end up that way he didn't say anything.

"Maybe it is both," Tanner said. "Think about it. Perhaps this Brent is obsessed and wants Kaylee because he wants to be a part of what she has. As her boyfriend, he would belong to her world so to speak. Then he could systematically destroy her career from the inside out due to his jealousy."

"Or try and take credit for her work. The whole man behind the woman thing," Griffin offered. "Either way, it's not a healthy mental state for a human being. Have you thought about trying to lure him out?"

"There's an idea," Jared agreed. "Set a trap."

Reed stroked his chin in thought. "I like the idea of being on the offensive rather than the defensive. What are you thinking, Griff? We announce she won some kind of award maybe?"

"I'm thinking a little *Thin Man* action."

Reed snorted. He'd never seen that movie and he was pretty sure Griffin hadn't either until Jazz moved in a few months ago. "Pretend I'm not living with an actress and explain that remark to me please."

"Gladly," Griffin chuckled. "Jazz has me watching these old movies and I have to admit they're really good, especially this one. William Powell is a retired police detective and one of his friends ends up dead. At the end of the movie he invites all the suspects to dinner so they're all in one room."

"Ellery Queen does that too," Tanner interjected. "Love those stories."

"I think Agatha Christie does it as well but William Powell drinks martinis while he solves crimes. So now that he has everyone there he starts to tell them why each of them make a great suspect. He says something provocative and the killer reveals themselves," Griffin ended triumphantly. "Everyone thinks he knew who it was before but he really didn't. He only had theories. He needed them all together to find out for sure."

"So I should invite her writing club here and grill them like criminals? Kaylee will love that," Reed said dryly. "But perhaps it could work…with a few technological modifications. I could plant more cameras and listening devices around and see if anyone tries to leave her a letter or picture. Or maybe take something personal of hers as a souvenir. I've seen quite a bit of that in stalker situations."

"Sounds like you have a plan," Seth approved.

"There's only one problem with it," Reed warned, already thinking of the downsides. The problem with taking up the offense was it tended to be riskier.

"What's that?" Griffin asked.

"Kaylee," Tanner answered for Reed.

"Kaylee," Reed echoed. "I'd be using Kaylee for bait. I'm not sure how I feel about that and it might send Ava into labor or something. Is Logan with her today?"

"He is. He had a deputy out sick for a few days so he hasn't spent much time with her," Tanner explained. "I have his report for the meeting."

Reed owed Logan a call anyway. He'd tried to phone the day after Reed and Kaylee had first ended up in bed together but had only reached Logan's voicemail.

"I'd feel a whole lot better about trying to set a trap if you guys were here." An idea struck Reed and he sat up straight as the details began to formulate in his mind. "You actually can kind of be here with me. You could have your eyes and ears on the cameras while I stick with Kaylee."

"Not bad thinking for a guy who is on vacation," Jared laughed. "If I can juggle my schedule, I'm in."

The other men echoed Jared's response and Reed was breathing much easier about the idea. "I'd like to wait a little while longer though. This would be the plan of last resort. I don't want to put Kaylee directly in the line of fire if I don't have to."

"Agreed," Tanner said. "Keep us posted. So what else do we need to discuss today? Griffin, is everything quiet again in your town?"

The meeting proceeded as each man made his report. Except for a few minor drug charges and some domestic issues, things seemed quiet in all the towns which was a relief. Reed had already talked to his deputies, who seemed to be having a fine time without him, and everything was under control there. Of course the guys were probably skating by on the very minimum of paperwork which Reed would need to sort out when he returned home.

Home. The sooner, the better. It would hurt him to leave Kaylee but each passing day would only make it worse. He still wasn't sure he had anything to give her beyond sex and friend-ship, and he wasn't sure he ever would.

Kaylee snapped her laptop lid shut. She ought to be writing but her mind was too jumbled to make much sense. In desperation, she called Ava who always managed to set Kaylee back on the writing path.

"How are you feeling?" Kaylee asked Ava. "Is your blood pressure normal?"

"No," Ava growled. "It's still too high, and I'm sick of lying in this bed contemplating the universe. A woman can only write so many words a day you know. Especially while Logan or one of his minions is hovering over me as if I'm going to explode at any minute."

Giggling, Kaylee propped her feet up on the desk. "Minions? Logan has minions? Since when?"

"Presley and her little one, Bennett, come over when Logan can't be here. When she has things to do Jazz comes over or Madison." Another groan. "And I feel so damn guilty when Madison is here. I found out she and Tanner have been trying to have a baby with no luck. She's been diagnosed with severe endometriosis and the chances of her getting pregnant are low. I feel so badly for her and then she comes over here with nothing but a sweet smile and is so nice. It has to be hard for her."

"How did you find out? Did Madison tell you?"

"No, Tanner admitted it when he picked her up the other night. She was in the bathroom and he wanted to warn me in case she got emotional. Heck, she's been awesome. Jazz, too."

"You haven't talked too much about Jazz. What is she like?"

"She's a hoot and a half. She has great stories from her time in Hollywood and she just adores Griffin. They've decided on a long engagement since they've only known each other for a short time but she's definitely settling into small town life. Her actress friend Caitlin has decided to pull of stakes and move to Hope Lake as well. They're going to open a theatre group together. Give acting and singing lessons, have a children's theatre and so on. You know how much parents love to see their little darlings in a play. It sounded pretty fun."

"In no time at all you and Logan will be watching your two kids up on stage. I know Logan will film it. You'll have to post it so I can see it."

"I hope they don't have my drama skills. I had two lines in the *Santa Claus for President* school play and I was so scared I couldn't even get them out. But enough about me. How are things with you and Reed? Did you take my advice and go for it? Please say yes. I'm living vicariously through you. I'm on complete pelvic rest and don't ask what that is. It's too depressing to even talk about."

Kaylee had a pretty decent idea what it meant and was glad it didn't apply to her. "How can I answer that…no comment?"

"Yes," Ava hissed with glee. "Good for you. Is he as good as he looks?"

"Better," Kaylee sighed reluctantly, visions of this morning dancing in her head. "Much, much better. But he has issues, you know. He's carrying a lot of baggage."

"You're not going to marry him," Ava stated, and Kaylee was glad that her face couldn't be seen through the phone. If Ava had seen it she'd know that Kaylee had fallen badly for the emotionally tortured cop. "Just enjoy the fun and don't think about tomorrow. Except for your next book, of course, and congratulations on the release—it looks like another hit. I'm still reading the last one but as soon as I'm finished I'll start on the new one. I have a lot of time on my hands these days."

"Enjoy it. I don't think the babies will let you read again for maybe ten years or so."

"I think you're being wildly optimistic," Ava laughed. "But that's what I love about you. Your glass is always half full."

"And what I love about you is that you can get me back on track. I seem to lack writing motivation today."

"Put the laptop away and pick up a notebook and pen. That always makes things better for me when I have to slow my thoughts down enough that my hand can keep up. Give it a try."

Kaylee had already closed her laptop so it was worth a shot. "Why not? Worst case scenario I end up outlining another book and putting that in my backlog."

"Just how many do you have in reserve?"

"Dozens. At the rate I'm going I'll need to live to be a hundred and ten to be able to write them all and that's if I don't come up with any more."

"Then I better let you get to work. Call me in a few days and let me know how things are going."

"I will. Take care and get some rest."

After ending the call, Kaylee stood and headed into the kitchen. Maybe some baking would help with writer's block. It couldn't hurt and even if it didn't help they would still have cookies to eat. It was a win-win in her book.

Rummaging through the cabinets, she checked her ingredients. She was going to need a trip to the store. She snuck a peek outside and Reed didn't look like he was on his call anymore so she rapped on the window to get his attention.

"I'm going to the store," she mouthed, picking up her car keys from the counter and holding them up. "I'll be right back."

Reed frowned and shook his head. Not paying him any mind, she slung her purse over her shoulder and mouthed again, "I'll be back in a few."

This time Reed set his laptop on the glider cushion and pulled open the door between the porch and the kitchen.

"You're not going anywhere by yourself, remember? If you need to go somewhere I'll take you."

He had that "I am God, don't argue with me" tone she'd grown used to and wasn't intimidated by in the least. But he did have a damn point. Someone wanted her dead enough to try and run her down. She didn't really want to become road kill in the parking lot of the Schnucks.

"Fine," she conceded. "Can we leave now?"

"Sure, and we'll take my truck."

He didn't like her cute little economy car? He did probably feel like a giant in it.

"Whatever," she said with a long-suffering sigh. "Can we just go now? I have a craving for cookies."

A grin spread across his face. "Why didn't you say so in the first place? Cookies? Let's go."

Kaylee smiled back, glad that they could be still be natural around each other after last night. She could only hope that their talk was the first step on his long road to healing.

Reed pulled the truck into the driveway and Kaylee dug into her purse for the house keys. They'd ended up doing more than cookie shopping. Since they were at the store they'd shopped for the whole week. Since they hadn't heard anything from her stalker since Friday night, it looked like Reed might be here for quite a while.

Kaylee was just fine with that.

"I'll carry the groceries in," Reed offered. "Why don't you get the mail?"

"Chauvinist," she joked, sliding out of the truck and unlocking the front door while Reed grabbed the bags. "I'm perfectly capable of carrying some groceries."

"Aren't you lucky that you don't have to," Reed shot back with a grin as he brushed past her into the kitchen. She giggled and sauntered back down the driveway to the mailbox. She wasn't a big fan of snail mail, most of it junk. She paid her bills online and didn't subscribe to any magazines.

She grabbed the mail and walked toward the house, sifting through the usual contents.

Advertisement. Another advertisement. Paper bill for something already paid online.

Shit. Shit. Shit.

The same blank envelope except for her name in block letters. Sliding her trembling fingers under the flap, she pulled out the single sheet of white paper. This letter was brief and succinct.

Your time has come. The day of reckoning is nigh, sinner bitch.

Taking a few calming breaths to slow her heart, she walked into the house where Reed was already unpacking the groceries. He'd become such an integral part of her world in so little time. She cleared her throat and held out the paper and envelope.

"I got another letter."

Anger kindled in his eyes and his jaw tightened ominously. "Set it down on the counter. Let's keep as few prints on it as possible although there wasn't any to be found on the other letter."

She placed it in front of him and he perused the small amount of contents, shaking his head. "Son of a bitch. We'll need to call the cops again of course." He exhaled slowly. "I wasn't going to mention this right away but I talked to the guys this morning and we floated an idea of setting a trap to flush this guy out."

Kaylee had heard Ava talking about the group of local sheriffs who met to help one another enough to know who "the guys" referred to. But what about this trap? It sounded a little Scooby Doo.

"A trap?" she repeated. "What did you have in mind?"

"If Brent is obsessed with you because of your career it might bring him out if we had some sort of get-together to celebrate your latest book."

"If it's Brent," she countered. "And if that's the reason someone is stalking me."

"He's our best bet right now. He's not accounted for when that car tried to run you down. But you make a good point. It may not be professional jealousy—it may be good old-fashioned jealousy. So for good measure I would stick close to you and make sure everyone knew we were a couple."

"Are we a couple?" she challenged, the words coming out of her mouth before she could stop them. It was an incredibly stupid thing to ask but there it was.

"Considering the things we did together yesterday and this morning I would say yes." His eyes narrowed dangerously. "Just because it's not 'til death do us part doesn't mean we aren't together. Unless I've missed something."

"Nope." Kaylee shook her head, feeling better than she had all day. He truly cared about her and it did make her feel special. "So you want to throw a party? For my book? I don't usually self-congratulate like that."

She didn't like drawing attention to herself.

"Let's make an exception this time. Plan something that will get people here. I'll set up the surveillance system."

"More cameras." Kaylee sighed in resignation. "How can you watch them and be a doting boyfriend at the same time?"

"I've got friends," Reed replied enigmatically. "Good friends. So are you okay with this plan? I don't want to put you in danger, honey. If you don't feel comfortable doing this we'll find another way."

She'd trust Reed with her life, didn't he know that?

"No, I think it's a good idea. I'm not scared as long as you're there with me."

"I'll never leave your side for one second. I promise," he vowed. "Your safety is the most important thing to me."

"So we plan a party?"

Reed smiled and laughed. "You plan a party while I set up the equipment. I don't think I'd be very good at selecting piñatas and finger sandwiches anyway."

One party to catch a stalker coming right up with a side of surveillance. She'd have to put this in a book someday.

Chapter Twenty-Four

Reed was standing in the middle of the living room watching Kaylee greet their guests. Friday night was a good time for a party and the house was filling up with people—some Reed had met, and some he'd never seen.

"Can you hear me?" Jared's voice came through the earpiece Reed was wearing in a hopefully discrete manner. If anyone noticed, he hoped they would think it was a hearing aid and not remark on it. "Just nod your head if you can."

Reed nodded and glanced up at the camera in the corner. Every inch of the house and yard was covered. He'd spent the better part of the week setting them up, making sure the angles were perfect. Now his buddies a thousand miles away were sitting in their homes and offices watching the footage while he kept his eye on Kaylee.

He let his gaze linger on her curvy form and bright smile. Damn, she was beautiful. He was used to the tightness in his chest now and the way his mind went all mushy when she was close to him. He liked the scent of her skin after a shower and how she frowned at her laptop when she was writing. He liked the cookies she made and the way her lips tasted of sugar and vanilla. He especially liked the way she sighed in her sleep and cuddled close to stay warm on chilly nights.

He liked pretty much everything about her, and it was going to hurt like hell when he left. Funny how a few weeks ago he hadn't felt much of anything. In a way it was like waking up after being in a long, deep sleep. The world looked brighter and sharper and his senses were far more attuned to everything around him. He still felt the pain of the past but also the contentment of being here with Kaylee. He wouldn't lie though and say he wasn't tempted to go back and shut himself off again. Life had been in many ways much easier then.

"You're scowling again." Kaylee was standing in front of him with a smile on her face and her hands on her hips. "Any particular reason?"

"The usual ones," he responded, knowing it would make her laugh. She was more in sync with his moods than he was. She seemed to know instinctively when he needed to be alone and when he wanted company but perhaps all women were more sensitive than men. Or at least him in particular. Or maybe he was simply that transparent. He'd have to remember to ask her later.

"Well, wipe it off of your face and paint on a smile. I don't like being the center of attention for all these people either but we need to make the best of it."

They were so alike—he and Kaylee. Neither of them wanted to spend the evening making vapid small talk with semi-friends and acquaintances. A much smaller group of people to dinner would have been preferable but wouldn't have given the stalker as much opportunity. With all this activity it would be easy for him to slip in and out of rooms. Reed had his fingers crossed for another letter or picture tonight.

"Is our friend Brent here yet?" he asked, watching Walt pour himself a glass of wine at the kitchen island that was doubling as a bar tonight. Reed's gut was telling him that Walt was an odd duck but had nothing to do with Kaylee's stalking and attempt to run her down.

Shit, call it what it really was. Attempted murder. Some asshole had tried to murder his woman. Reed sure as shit wasn't going to give them another fucking chance.

"I haven't seen him yet. Maybe he won't come." She sounded kind of hopeful but Brent wouldn't be able to stay away. Reed had recognized the want in the man's expression that first day at the writer's group. Brent wanted Kaylee.

Glancing at his watch, Reed waited for his friends to check in. Every fifteen minutes on the dot.

"Nothing to report," Jared said. He was watching the kitchen and living room.

"Nothing here," Griffin chimed in. He'd been assigned the exterior of the house.

"Not a thing," Seth agreed. He had Kaylee's bedroom and bathroom.

"Nothing," Evan reported. He was observing the office and spare bedrooms.

Tanner, Dare, and Logan were all on duty. Reed had finally been able to talk to Logan about everything that had been happening and it had gone better than expected. Ava had prepared her husband well apparently for the news that Reed and Kaylee were an item. Logan had growled a few times but had eventually said that he was glad that Reed was there to take care of Ava's friend.

Reed had "cared" for Kaylee twice last night and then once more this morning in the shower. It just kept getting better and better. Last night they'd played doctor and naughty nurse.

"Kaylee!" Turning in the direction of the squeal, Reed inwardly groaned at the entrance of Linda and Cheryl. The two women, seemingly joined at the hip, had come over earlier in the week to talk to Kaylee about what they should wear to the party and if they could bring any food or drink.

"Congratulations on the new book! It's really zooming up the charts," Linda gushed, batting her eyelashes that were too thick with mascara. "I was bragging to my hairdresser only yesterday that I know a famous author."

Kaylee's cheeks turned a deep red and he slid his arm around her waist and pulled her close so she wouldn't bolt. She hated this shit and today wasn't going to be easy for her. He'd promised to never leave her side and he'd meant it.

"Thank you, Linda. That's so sweet but I'd hardly call myself famous. Stephen King is famous. Hardly anyone knows my name and I'm fine with that."

"This is only the beginning," Cheryl raved, hugging a clearly uncomfortable Kaylee. "The name Kaylee Blue is going to be known everywhere."

Kaylee thanked Cheryl and the three of them launched into a spirited discussion of what cover elements sold books and what turned off buyers.

"I do like a hunky man on the cover," agreed Linda. "But I don't much like women with them. I don't know why but I like to just look at the male."

Cheryl eyed him over her wine glass. "There's nothing like a hunky man." She turned to Kaylee with a sly smile. "So will Reed be moving here or are you moving to Montana? Isn't your friend there as well? He'd be a man worth relocating for."

Reed slid his hand around her shoulders and under her long hair, his expression full of adoration. "Kaylee and I have a lot of decisions to make. I'm sure we'll find a way to make things work."

Linda and Cheryl looked impressed by his smitten display and Kaylee was breathing easier although she looked like she wanted to laugh out loud. Perhaps he'd overdone it but the women bought it hook, line, and sinker.

"I've got movement in the back of the house," Griffin's voice sounded in Reed's ear. "A man with dark hair, mid-thirties. Blue suit and tie. He's carrying a small bouquet of flowers and what looks like an envelope. Moving to the back door but staying behind a crowd of people. Jared, are you picking him up yet?"

Adrenaline coursed through Reed's veins and his pulse pounded at his friend's pronouncement. It was fucking working and the description sounded like Brent. They would catch the little bastard red-handed.

"I've got him," Jared answered. "He's moving toward the stairway very slowly, and trying not to garner any attention. Evan?"

Reed glanced casually over his shoulder but the stalker was keeping hidden very well. Even at his over six-foot height Reed couldn't see him behind the crush of bodies. His grip tightened ever so slightly on Kaylee's shoulder and she turned to give him a strange look. He raised his eyebrows and her own eyes widened in surprise as she realized what he was trying to communicate.

"I got him," Evan stated. "He's at the top of the stairs and heading down the hall to one of the bedrooms. I'm guessing Kaylee's. Seth?"

Reed was already bounding up the stairs, his hand under his suit jacket where his service revolver was nestled in his shoulder holster. Pulling the weapon, he waited outside the door for Seth's signal.

"He's just placed flowers and an envelope on Kaylee's bed. Move in."

Reed shoved open the door so it banged on the wall. Brent whirled around, his expression going slack and his eyes going round. Putting his hands up, he began to step away from Reed.

"Freeze and don't move." Reed pointed the gun at Brent who had gone pale with sweat popping out on his forehead.

"Hey, man. I was, um, just leaving Kaylee a present."

Brent's voice had gone up at least an octave and he lowered his hand as if to reach for something.

"Don't fucking move," Reed snarled again. Kaylee was at his elbow and he never took his gaze from Brent, letting the man know this was fucking serious. "Kaylee, call the police. Brent can explain it to the cops why he was sneaking around your house and in your bedroom."

"I told you, I was just leaving her—"

"Save it," Reed cut in, keeping the firearm trained on the man who seemed to have absorbed what was happening and was now shaking like a leaf. "Put your hands on your head and turn around."

Brent hesitated but then complied, placing his hands on his head and facing the wall. Reed holstered his weapon and retrieved his cuffs from his back pocket before cuffing the man's hands behind his back. After checking him for weapons, Reed stepped back and pressed Brent in a chair near the bed.

"Why have you been harassing Kaylee? Are you in love with her?"

Brent's face turned bright red and he shifted uncomfortably in the chair. "I like Kaylee a whole lot. She's always been real sweet to me."

"But you didn't tell her about your drug conviction?"

The man scowled now, his lips twisted in anger. "How did you know about that? I never told anyone."

"No such thing as a secret anymore," Reed countered. "Why were you trying to scare Kaylee?"

"Reed." Kaylee placed her hand on his shoulder. "The police are on their way but what am I supposed to do with all those people in the living room? Walt is holding them at bay but they all want to come back here and see what's going on."

Reed glanced over his shoulder and Kaylee was flanked as usual by Cheryl and Linda both looking shocked. Reed on the other hand was feeling triumphant. He'd finally caught the rat in the act of leaving a letter.

"Send them all home," he answered grimly. "The party served its purpose and is over."

"I'm not sure they'll leave," Linda breathed softly. "Most of them just got here."

"I'm sure you ladies know how to clear a room," Reed said before turning his attention back to Brent. "Answer my question. Why were you trying to scare Kaylee?"

"I wasn't, I swear. I really like her and wanted her to notice me, I guess. Since you came here she doesn't have time for anyone else."

"And that made you angry?" The question came from behind Reed and he turned to see one of the officers that had been on duty when Kaylee had almost been run down. "Angry enough to try and kill her?"

The police weren't going to let Reed continue his interrogation. He was probably going to get scolded for putting Brent in handcuffs too but it had been worth it. Brent was out of the stalking business.

"Can we get you folks to step out here so we can get your statements?" the other officer asked. "We have several questions."

Reed bet they did. He nodded and put his arm around Kaylee and they walked down the stairs to the office. Pulling the earpiece off, he sank down onto the couch, his hand still holding hers. It was going to be a long night.

"Can you start from the beginning?" the cop requested, taking out a notebook and pen. "How did you know the suspect was in Ms. Carter's bedroom?"

Reed leaned forward, his elbow on his knees. "It's like this. I'm a sheriff in Montana who came here to help find this guy and protect Kay–, I mean Ms. Carter. I rigged the house with security surveillance in every nook and cranny. Then I had some of my colleagues watching the tape while I was in the party with Kaylee. They alerted me to the suspect sneaking in the back door and hiding behind guests." He held up the ear piece. "I could hear them with this."

The officer stopped writing in his notebook and shook his head in confusion. "Wait a minute. Maybe we should back up further. You did what?"

Yep, a long night indeed.

Chapter Twenty-Five

Kaylee slumped over her coffee the next day and yawned. They'd spent hours talking to the police and the detective that had been assigned to her case. Angry at first at what Reed had done to trap Brent, they'd threatened to arrest him but she still wasn't clear on what the charges would have been. Reed had been here at her own behest and he hadn't hurt Brent at all, only handcuffing him. Reed in turn had been calm and professional with them, eventually winning them over as they swapped cop stories.

Brent had been taken down to the police station for questioning but he was denying his guilt even as they escorted him out. Not one person had left the party, too curious as to what was going on. In fact, they'd stayed and eaten her food and drank her beer and wine until quite late. Some friends she had.

It had been after two in the morning when she and Reed had stumbled to bed, bleary eyed and exhausted. He'd been up early but she'd slept in until ten. Already showered, he was too damn awake and cheery.

"You need more coffee."

Kaylee drained her cup and held it out. Laughing, Reed refilled it before taking care of his own. He was a morning person, dammit. So annoying. Kaylee didn't like mornings and had never seen the appeal of watching the sunrise or being the early bird. Who likes worms?

"Can you stop being so...awake?"

"Doubtful. How many of the cameras do you want me to leave up? You should have some for security."

Rubbing the sleep from her eyes, Kaylee scowled at her man and houseguest. "You know I can't make decisions until after a couple cups of coffee."

Reed smiled indulgently. "Then I'll decide for you. The weather report said it was going to rain later. If I want to do anything outside, I better get it done soon."

"I like to write to the sound of the rain."

But first she needed a shower to wake the hell up.

"Is that the plan for the day? Writing?"

The caffeine was beginning to kick in. Did Reed have some fun planned? Perhaps some afternoon delight? Now that her stalker was caught, it felt as if the weight of the world has been lifted off of her shoulders. Of course, it was sad and disturbing that Brent had done those things. She didn't understand what had driven him. He'd always seemed nice and polite.

"Do you not want me to write today? Did you have something else in mind?"

"I thought it would be nice to spend the day together." He fiddled with the handle of his coffee mug. "Since it's my last day here and all. Now that Brent's been fingered I can be getting back to my vacation."

She was wide awake and not liking what she was hearing. It hadn't even occurred to her he would leave immediately. She'd thought he might spend the rest of his vacation with her. Or maybe she'd just hoped it.

"I wouldn't want to keep you from your vacation." Kaylee got up from the table, the chair legs scraping the tile loudly in the quiet. "Are you leaving in the morning?"

He was looking at her again with that narrow-eyed gaze as if he was assessing not only her physical appearance but her state of mind.

"You sound mad," he said flatly.

"I'm not mad," she denied, warming up her coffee even though it was already hot. She needed something to do with her hands or she was going to throw the pot at his thick skull.

"You aren't happy." He got up and came around the table to where she was standing and leaned against the counter. "I didn't want to assume anything, honey. I did what I came to do. Our deal was that I would leave afterward. But if you don't want me to just say so."

"You want to leave," she accused, her voice low. "You can't wait to get to Florida."

He took a few steps forward and backed her into the cabinets, his imposing frame filling her line of vision. He smelled like soap and man and dammit, he shouldn't smell so good when she was angry with him. "I don't even like sand. And I'm not planning to go there anymore. I was just going to point the truck in some direction and see whatever there is to see. Now, if I had something else to do that would be fine. Do I?"

A flash of anger ran through her. He'd said he liked being the aggressor in the relationship but then he expected her to take all the chances. "I don't know, Reed. After everything that's happened I thought you might stay, but don't fucking do me any favors."

She twisted away to get around him but his superior strength easily held her in place. "Relax, honey. That's not how things are and you know it. I'd like to stay for awhile but I didn't want to assume that you wanted that too. Why do you think I mentioned leaving so early in the damn morning?"

"To piss me off." The words were out of her mouth before she could stop them.

"Kind of," he admitted with a grimace. "I wanted your real reaction, not a polite one. I knew if I caught you before your third cup and a shower I'd get an honest answer."

She'd given him one. She knew that he had to get back eventually but he'd only spent two weeks of his vacation so far. She'd simply been too proud to admit she wanted more. It was hard to remember that he didn't know she loved him.

"Do you like history?" she asked, already thinking of things they could do together. Most of them involved being naked but a few did require clothes.

"I do," he affirmed. "What did you have in mind?"

"The Abraham Lincoln Museum is in Springfield. He's kind of a hero of mine and it's pretty cool. We could go there."

Reed nodded. "Sounds like a plan. I'll clean up in here while you shower." She placed her coffee cup in the sink and moved toward the stairs, but he caught her hand. "And Kaylee? Make no mistake. I'm looking forward to spending some time with you."

Heart squeezing in her chest, she dashed up the stairs with a smile on her face. He might not love her but he cared. She could work with that.

"That museum was impressive," Reed said as they unlocked the front door and collapsed on the couch. "And the technology made it even better. Going there was a great idea, honey."

They'd had a terrific "date" day, laughing and talking the entire time. Kaylee didn't push things and was simply content to have fun while he was here. It made her even more precious to him if that were possible. What he felt for her made him feel weak and strong all at the same time which only served to confuse the fuck out of him. But not enough to make him leave.

"I'm full of great ideas." Kaylee had a mischievous gleam in her eye and suddenly he didn't feel so damn tired. "I have one right now as a matter of fact."

"Do you?" She straddled him and ran her hands up his chest, her lips brushing his. His heart tripped and his breath hitched in his chest. "I think I like this idea. What fantasy are we living out tonight?"

"Hmmmm…I've been thinking about that. How about master and slave?"

Kaylee giggled and his chest tightened painfully. Her green eyes were twinkling and her cheeks were pink with excitement. This fantasy must be a good one if she looked like this and he'd barely kissed her.

"Tell me about this master and slave fantasy. How does this one go?"

"Well…I was thinking it would be fun if you tied me to the bed so I'd be at your mercy. I'd have to do whatever you wanted, you know, like a sex slave," she said, already breathless with anticipation. He bet if he checked her panties they were damp with arousal as well.

His cock liked the idea just fine, pressing painfully against the buttons on his fly. He'd played dominant/submissive games in the past and the thought of Kaylee bound for his pleasure was an intoxicating one. He had a few ideas of his own to make this fantasy even better.

"Then head upstairs and strip off your clothes. Sex slaves are supposed to be naked."

Deliciously naked. Kaylee was self-conscious when un-clothed but he thought she looked incredibly fuckable with her round breasts and curvy hips. Her ass cheeks were perfect for spanking and she definitely needed one tonight.

She flounced up the stairs, trying and succeeding to arouse him further. It wasn't easy but he made himself wait a few minutes instead of panting after her like a dog in heat. He wanted to make this night last. With Kaylee bound to the bed, he could make her come as often as he wanted before fucking them both into oblivion.

The anticipation was too much. He bounded up the stairs and into the bedroom thinking she would be laid out on the bed like a buffet. Instead she was kneeling by the bed looking very submissive indeed.

But he knew better.

Fighting a grin, he kept his features set in a stern manner. If she wanted the whole experience he was happy to give it to her.

"So this is the new sex slave." His voice boomed in the si-lence and he swore she was holding back a smile and a giggle as well. "I think I'll sample what she has to offer before we go any further."

He'd get her to help him let off a little steam so he would last longer later.

Standing in front of her, he placed his hand on her head. "Service me, slave. Show me what pleasure you can give me."

There was a definite smirk on her face, but it would be gone in moments because her fingers were fumbling with the buttons on his jeans and tugging them down his thighs. His cock sprang free when she pulled down his boxer shorts and his balls tight-ened as he watched her tongue snake out and wet her full lips. That tongue and mouth needed to get busy.

Her hand surrounded him while the other cupped his sac with fondling fingers. He sucked in a breath as her wet, hot lips engulfed the head of his cock and he groaned as her tongue fluttered around the sensitive underside.

Shit. Damn. Fuck.

Squeezing his eyes shut, he recited crime statistics to keep from blowing too soon, wanting to enjoy her erotic ministrations a little while longer. Her lips tightened and the suction was almost more than he could take. The pressure built in his lower back and he pulled away but she followed him, her mouth never leaving his cock.

"Honey," he said, his voice hoarse and tortured. "Pull off, baby."

Of course his little slave didn't listen to him. Instead she rolled his balls in her clever hands and flitted her tongue around the head. He felt his cock swell and then his hot seed was filling her mouth. She sucked him dry and then sat back on her heels, looking pleased with herself while he tried to pull himself together.

Naughty.

"I told you to pull off, little slave. Not obeying your master is grounds for punishment. Stand up and place your hands on the bed."

Reed was going to spank her. Kaylee had known defying him in the bedroom at any time, let alone during a game of master and slave, was a reason for a good spanking. He was all alpha when it came to sex and that was just fine and dandy.

Now she was going to get the punishment she wanted so badly.

"Yes, Master," she said as meekly as she could manage without looking triumphant.

Rising to her feet, she bent at the waist and placed her palms on the mattress. Her legs were braced wide apart and her thighs were sticky with honey. She could hear the hammer of her pulse in her ears and she relaxed her entire body as she waited in heavenly anticipation.

His hands rubbed her ass cheeks, warming them up and her body hummed in appreciation of his touch. There wasn't another man in the world she would do this with but with Reed it seemed almost natural to play with their sexuality and explore their long held desires.

"This is for your disobedience," Reed intoned, his voice sending shivers up her spine. She closed her eyes, wanting to savor every moment of his mastery. He didn't make her wait, bringing his palm down on her bottom sharply. The heat on her ass simmered as he peppered the cheeks with slaps designed to raise the temperature on her skin gradually. The warmth grew and spread to her pussy and clit, her feet shifting as her arousal grew.

The spanking stopped abruptly but his fingers stroked the abused flesh gently. "I hope you've learned your lesson, little slave."

She had to remind herself to breathe before she could answer. "I have, Master. I'm very sorry for my disobedience."

It was a boldface lie because she'd do it again knowing her ass would be red-hot and her pussy drenched when he was finished.

"Lie on the bed on your back," he commanded and she scrambled to do his bidding, but first she had to move the tethers she'd dug out of the back of the closet. He frowned and picked up the straps with fur-lined cuffs at the end.

"Slave? What are these?"

She could feel her deep-red flush from head to toe. "Um, I ordered them for research. I've never actually used them but I needed to know how they worked for a book," she said, breaking character for the explanation. "Are they okay?"

Holding her breath while he examined them closely, she exhaled when he smiled. "These will do nicely. I thought we'd have to use socks or something. This is much better." He straightened up and went immediately back into fantasy-man mode. "Arms over your head, little slave."

She lifted her arms and he wrapped one end of the tether to the brass headboard. The other end had the two fur-lined cuffs. Those he wound snugly around her wrists and fastened them with velcro straps. She tugged at the bonds and found they were secure but comfortable. The padding and lining would keep her skin from being bruised and marked but the tether would keep her firmly attached to the bed.

But he wasn't done. Attaching one of the other straps to the side bar of her bed, he lifted her leg and wrapped the cuff around her thigh before repeating the process on the other side. He sat back on his heels and grinned at her predicament. He'd bound her legs wide apart and pulled high so every inch of her pussy was wide open for his inspection.

"Now this is a slave bound for my use. And I do intend to use this slave well."

"This is obscene," she hissed, trying to pull her legs together. "You can see—well, everything."

Reed nodded and stroked his chin, still smiling. "I do like to look. So pretty and pink and all wet. Just for me." He leaned down and whispered in her ear. "Relax, baby. You're beautiful everywhere."

She wanted to believe him, but there was that spot of doubt deep inside that kept her from enjoying this. He seemed to recognize it because he nodded as if he'd decided something important.

"I see you don't believe me. You're right, words are meaningless. I'll show you so you never forget."

He bent his head and ran his tongue from opening to clit and then back again. Callused hands on her quivering thighs, he explored every centimeter of her pussy before tongue-fucking her until she had to bite back her screams. With no mercy he'd taken her right to the edge of orgasm. No build up, no teasing. Simply pure unadulterated ecstasy.

Running his tongue around her clit in ever-decreasing circles, he chuckled as she spat out several four-letter words in frustration.

"What a naughty mouth for a slave. But I know what to do. Time to come, Kaylee."

His mouth closed over her clit just as he smacked her already sore bottom. The pleasure and pain sent her over immediately, her climax so powerful it seemed to turn her inside out. He continued to spank her as his tongue sent her higher, not letting her come down from the first orgasm. She'd barely caught her breath when the second one began.

Lost to the waves crashing through her, she tugged at her bonds only to be assured she was still his helpless prisoner. The mere thought of being at his mercy amped up her arousal all over again even as his fingers sought and found her nipples. Plucking the hard buds, his mouth never ceased its efforts to send her higher and she shot into climax number three as she called his name in a voice she barely recognized as her own.

The pleasure was simply too much. Pleas for mercy came tumbling from her lips as she sucked in air to her aching lungs.

Her pussy clenched, needing to be filled and her body trembled as her orgasm slowly gave up control.

The bed shifted and she opened her eyes to see Reed stripping out of his clothes. Piece by piece his magnificent body, honed to perfection was revealed to her gaze. She relished every moment not knowing how much longer she would have with him. She wanted to make every minute count.

She let her gaze travel from his square jaw to his wide, muscular shoulders, then down to his ridged abs so flat you could bounce a quarter off of them. His powerful thighs were revealed as he pushed down the denim fabric of his jeans and she couldn't help but stare at the impressive cock jutting from between his legs. The first time she'd taken it she thought it might break her in two. Even now he stretched her muscles each time but in the most pleasurable way possible. She loved the feeling of fullness he gave.

"Fuck me," she breathed, wanting and needing him more each day. Dark thoughts of his departure began to fill her head but she ruthlessly pushed them away. There would be time for that later. Now was all about the pleasure they created together.

"What a demanding slave," Reed chuckled as he ripped open a condom. "Lucky for her I'm about at the end of my rope too."

He didn't look it, his expression cool but she knew the mask would drop away soon enough. He couldn't keep the facade going once he was inside of her. Then and only then did she see his raw emotions on display.

He braced himself above, his palms planted on either side of her. Bound this way, she had no control as he entered her slowly, drawing out the sensations. Pushing forward and pulling back. Each stroke sending him deeper into her cunt until he was finally in to the hilt.

Pausing for a moment, he let her get used to his invasion but she was already impatient. She swayed her hips and he cursed as her pussy tightened on his cock.

"Naughty slave."

His hands gripped her thighs and his weight pinned her hips to the bed as he powered into her, each thrust sending tremors of delight all the way to her curled toes. Mindless with pleasure, the room tilted and blurred as unbelievably her body climbed toward another release.

"Don't be afraid of it, baby. Let it happen," Reed encouraged, his mouth nipping at her shoulder. "Give it to me."

Trusting him as she had no other man, she stopped fighting the urge to fall and let herself float like a feather on the wind. Her body didn't belong to just her anymore, he owned it in the most elemental way a man could, her body capable of erotic pleasure as she'd never known it. Every sense was alive as she felt the rough hairs on his thighs and his breath on her neck. She could hear him pant with exertion and see the corded muscles in his arms as he held himself above her.

He pistoned in and out of her like a metronome, each stroke rubbing that secret spot on the inside and her swollen clit on the outside. The twin sensations were too much and she exploded in a flash of brilliance. White and colored lights danced in front of her eyes as the swell of pleasure carried her away. Groaning, his own release took him. She could feel his cock jerk inside of her and the flush of heat as he emptied his seed into the condom.

When it was over not an ounce of strength was left in her body. Reed quickly released her from her bonds and cradled her close as the sweat dried on their skin.

"I'll be right back," he promised softly before padding into the bathroom. He returned with a warm washcloth and tenderly ran it over her still quivering flesh. After tossing it in the hamper, he pulled her close and rubbed his chin on the top of her head.

"Sleep, honey. We've got all night to live out your fantasies."

What she could never tell him was this was her greatest fantasy. That he would hold her like this forever.

Chapter Twenty-Six

R eed was in the kitchen the next morning nibbling at the leftover bacon when the phone rang. Since Kaylee was in the shower he reached for the receiver automatically.

"Hello?"

"Mr. Mitchell? This is Detective Dale French. Is Ms. Carter available?"

The detective had turned out to be a knowledgeable lawman and a pretty good guy. He'd taken Kaylee's case seriously and appeared to be determined to bring the offender to justice.

"She's not available to come to the phone," Reed replied, not sure if Kaylee would be okay with him saying she was in the shower. Women could be funny about those things. "Can I take a message?"

The detective hesitated for a moment but then must have decided it was okay. "Sure. I know this isn't going to make you very happy but we didn't charge Brent Sharp last night. Frankly we didn't have enough evidence to do so. When we looked at the note the handwriting didn't match any of the other letters. Plus, his fingerprints were all over the paper and the envelope as if he wasn't trying to hide his identity like the other ones. Listen, after talking to him I just don't think he's our guy."

Bitter acid filled Reed's throat and he had to swallow hard to keep the disappointment at bay. "Are you sure? He definitely wants Kaylee."

And hadn't bothered much to hide it even when Reed came on the scene.

"He admitted he's had a crush on Ms. Carter. He also admitted that he felt like he needed to make a bold move now that you were dating her. I told him that it probably wasn't the brightest thing to do since she's being stalked and he agreed. He offered up his DNA to match to the adhesive on the envelopes without a fight. In fact he seemed to welcome it. He said it would exonerate him once and for all. I know you wanted it to be him but he sure as hell didn't act like any stalker I've ever talked to."

That meant Reed was back at fucking square one with no suspects and no leads. It was a goddamn nightmare but more for Kaylee than for him. She'd been so carefree since the police had led Brent away in cuffs.

"It sounds like you're right," Reed admitted, hating every second of this conversation. Kaylee was going to be devastated when he told her. "The fingerprints are a telling piece of evidence. He wouldn't change MOs after all this time. I appreciate you calling personally, Detective. I'll let her know."

"What will you let me know?"

Kaylee breezed into the kitchen as Reed hung up the phone. He wasn't the type to sugarcoat news and she deserved the unvarnished truth. There would be a part of her that was relieved it wasn't her friend Brent.

"That was the detective leading up your case. They didn't charge Brent last night. The detective said there was not enough evidence, and in fact the evidence made him look innocent. They let him go."

Her eyes went wide and then went bright with tears, her lips trembling. "It's not over? Someone still wants to hurt me?"

He couldn't stand the fear in her expression. Pulling her into his arms, he stroked her hair as tears spilled over and onto her cheeks.

"I'm so sorry, honey. Brent's fingerprints were all over the note and envelope. That's not at all like before. In addition he offered to give his DNA without any issue. It just doesn't look like he's the one."

She leaned back so he could see her tear-stained face. "But you said it was him. So you were wrong? I thought you were some great lawman, but now I find out you have no idea what you're doing."

The arrow she'd shot pierced him right in the heart as she'd known it would. He prided himself on being a good sheriff and until a few days ago it had been the most important thing in his life.

"Sometimes we get it wrong. But I can assure you I do know what I'm doing. I can keep you safe until we find the right person. I promised you that before and I promise it again. Have you stopped trusting me?"

"No. I trust you," she answered softly. She'd had so many people abuse that trust and he hoped to hell she hadn't placed him in that dubious company. "I'm just disappointed, that's all, and took it out on you. I'm sorry."

He'd fucked things up royally but it wasn't too late. He'd do what he always did when a case took a turn like this. It was back to the basics. Evidence. Motive. Opportunity. He needed to widen his search of suspects to casual acquaintances and perhaps even strangers. It was unlikely but he had to cover all the bases.

"I won't let you down. We'll find this guy, and in the meantime I'll make sure you're safe."

She swiped at her cheeks and nodded. "I know you will. I was just so happy it was all over."

"Look at the bright side. Brent didn't betray you," Reed pointed out, although he still wasn't a fan of the guy. Any man who would come on to another man's woman wasn't the stand-up type.

"That's true." She grabbed a tissue from the box on the counter. "I was so angry with him last night I couldn't even speak to him. I wanted to scream and yell but in the end I didn't say anything."

"I was glad you didn't. Between my questions and the police we didn't need anyone getting emotional. It was best that it stayed professional."

"So what do we do now?"

"Look at the evidence again. Look at the statements of the people at the party especially. Maybe people assumed someone was in the house when they really weren't. We need to look at opportunity closely. We'll also take another look at that first list of people you've had contact with, see if there's anyone you might have missed."

"It sounds frustrating. How can you do this every day?"

"I don't do this every single day. Just some days. Tough cases like this are a bitch to solve but when you do…it makes you feel ten feet tall."

That got a smile from her. "Explains your bossy, alpha male attitude."

"Naw," he shook his head. "I was born that way. Comes natural."

"You don't have to sound so proud of it," she retorted, back to her usual exuberance. "It's not something to crow about."

"I'm certainly not ashamed. I told you in the beginning if you just did as I told you to everything would be a lot simpler."

Kaylee rolled her eyes over her shoulder as she pulled open the refrigerator, snagging two sodas. She handed one to him and popped open her own. "I was not put on this earth to make things easy for you."

"In no way would I ever call you easy, honey."

She looked up at her through her lashes. "Are you sure? I did sort of come on to you when you first got here."

"Did you? I don't remember."

"Damn, you are good. That was the perfect answer." She giggled and took a drink of her soda. "So what do you want to do today?"

"Work," he replied, crossing his arms over his chest. "You need to write and I need to look at everything. No fun and games today." He leaned down and kissed her on the tip of her adorable nose. "But tonight is a whole different story."

He had a few fantasies of his own he wouldn't mind living out with Kaylee. Of course one involved a boat but the other was completely doable.

He wanted to eat dessert off her delectable body.

"You worry too much," Kaylee scolded Reed. "I'll be fine here with Cheryl. Go for a walk, or get a cup of coffee at the shop at the corner. Maybe go to the mall or something."

Kaylee needed some quality writing time and Reed wasn't making it easy. He'd driven her crazy all day yesterday with his questions every five minutes about the people on her list. At this rate she was going to launch a heavy object at him by dinner time.

Reed shook his head, the set of his jaw stubborn. "I don't like the thought of leaving you."

"You're not leaving me." Kaylee used her most reasonable tone but she was fast losing patience. "Cheryl will be here and you've already cleared her as a suspect, right?"

Reed nodded but his jaw was tight. "Sure I did. She was in the house when the car tried to run you down."

"Exactly. So if the two of us are locked in Fort Knox, oops, I mean my home, everything should be fine?" He still didn't look convinced. "Listen, I'm at an important juncture in the book. I need some quiet writing time badly."

"Cheryl will be here," he argued. "That's two people, not just one. It should be twice as bad."

"Except she'll be working too. We'll do writing sprints and I'll get tons done." She softened her tone. "I need to feel like there's some normalcy in my life, that I'm not in prison. I don't want to let this guy make me feel that way."

"Fine," he conceded, although clearly not happy. "But don't answer the phone or the door and stay away from the windows."

"Do you really think a stalker is going to ring the doorbell?" Her tone came out sarcastic but she couldn't help it. He was acting like she was a total idiot. "This guy has gone to great lengths to keep his identity a secret. I don't see him walking up to the house and announcing himself."

Reed said something under his breath she couldn't hear but it sounded something like "stubborn, mouthy woman."

Yes, she was.

"I don't know what this guy would do and neither do you," he argued. "Until we have a better handle on this I think we should err on the side of caution." The doorbell rang interrupting him, thank heaven. He'd just been warming up and she would have been the recipient of quite the lecture. "I'll get the door."

She sighed as he checked the camera feeds. It was Cheryl, of course. He strode to the door and let her visitor in, greeting her with friendliness despite his opinion. He found Cheryl a tad too obvious in her interest in him.

Cheryl set up her laptop while Kaylee walked with Reed to the door. "Be sure to take my house keys so you can let yourself in. Since I'm not allowed to answer the door and all."

She smiled to soften the words and it seemed to help. The side of his mouth quirked up and then a full smile. "Am I being overprotective? I just don't want anything to happen to you, honey."

"The only thing that might happen is me getting a little tipsy if the two of us have a good word count and we decide to open a bottle of vodka." She leaned forward so only he could hear. "And you know how I get when I drink."

"Sounds promising. I've got one or two fantasies we could work on."

"I'm all ears."

Reed looked up and she followed his gaze to Cheryl watched them intently. She probably couldn't hear anything being said but her and Reed's body language spoke volumes.

"I guess I'll go up to the coffee shop at the end of the street. I've got some calls to make and I can take the file up there too."

"See," she teased. "You do have somewhere to go. Don't worry about me. We'll be working for hours."

"I won't be gone that long," he warned before heading to his truck. "Two cups of coffee and a couple of phone calls and I'll be back." He waved as he swung into the driver's side and fired up the engine.

"Where is Reed going?" Cheryl asked as Kaylee watched Reed drive away.

"He's headed to the coffee house up the way to make a few calls. Hopefully he'll stay out of our hair for awhile."

Cheryl smiled but it seemed off in some way, not reaching her eyes. "That's good news."

She reached into her laptop bag and pulled out a handgun, pointing it at Kaylee. "Have a seat. We have so much to do. This has been a long time in coming."

Stiff with shock, Kaylee stood rooted to the spot, her mind unable to process what was happening.

"Do it and things will go nicely for you. Give me trouble and—well, this will get ugly."

Somehow her feet unstuck from the floor and she made it to the couch on trembling legs, still staring down the barrel of a gun. Held by a supposed friend. And she'd just kicked Reed out of the house for what could be hours.

Write yourself out of this one.

Her brain was beginning to work again and her stomach knotted and churned as she realized what was happening.

Brent wasn't her stalker. It was Cheryl.

"Why?" Kaylee asked. She had an idea but she wanted to hear it from Cheryl's own lips.

She smiled and sat down across from her, the gun pointed directly at Kaylee's chest. "There are so many reasons but mainly the fact that you don't deserve what you have. You write that filth and it sells a hundred times what I sell. It's wrong, and the more I thought about it the more I realized that I needed to do something about it. I needed to make things right."

"How will killing me do that?"

Kaylee's heart was racing and sweat was pooling on the back of her neck and under her arms. She needed to keep Cheryl talking as long as possible. Perhaps Reed would come back early as he'd threatened. She crossed her fingers and hoped.

"That's only the first part," Cheryl said, waving her gun and making Kaylee queasy. "Killing you is just the added bonus, really. Always so sweet and innocent. Everyone loves Kaylee. Everyone wants Kaylee's advice," Cheryl said with a bitter tone. "You write that crap and everyone worships at your feet. It's not fair. Just like everything else in my life."

"Everything else? Killing me won't change anything else that's happened."

"You have no idea," Cheryl spat. "The things I've put up with. Selfish men who didn't appreciate me and now readers who don't either. But I'm finally going to even the score. I'm going to make sure I get what I deserve."

A one-way ticket to the funny farm? Life in prison?

"What is it that you deserve?"

Keep her talking. Stall.

"Why, everything," Cheryl said as if it should have been obvious. "My mother always said I was meant for better things. When I married my husband I thought I'd found that."

Kaylee remembered Reed's background check on Cheryl. "You've been married more than once."

Her eyebrow rose. "Your boyfriend's been thorough I see. Yes, none of the men in my life have been able to give me what I deserve. I've finally realized that it's up to me. I have to do it."

"By killing me?"

"Sadly, yes. But I've made sure you won't be missed."

Once again Kaylee had put her trust in the wrong person and sent away the one person she did trust. If Reed were here he would have protected her. But she wasn't giving up.

"If you wanted to kill me, why didn't you just do it instead of sending me letters and pictures?"

Cheryl's face was all smiles. "Because it was fun. It made things much more dramatic don't you think? I did the same in my third book. The killer played a lovely cat and mouse with the hero. Of course this is going to have a much different ending."

Her mind racing, her gaze darted back and forth between Cheryl and the exits.

Think. Think. Stay calm. Don't show any fear.

Sitting in the living room, the front and back door were both more than ten feet away. She'd never make it if she tried to run.

The stairs? No, she'd be shot on the way up.

The hallway to the office? Kaylee doubted she would make it before Cheryl shot her but she couldn't just sit here and wait to die. She didn't want to die. She wanted to live and spend more time with Reed and maybe even see him open up a little more. She wanted to love him.

"Because you hate me?" she asked, still trying to stall. "And you're jealous?"

Apparently it was the wrong things to say. Cheryl's expression turned venomous and her eyes shot daggers of hate. "I am not jealous. I am simply righting the wrongs of the universe."

Riiiigggghhht.

Wait. The mystery party. Cheryl was in the house. Was there another person in on this?

"Who tried to run me down when you were in the house? Did Brent do it?"

Beads of sweat ran down her back under her t-shirt and she pressed her damp palms to the denim of her jeans. Funny how she could hear her own heartbeat just as she'd written about it in her books, but this was actually happening. She needed a real solution to this non-fiction problem.

Cheryl waved the gun and laughed.

"Brent is sweet but he worships the ground you walk on. Hardly killer material. But I thought he'd be fun for the red herring in this little story." Cheryl's lip curled in a sneer. "He was so pathetically easy to encourage. I told him that you were secretly attracted to him and that your friend Reed would soon be gone and out of your life. The fact that your sexy boyfriend glommed on to Brent was exactly what I'd hoped. His questioning of Walt was just a bonus."

"And don't you worry about Reed when this is all over," Cheryl trilled. "I'll be happy to console him in my own special way. I doubt he'll mourn you long." She tapped her chin. "But as to who drove the car? That was me. Linda innocently provided my alibi by saying I was in the house when of course I wasn't. She asked me where I was and I said I was upstairs. She's as dumb as you are and believed me. But my aim was never to kill you. I just wanted to scare you. It was the third act pinch point, you see. The emails were the inciting incident. The first letter and picture the gateway to act two. And so on. It really is my best work by far."

"And this is the final act? The black moment? You're going to shoot me and walk away. What if you don't get away with it? Reed's a good cop and he'll know it was you that shot me."

Cheryl pulled something from her pocket and placed it on the coffee table between them. "I'm not planning to kill you, Kaylee dear. You're going to do that yourself. Reed won't be looking for a murderer when there's been no crime. You see, this is the final act plot twist."

A large prescription bottle sat between them and Kaylee swallowed the lump that had formed in her throat.

"And why would I do this? And why would anyone believe it?"

"Your horrible guilt about stealing my stories drove you to it." Cheryl kept the gun trained on Kaylee as she used her other hand and pulled a piece of paper from the laptop bag, slapping it on the table. "This letter details the whole thing. How you stole my work and put your name on it. How you published it and profited. Finally you couldn't take the guilt any longer. So sad. Everyone will know you for the cheap hack that you are. And me? I'll be the victim. People love a victim."

Kaylee had to give her credit, she'd thought it through. Mostly. But not quite.

"No one will believe I did it. No one will believe my books were written by you. We have completely different styles."

"They'll believe it if you say it. Everyone believes every word out of your precious mouth," Cheryl snarled. "Let me get you a pen to sign the note and some water for your pills. By the time your boyfriend returns it will be too late."

"How are you going to explain that you sat by and watched me steal your work?" Kaylee needed to slow everything down. There was no way she was going to swallow those pills. She'd make Cheryl shoot her first. Kaylee didn't know how experienced Cheryl was with a gun but hitting a moving target was never easy. And Kaylee was determined that she wouldn't be stationary if Cheryl decided to pull the trigger.

"You were threatening me, of course. You said you'd tell everyone I'd stolen your work. You know as well as I do that reputation is everything in this business. No one would take my word over yours." Cheryl stood and walked to the kitchen, but the gun never wavered. "Now let's get you a nice big glass of water. You're going to need it to take all those pills."

Chapter Twenty-Seven

Reed found a quiet, out of the way table at the coffee shop and sat down with his black coffee and the large stack of background checks and copies of the original emails and letters. He'd spend some time looking through them but first he needed to call Logan and see how Ava was doing. Reed pulled out his phone and had Logan on the line in seconds.

"How's it going? Are you taking good care of Kaylee?"

Reed was relieved to hear Logan sound in such good spirits. He and Ava had been having such a tough time of it with this pregnancy.

"I'm trying to, how are things there? Is Ava still at home?"

"She is and her blood pressure is down but the doctor is being cautious. But I know one of the reasons she's so calm is that you're there dealing with this situation. She knows you won't let anything happen to Kaylee."

"Nothing will happen on my watch," Reed vowed. "She's safe as a kitten. Actually she's got a friend at the house right now and they're working."

"She kicked you out, didn't she?" Logan chuckled and Reed figured that the same must have happened to his friend. "They get all prickly when they get to certain points in the book. Best to give them some space."

"I gave her about one mile which is as far as the coffee shop is from the house. Plus I can check on her anytime with all the cameras I have installed. I can pull the feed right up on my phone."

"Now that is an idea," Logan declared. "But I'm not sure I would tell Ava that they were there. She might not appreciate my concern."

Ava might be the only woman in the world that could handle Logan. She gave him hell and he gave it right back, but the whole damn thing seemed to work.

"So Presley and Madison were here yesterday and talked to Ava about a baby shower. A dozen or so women, cake, punch, and crepe paper streamers. I'm not sure I can take this. You need to get back here soon and save me," Logan laughed.

"What did Tanner say?"

"He slapped me on the back and said to take it like a man. That this stuff was small potatoes compared to actually raising a human being. Hell, he's probably right."

Tanner usually was which is what pissed everybody off. It was like hanging around with that Yoda character from Star Wars.

"Anything else I need to know?" Reed loved being with Kaylee but he had to admit he missed the day-to-day goings on at the station. It was the one place where he knew what to do. No messy emotions involved.

"There was some party over at the Perry spread," Logan replied. "Seth had to go down there and break up what looked like a damn riot. Everyone throwing punches at each other for no other reason than they liked to hit things. It was a fucking mess. Seth ended up with a couple of stitches on his hand and a piss-poor attitude. He's had it with the Perrys. And you know Presley—hell, she's fit to be tied about the whole thing. Clucking around him like a mother hen and muttering about how Bennett isn't going to be a cop."

"Glad I wasn't around for that. Anything else?"

"Naw, everything is pretty quiet. Crime will gear up for the holidays though. It always does. It's just taking a breather right now. Is there anything I can do for you to help find this guy?"

Reed stared down at the stack of papers in front of him. "I'm going back to the beginning. Looking at motive and opportunity while we wait for the bastard to strike again."

"Send me copies of what you have. I'll take a look at them. Maybe a fresh set of eyes will help," Logan offered.

Reed rubbed his temple. "Couldn't hurt at this point. I'll send them to your office."

"Oh hell no. You know how Jillie is. She'll print out every goddamn piece of paper and carry it into my office one at a time. Shit. She's terrified of technology. Send it to my home email. I'm working quite a bit from here anyway to spend more time with Ava and I'll be looking at the evidence in the evenings."

"Let me get something to write with. Hold on." Reed didn't have a pen on him but he spied one sitting on a table near him where a man was reading the paper and doing a crossword. "Excuse me, can I borrow that pen for just a minute? I need to write down an address."

The man barely looked up but nodded and handed the pen to Reed while he worked the puzzle in pencil.

"Shoot." Logan rattled off the address and Reed scratched it in the margin of one of the papers. "Let me make sure I've got this. 'LAW RIGHT'? Is that it? That's interesting and easy to remember."

Reed handed the pen back to the patron and stared down at the email address. Something was bugging him but he couldn't put his finger on it.

"It's our names, Einstein," Logan laughed. "L for Logan, A for Ava, Wright for our last name of course, but then to make it easy for people to remember it spells 'Law Right.' Ava made it up. You know writers and the way they like to play on words."

Reed frowned, still staring at the words he'd scrawled. "Listen, I need to get off the phone. I've got a lot of work to do. I'll send you those copies when I get back to the house."

Bidding Logan goodbye, they promised to talk again the next day when Logan had had a chance to review the documents. Reed picked up the paper and stared at it, oblivious to anything going on around him. He could only hear the buzzing in his head as his brain put the puzzle pieces together.

"Bookchiller," Reed said out loud, things finally starting to make sense. "CHILL stands for Cheryl Hill. She did what Ava did and made a play on words."

Son of a fucking bitch. Hopefully he wasn't too late.

Adrenaline shot through him and fear chewed at his stomach, acid building in his throat. His woman—the woman he goddamn loved—was alone with someone who was obviously twisted from the emails and letters. He should have never left her. If anything happened to her he would never forgive himself.

She would be the second woman he'd failed.

But first he needed to calm the fuck down and use his head. Running back to the house with guns blazing would only serve to get Kaylee killed.

His heart pumping, Reed quickly accessed the cameras even as he headed to his truck. The outside of the house looked clear. The bedroom? The same. His chest tightened so painfully at the live feed of the living room it almost took his breath away. Cheryl was standing there with a gun pointed at Kaylee.

To her credit, she didn't look cowed or afraid. The two women were talking and Reed could only hope Kaylee could keep it up.

He wouldn't let anyone take her from this world.

"That's right, honey. Stall her just a little longer. I'm coming."

Reed pressed his body to the side of the house hoping Cheryl hadn't turned on the camera feed. If luck was with him, she'd feel so comfortable with him out of the house she'd never think to check if anyone was coming. He'd parked his truck down the block so she wouldn't see it and he had come around the back of the neighbor's to keep out of the living room's line of sight. He'd also called Detective French and he was on his way but Reed had made it clear he wasn't waiting. Kaylee's life was held in the balance.

A quick check of the camera feed before he'd exited the truck had told him Kaylee was still alive but Cheryl's expression was growing darker. He didn't have much more time.

Using the keys Kaylee had insisted he take, he pushed the key into the door off the basement, holding his breath that it would indeed work. Although he'd seen the entrance when he'd come down to the basement for Halloween supplies, he'd never actually used it. He wasn't even sure if any of these keys were to this door; he could only hope that all the doors were keyed the same.

Turning the key as quietly as he could, he heard the click as the lock disengaged. He exhaled slowly in relief but then held his breath again as he twisted the doorknob and entered the dark basement cautiously. He left the door open to let in enough light to see the stairs that would lead him to the kitchen.

Sweat had gathered on his forehead and back even in the chilly autumn air while his heart pounded in his ears. Going into warrior mode, he turned off his emotions, letting his instinct take control. Messy emotions became even messier missions. Thinking too much didn't help either. In fact, it could get a man killed in a hurry.

He pushed away any external distractions, focusing solely on the sounds coming from the main floor as he crept silently up the steps. As usual, the door at the top of the stairs was closed and he would need to go through that door at exactly the right moment. Not too soon and not too early.

Pulling up the camera feed but keeping the sound on mute, he cursed as Cheryl walked closer to Kaylee. He needed Cheryl to step away if only for a moment. Anticipating her movements was key to taking her down. He pulled his weapon from his shoulder holster and held his breath as the blood roared in his ears. How Kaylee had become the absolute most important thing in his life he didn't know, but she had and he'd die before anything happened to her.

She was everything.

"I'm not going to sign this letter or take those pills," Kaylee said, trying to act as calm and strong as she could despite the fear swirling inside. "You're going to have to shoot me and then everyone will know that I'm the victim, not you."

"I'll just put the gun in your hand," Cheryl scoffed. "It will still look like a suicide. They'll find the note whether you sign it or not."

Kaylee had to take a few breaths before she could speak again. Inside she was trembling, terrified of the gun pointed directly at her, but outwardly she was trying to channel Reed's cool façade. "You haven't thought this all the way through, have you? If you shoot me the forensic evidence isn't going to match up. They'll know I didn't pull the trigger. And once they examine the letter they'll know it wasn't produced from my printer. Really, you're fucked," she said bravely. "If I were you I'd give this up. You'll end up in prison for a lifetime and everyone will know what you really are."

Kaylee's breathing was labored and she had to concentrate to keep her legs from visibly shaking. Her once friend and now enemy was becoming less and less talkative, clearly wanting everything tied up and done. Pressing her lips together to keep from screaming, her fingers gripped the flesh of her thighs until the knuckles were white.

Cheryl took a few steps back and raised the arm that held the gun slightly higher pointing it directly at Kaylee's heart. "Enough talk. Time to—"

Whatever she had been about to say was obliterated by a flash of light and what sounded like an explosion. Kaylee's ears rang as Cheryl dropped the gun she'd been holding and her hands pressed against her abdomen where a large red stain was blooming on the white fabric of her blouse. Her entire body crumpled to the floor in a heap.

Kaylee sat frozen on the sofa as her mind tried to make sense of what had happened. She was alive and Cheryl was shot and possibly dying. That had been the sound and light Kaylee had seen and heard.

She was alive.

Sirens wailed in the distance but Kaylee didn't have time to process what that meant as she was lifted by two muscular arms into a crushing embrace.

"Are you alright? Tell me you're okay, baby." It couldn't be Reed's voice she was hearing. It sounded too anguished, too pained. It sounded like a man who thought he might lose the woman he...loved. He was far from the calm, cool, and collected lawman Ava had described and Kaylee had met only a few weeks ago.

"I'm okay," she answered but her voice came out as a croak. Pressing her palms against the hard wall of his chest, she leaned back to look up into his face. It was the expression of a man in love. Fear, pain, determination, and tenderness were all etched in his handsome but haggard features. "I can't breathe. You're cracking my ribs."

She'd almost been killed but somehow the only thing that mattered was this one true thing.

Reed loved her.

His arms slackened and he shook his head. "Sorry, baby. I'm just so damn glad you're okay."

The adrenaline that had been keeping her going was beginning to ebb and her knees seemed to give way. Seeing her fade, he picked her up and placed her on the couch as streams of people began filling her living room, first from the basement and then from the front door. EMTs crouched around Cheryl while Detective French strode over and knelt beside Kaylee.

"Looks like we missed the action. What happened?"

"I came in the basement entrance just like I told you I would," Reed said, never taking his eyes from Kaylee, his hands clutching her own. "I watched the camera feed on my phone for the just the right moment, but once I saw Cheryl lift her gun and aim I couldn't wait any longer. Luckily she'd separated just enough from Kaylee that I was able to throw open the door and get one quick one off before Cheryl pulled the trigger."

"Good shooting." The detective glanced at Cheryl lying on the floor motionless and surrounded by paramedics but the stench of blood turned Kaylee's stomach. "They'll get her to the hospital. I assume we can have all the camera footage for the trial? From what you said she was admitting everything."

She gulped in some air and leaned her head back on the couch as her brain tried to catch up to everything that had happened. Reed had actually saved her from certain death. Cheryl had wanted Kaylee dead. Dead. She still couldn't quite wrap her mind around it.

"How did you know what was going on? Were you watching the camera feed while you were at the coffee shop?"

Reed shook his head even as he was tucking strands of her hair behind her ear. "I figured out it was Cheryl from the email address. 'Bookchiller.' 'CHILL – C. Hill.' It was Logan and Ava's email address that got me thinking it. So I checked the feed and saw she had a gun pointed at you. I hoped you could stall long enough for me to get to you. I was only two blocks away at the coffeehouse."

She cupped his face in her hands, tears spilling over as the enormity of the day began to sink in. "I just kept thinking that I needed to keep her talking…I trusted that you would save me if you could."

His body trembled under her palms and she knew he understood what that word meant to her. She would always place her trust in this man.

The detective cleared his throat, bringing her back to earth and the present. "I apologize but I do need to get everyone's statements. There's going to be paperwork here. Someone was shot and that means we need to dot all the i's and cross all the t's so Mr. Mitchell can be cleared of any wrongdoing. With everything on film it shouldn't be a problem, but the sooner we get started the sooner it will be done."

Reed had shot another human being to protect her. How did you thank someone for something like that?

"Then let's get this over with," Kaylee said. "I want to get on with the rest of my life."

She wasn't sure if she would be lucky enough to spend it with Reed, but she wouldn't give up on him. She'd realized today he wasn't like the men in her books.

He was ten times better…because he was real.

Chapter Twenty-Eight

"Can you stay for a few days?" Kaylee asked as they sat on the back patio late that night. The air was cold but the heater and a flannel throw kept them both warm. Her head was pillowed on his chest and he was playing with her long silky hair.

They hadn't spoken much today. At least to each other. They'd talked to the police, repeating the same details again and again until they'd finally heard enough. News trucks had shown up at some point but they'd both refused to talk to the press. Of course Brent, Linda, and Walt hadn't shown such restraint. They'd been on both the six and the eleven o'clock news saying they'd never seen any sign of Cheryl's behavior.

Reed inwardly predicted people would be coming out of the woodwork soon to talk about how they had seen Cheryl's obsessive personality before. Something like that didn't happen overnight but had probably been simmering for years.

Now he and Kaylee were finally alone. Her tears were dried and some of the shock had worn off. The police had suggested she see a victim's counselor and Reed whole-heartedly agreed. She'd need help making sense of the events and not blame herself for what had happened to Cheryl, because as soft-hearted as Kaylee was, she would think it was somehow her fault.

And there was no one else at fault here except for Cheryl herself. Her actions and decisions had all led up to today. She'd put Kaylee in a life or death situation where only one of them would come out okay. For Reed there had only been one possible outcome. Kaylee.

So now there was no reason for him to stay any longer with Cheryl in custody.

Unless he simply wanted to. It probably wasn't a great idea but he did want to spend more time with her. He had more vacation to burn and any desire he had to visit Florida or anywhere else had faded away. If he wasn't going back to work, he wanted to be with Kaylee.

"I have more time before I go back to work," he admitted. "The mayor made it very clear that I had to take at least six weeks."

"Does he know that you've been calling your deputies almost every other day?" she teased, her hand warm on his chest.

"No, and neither was anyone else to know. Have you been listening in on my conversations?"

"The walls must be thin, or maybe it's the bossy tone you use when you talk to them that permeates the entire house."

He couldn't argue with the remark. He ran a tight ship and didn't mince words with his deputies. The men he employed liked it that way and appreciated the no-nonsense way he ran the station.

"I *am* the boss. If you think I'm bad you should see Jared. Perfection isn't good enough for him. He has a tough time keeping deputies when he has that high of standards."

"He doesn't sound very nice."

Nice wasn't a word most women used to describe Sheriff Jared Monroe. Sexy, brooding, alpha, stubborn, handsome, implacable might be a few. Men described him as a tough son of a bitch who didn't ask anyone to do anything he wasn't willing to do himself—men who were willing to put themselves out there and see what they were made of. Any man who wasn't willing to push further and ask more of himself than he'd thought possible? Well, he need not apply.

"Actually Jared is one of the nicest guys around. He'd do anything to help a person and has been known to walk miles through a blizzard to help stranded motorists or work forty-eight hours straight so one of his deputies could have time off to be with his newborn. He just has incredibly high standards for himself and the people around him. He can be tough to work for. Hell, he's toughest on himself."

"Then he sounds driven and tortured."

Jared was definitely driven to be the best. Was he tortured? He didn't act it, but then Reed didn't know what drove most of his friends. He was only now figuring out what tortured him.

And because of that they needed to lay down a few ground rules before Reed agreed to stay here.

"If I stay it's not a promise, honey." The words came out awkwardly but he didn't know any other way to say it.

She didn't raise her head to look at him. "I know. I'm not ready to say goodbye yet though."

"Me neither. I'm not sure I ever will be but I know that I'm not ready to talk about the future. I've got a lot of baggage I need to deal with."

And he did intend to deal with it. When he'd admitted to himself that he loved Kaylee he'd known that he had to face his past and wrestle his demons. But he wasn't sure how.

"Do you want to?" Her hand had slid down his chest and her fingers had entwined with his. A warm feeling of contentment spread straight to his bones. It felt good and right but also fleeting. If he reached out for it, would it elude his grasp?

"I do," he said with firm conviction. "You've shown me it's time to face up to everything that's happened, although I'm not sure how to even start."

Kaylee sat up and pulled away from him slightly so she could look into his eyes. "I've agreed to see a counselor, maybe you should too. You're as much of a victim as I am."

Reed shook his head, his first gut reaction a resounding *no*. "That doesn't sound like something I could do. I need to handle this on my own."

Kaylee raised her brows and smiled. "How's that working out for you?" she asked in a saccharine sweet voice.

Got it. Sarcasm.

"Not very well I'll admit, but to be fair I wasn't exactly trying to deal with things. I've experienced more emotions in the last two days than I have in the last fifteen years combined. I gotta be honest, honey. I'm not sure I like it."

He loved her but it didn't mean he was good at it or that it was enough to make her happy. The way he was now he knew he couldn't make it work for the two of them. He'd always be looking over his shoulder.

"I want you to get better. Even if..." Her voice drifted off for a moment but came back stronger. "Even if you and I don't happen after this time together, well, I want you to find happiness. It's not just about you getting better for me. It isn't like that."

She sounded defensive but she needn't have. He knew she wasn't being selfish although he wouldn't have blamed her if she had been.

"I'd like to get better…for you, baby." He couldn't even begin to express how true that statement was. "I care more about you than anything else in my life."

It was as close to saying "I love you" as he could get at this moment and amazingly she seemed satisfied. Of all the people on this earth, she understood how hard it was for him to care for anything or anyone, let alone this much.

"I feel the same. Let's just take it day by day. I won't ask for commitments or promises and you try and get better."

She held out her hand as if she wanted to shake on the deal, but he had a better plan. His hand curled behind her neck, caressing the satiny skin, and he drew her close for a long, hot, satisfying kiss.

"That's a deal, honey."

For now it was all he could promise.

✧ ✧ ✧ ✧

I will not cry. I will not cry.

"Did you get your razor from the shower?" Kaylee asked Reed as they stood in her bedroom while he packed up his things four weeks later. They'd spent practically every moment of that time together and if anything she had fallen deeper in love with this man who was in so much pain.

They'd both kept their promises. She didn't ask him for anything past this time and he opened up more. Neither of those things had been easy. Right now she wanted to throw herself to the floor and hang on to his leg so he couldn't walk out of the front door and climb into his truck.

"I did, and all my clothes from the closet and drawers. I think that's it."

He stared down at the bag but didn't zip it shut. There was a part of him that wanted to stay, Kaylee knew that. She also knew there was a part of him that couldn't wait to get back to Montana where he could fall into old habits and return to being the man that never felt anything or cared about anyone.

"Kaylee—" Reed began but she cut him off.

"How long will it take you to get home?" she asked brightly, not wanting to hear him talk about how sorry he was that he had to go or that he couldn't love her. The last month had been the best of her life but it was over. She'd vowed to see the good side of this situation, that she'd had any time with him at all. No crying or whining.

"About twenty hours or so," Reed answered shortly. "You're not going to stop me from talking. I'm not leaving until we do this."

Then she never wanted to talk about it, except that wouldn't be fair to him.

"So talk." Kaylee dropped down to the bed and sat cross-legged on the mattress. Composing her features, she looked up at him and waited for what was sure to be a well-rehearsed speech about how it wasn't her but him.

It's not you, it's me, baby.

"I'd like to ask you for time, but I'm not going to. It wouldn't be fair. I have a lot of work ahead of me turning all this emotional shit around and asking you to wait while I do it is a selfish, bullshit move. Especially as I have no idea how long it will take or if I'll even be successful."

He would be, she was sure of it. He was that type—good at everything and so damn smart. But she didn't know how long it would take either. He'd been like this for years. It might take the same to deal with the past.

"I want to tell you I'll wait, but you're right. It's not fair to me or you, really. Your feelings could change in the future but you'd feel obligated to me. And waiting around for you isn't a healthy thing to do. I can't put off my future because you aren't in it."

She sounded so practical and calm but inside she was slowly dying, like a dagger had been plunged straight into her heart and being twisted ever so slowly to draw out the pain. It made simple things like breathing feel like a great effort.

Reed nodded and rubbed the back of his neck. "I doubt my feelings are going to change. If I haven't found anyone else that makes me feel this way in fifteen years, I think I'm good for at least another fifteen or twenty or more. But you made an excellent point. It's not right for you to base your decisions on me."

She wanted to smack him and make him say the words he'd studiously avoided saying for the last month even though she knew he felt it. He showed his love every single day in every action and touch. Every word and deed. Did he think she was stupid? She wrote romance for fuck's sake. She knew when a man was in love. Why couldn't he throw her a bone before he left and just fucking *say it*?

"So we're making a clean break," she said instead, taking a shaky breath and swallowing the lump in her throat. "What we had was great but now it's over and we start our lives separately. Except maybe text me when you get home so I know you made it okay?"

She sounded so damn needy but she'd worry every hour he was on the road. Reed didn't seem to mind though. He smiled and chuckled before reaching down to finally zip the leather bag closed.

"I will. I'll text you when I stop for gas or food so you know I'm okay." He pushed the bag aside and sat down next to her, pulling her into his arms. She took a deep breath so she could memorize his scent. She wanted to imprint the way he felt into her brain so she would have the memory whenever she needed it, some dark, lonely night far into the future. "You know, it's okay for us to care about each other. It's okay if you want to stay in touch or something. I'm going to miss you and I hope you'll miss me."

"I will." She nodded and rubbed her cheek against his chest. She could hear the steady thrum of his heart but this time the rhythm didn't calm her down. It served only to make her more aware that the real live hero she'd met would soon be gone from her life. "You could send me an email every now and then or something."

"You too. Let me know when the book comes out or what Santa Claus brings you."

Kaylee slapped her forehead with the heel of her hand and pulled reluctantly from his warm embrace. "Shit, that reminds me. Since you weren't going to be here for Christmas, I bought you a present."

They'd had Thanksgiving dinner together last week, just the two of them, fixing the meal as a team and watching football. It had been one of the best holidays she'd ever spent as an adult.

His brows shot up. "You bought me a present? But I didn't get anything for you. Fuck."

She went to her closet and dug around behind her shoes. She'd known he'd never look there. She hoped he liked the present and understood what it represented to her.

"I didn't get you a gift because I thought you'd get me one. I got you a gift because I wanted to. Here it is." She placed the red and gold wrapped box on the bed between them. "You can open it now or wait. It's up to you."

He picked up the box and fingered the elaborate bow she'd fashioned, hiding his expression. "Can I save it until Christmas?

I'm one of those that doesn't like to open before Christmas Eve."

She swallowed her disappointment and hoped it didn't show. "Sure. I'm just the opposite. I used to shake every package under the tree trying to figure out what was in it. I would have opened every present early if my mom and grandma would have let me."

"Then you wouldn't have anything to open on Christmas," he reminded her. "What then?"

She grinned up at him, determined not to show her pain at his departure. "Then I get a whole new set of presents."

"I never thought of it that way before. Smart." Reed laughed and unzipped his bag and carefully placed the box inside before closing it again. "I guess I should be hitting the road. The sun's up and it's a long drive."

Walking down the stairs and to his truck was like walking to her own execution, her legs shaky and her eyes burning from the tears she didn't want him to see. She shuffled alongside as slowly as she could but eventually they ended up standing by the driver's door. Reed stowed his bag in the back seat of the truck and turned to face her.

Those pesky tears simply couldn't be held back when she saw his own hazel eyes shiny with moisture. She choked back a sob and threw herself into his arms, holding him as tight as she could and not wanting this to moment to end.

"I want to say thank you." His voice was hoarse with emotion and he probably hated that. "Thank you for helping me to live again. Thank you for not giving up on me. You're without a doubt the best person I've ever known in my life, honey. The best. I wish I could be that for you."

She wanted to cry out that he could...except that he couldn't. Not yet anyway. He still felt that he'd done something wrong and that he didn't know how or deserve love. She'd helped him as much as she could but the rest of the work he had to do himself.

And that was the painful part. She had to let him go so he could do this alone. She'd only be in the way, a distraction.

"You already are the best person I've ever known," she assured him, her own voice trembling with all the love she felt spilling over like the tears sliding down her cheeks. "You are, Reed."

They kissed, briefly but tenderly, one last time before he climbed into the truck. He'd cleared his throat a few times and his usual in-control façade was cracked and worn as he held her hand through the rolled-down window. His fingers gripped her own tightly and there was no doubt he was as affected as she was. "If you ever need anything, Kaylee Blue, you call me. Night or day. Now or in thirty goddamn years, you hear me? Whatever you need, I'm there. Got it?"

She scrubbed at her wet cheeks and nodded. It took every ounce of strength she had not to declare her love right then and there but it was a burden he didn't need. He'd feel obligated and a bunch of other things. Besides, whether she said it or not he knew. He had to. She hadn't bothered to hide it, she'd only been careful not to say it.

"Got it. Drive careful. Text me."

Slowly their fingers loosened and her hand fell to her side. Reed put the truck in reverse and backed out of her driveway and then drove down the street. She stood there until his truck was out of sight and then walked into the house, closing and locking the door behind her.

It was a habit now.

Curling up on the couch, she pulled her knees close to her chest and wrapped her arms around them as the sobs began to wrack her body, each one deeper and more painful than the last.

How long she sat there and cried she didn't know. Rocking back and forth as if to comfort herself, she didn't stop crying until she had no more tears.

Sniffling and stiff, she stood and padded into the kitchen for a tissue and then realized she needed several. She blew her nose a few times and then opened the freezer and pulled out the stash she'd saved for this morning. She'd bought it at the store a few days ago.

One half gallon of chocolate marshmallow ice cream. One spoon. No bowl required, but she might heat up some of that hot fudge sauce in the pantry. She might have some sprinkles in there too.

She was allowing herself one day to wallow in misery. That was it. Then it was back to business and her life. She loved Reed but she'd learned something from him as well.

Life not lived is wasted.

Chapter Twenty-Nine

Two long miserable weeks later Reed couldn't take it anymore. He hadn't made any progress on not feeling like he'd failed Julie. He knew it was only a couple of weeks, but shit, he missed Kaylee more than he'd ever imagined. He wanted to be worthy of her love, to have some sort of future to look forward to.

Kaylee did love him.

She hadn't said it but then neither had he. He couldn't tell her until he could do something about it. Sure, he could go to her now and tell her he wanted to spend his life with her, but he knew how that would end. At some point guilt would swamp him and interfere in his life with Kaylee. He'd always feel unworthy or scared that he'd do something. Their entire life together would be tainted.

Because he was a fuck up.

At the end of his rope, he'd picked up the phone and called his former father-in-law. Sonny Tolliver had been happy to hear from him and had agreed to meet, which was how Reed came to be ringing Sonny's doorbell today.

"Come in and get out of the cold," the older man encouraged as the front door swung open. It was colder than hell with a good covering of snow on the ground, but then Christmas was not far away. Reed still hadn't opened Kaylee's gift to him but it sat on the table next to his bed where he could see it every morning and every night.

"Thanks, Sonny. It's damn cold and wet this morning." Reed stomped the snow off his boots and shrugged out of his coat and gloves, hanging them on the hooks in the front hallway along with his hat. He'd never been to this house outside of Gallatin, near the gateway to Yellowstone. The last time he'd seen Sonny had been at his wife Eleanor's funeral. At that time they'd been working a horse ranch near Billings.

"Get you some coffee?" Sonny's voice boomed, but then it always had. His short-cropped hair was now silver and his face had more lines, but he was still the barrel-chested foreman that Reed had always known.

"Wouldn't mind a cup." Reed followed Sonny into the kitchen-living room combination and let his gaze wander over the neat but spare furnishings. It was the home of a bachelor and Reed would know. Not like Kaylee's home with throw pillows and cute salt and pepper shakers. The only personalization Reed saw was a gallery of photos on the far wall.

He couldn't resist the pull and frankly, he didn't want to. He had a box of photos at home but hadn't dared to open them in over a decade. It had been too painful and Julie's passing still too fresh.

There was one of Reed, Julie, and her brothers on horseback. They couldn't have been more than sixteen but he didn't remember the exact occasion this was taken. Reed had been looking at Julie and she'd been smiling back as if he were her whole world.

Their prom photo. Julie looking so exquisitely young and beautiful in a dark blue strapless dress and Reed looking like a damn penguin in his tux. Shit, had they ever been that young and naïve? They'd thought they had the world by the short hairs.

"I like looking at the pictures." Sonny had come up next to him and held up a large mug to Reed. "I like thinking about the past. I'm not a big fan of the present. Too many people upset about things. Too many people staring at their damn phones and walking out in traffic. I guess I'm just getting old but I like reminiscing about the good old days."

Reed accepted the mug but couldn't stop the next words out of his mouth. "What about the days that weren't so good? What about them?"

"Ain't no way I know of to forget 'em." The older man shrugged. "When you get to be my age you realize the bad just makes the good all the better." Sonny grinned and chuckled. "And damn, we had some good. I could live off the memories until the day I die."

Reed didn't have one memory worth a shit from the last fifteen years. He'd been sleepwalking through life, throwing it away one day at a time as if it didn't matter. Because he was too chickenshit to feel the pain of loss.

"You want to talk about the good? Look at that picture, son. You, Julie, and the whole family out at Black Lake. I think you caught the biggest fish that weekend. Those days are worth remembering."

"I couldn't tell you the last time I went fishing," Reed replied, breathing through the heaviness that had descended on him. It wasn't so much a sharp pain now as it was a thick blanket that made him want to close his eyes and surrender to the loneliness.

Reed did remember that weekend at Black Lake. They'd had fun fishing and swimming without a care in the world that summer. It helped him inhale easier and it actually made him smile as he thought about how they'd tied a long rope to a tree and used it to swing out over the water and then jump in. Looking at those photos he hadn't realized he'd forgotten so much.

"I need to talk to you, Sonny," Reed finally said as they looked at the photos of the past. "I need to tell you something."

"Yep, I figured you had a bee in your bonnet, son. I haven't talked to you since Ellie's funeral, God rest her beautiful soul, so this must be important."

Reed flushed with shame and guilt. Sonny had deserved better, being like a second father to him all those years. "I'm sorry about that. I know I should have kept in touch."

"I talk to your dad every month, so I keep up on what's happening in your life. We're all real proud of you. I know Julie would be too."

Just when Reed thought he had himself under control, a dagger to his gut almost doubled him over with agony. "That's what I want to talk to you about. There's something I've never told you."

"You look almost green, son. Let's sit at the table and you can tell me all about it."

"I'm not sure where to begin," Reed said as he lowered himself into the chair, his hands cupped around the hot mug.

"I've always found it's best to start at the beginning and work from there."

The beginning. Where was that?

Reed took a sip from his coffee. "I loved Julie. More than you can imagine, but I let her down and I've never forgiven myself for it."

✧ ✧ ✧ ✧

Kaylee popped the cookie sheet into the oven and sat down at the island where her phone was perched on a box of baking soda.

"I'm worried about you," she said to Ava who had called this morning since Kaylee hadn't called in several days. Still hurting from Reed's departure, she'd buried herself in a new book. "What exactly did the doctor say again?"

"If my blood pressure doesn't stop creeping up he's putting my ever-growing ass in the hospital. If that happens I'll be almost an hour away from home and I'll only see Logan a few hours a day. I don't want that, although from what he said it's inevitable the further along I get. These two babies probably aren't going to wait the full forty weeks."

"Impatient just like their dad," Kaylee laughed. "You're not exactly patience personified either."

"But you are," Ava retorted. "I cannot believe you let Reed just drive away. Shit, why aren't you up here right now beating him over the head with a rolling pin?"

This was one of the reasons she'd only talked to Ava a few times.

"This is between me and Reed."

"Not anymore it isn't. He's here and you're not. So technically Reed brought the situation back here to Montana which means it now belongs to all of us. And all of us think you both have lost your minds. Logan saw Reed at the monthly meeting a few days ago and said he looked miserable. What are you two doing to one another? What's going on?"

"Ava, it's not my story to tell." Kaylee wouldn't talk about something he had told her in confidence. "It's Reed's story. But suffice it to say he needs time and space. He knows where I live, my phone number, and email address. He can get in touch with me if he needs me."

Other than a few texts from the road and one when he'd arrived at his home she hadn't heard a word from him. She'd thought he might go back to his old habits but if Logan said Reed looked miserable then he hadn't. It was the first good news she'd had in weeks.

"I just want you to be happy. Both of you."

"I am happy. I have a lovely home, good friends, and a great career. I even make awesome cookies which I need to pull out of the oven. Hold on for a minute." Kaylee jumped up, stuck her hand in an oven mitt, and pulled out the cookie sheet, setting it on the top of the stove. "Now if you're asking if I'm deliriously happy, then the answer is no. But I plan on being that way. I'm going to have a great life, Reed or no Reed."

"Reed's not happy," Ava countered. "I don't want him to be sad."

With a spatula, Ava carefully lifted each cookie from the sheet onto parchment paper laid out on the counter. "I know this sounds strange, but feeling sad is actually the healthiest thing Reed could do right now. Let him be sad."

Reed needed to finally grieve and mourn, something he hadn't let himself do all those years ago. Coming to grips with the fact he wasn't perfect and Julie wasn't either wasn't going to happen overnight.

"So it's over between you two? Done?"

Kaylee lifted a warm chocolate chip cookie to her mouth, letting it melt on her tongue. They were Reed's favorite and one of the reasons she'd baked them today. In a funny way it made her feel closer to him even though he was physically in another state.

"Who knows what the future will bring," Kaylee answered. She still had hope in her heart. The love she felt for Reed Mitchell hadn't dimmed in the least.

"You've gotten philosophical since dating Reed. It's a strange result."

Kaylee smiled, letting images of her time with him flicker in front of her eyes. "I guess it is. I need to run, but take care of yourself, okay? No getting thrown in the hospital. That's where they put the sick people."

"No kidding," Ava groaned. "But you take care too. I mean it. I want you to be happy."

"I'm fine. Stop worrying about me."

It was Reed they should be worried about. Kaylee couldn't help but wonder what he was doing this very minute.

Did he ever think about her?

Chapter Thirty

Reed's voice trailed off as he finished telling his story to Sonny. Instead of the shocked expression Reed had expected, the older man nodded and looked sad.

"Julie always was a handful of trouble. I'm surprised to hear that she asked you to do that because I know she wanted badly to live longer."

Reed shook his head in denial. "She wanted to die. She asked me twice, and when I wouldn't do it she was angry with me."

Sonny rubbed his chin in thought. "No, she wanted to live. She agreed to try that new treatment in hopes of prolonging her life. Don't you remember?"

Frowning, Reed couldn't understand why his father-in-law was saying these things. Julie had always been adamant about intervention.

"No, she never did," Reed repeated stubbornly. "She hated me because I didn't help her die. I let her down, Sonny."

"No, son, you didn't let her down. She agreed to try the experimental treatment but then she took a turn for the worse and they couldn't do it. That was in—oh, April I think."

Desperately, Reed casted back to spring of that year, trying to make sense of Sonny's story. "I don't remember that at all, and I was with her practically all the time."

"Well," Sonny said thoughtfully, "you weren't there when your dad had that heart procedure done. You were gone about a week or so. In fact, I don't remember you at that appointment with the doctor, but hold on. I can look it up."

"Look it up?" Reed repeated. "You have a record?"

Sonny was already rummaging through a desk drawer in the living room. "Here it is. Ellie kept track of everything, you know. It would be in here." He placed the large journal type notebook on the table between them and thumbed through the pages. "April 14th. 'Sonny, Julie, and I went to the doctor today and she finally agreed to try the treatment hoping for maybe six more months. I'd love to have more time with my baby girl and I pray the treatments won't make her sick or hurt worse. Reed is going to be so happy at the news when he gets back.'"

Staring at the pages, Reed shook his head again. "But no one ever told me."

"I doubt we had a chance. Or maybe Ellie thought I did and I thought she did. Anyway, Julie took a turn, and isn't that why you came back to Denver so quickly?"

Rubbing his forehead, memories of the past that he'd pushed away for so long had come rushing painfully back. Julie had only lived another month after that, each day growing weaker until she'd finally faded away.

"Yes, I remember now. She was back in the hospital by the time I came back. She was angry that I'd left."

"She was angry at everyone, son, although I'll admit she mostly took it out on you. But she was still difficult with her mother and me. It was partly her fury about being sick but the tumor was the other reason. It made her say things and act in ways she didn't mean. Not really. Reed, she didn't want to die and she sure as hell wasn't angry with you. She loved you. I'm an old man but I know that for sure."

His chest ached as he recalled how angry Julie had been, the things she'd say. But then she could also be sweet and loving too. At those times he'd felt like he had his wife back.

"She said I let her down, that I didn't love her. Kaylee said—"

"Kaylee?" Sonny interrupted, a grin spreading across his face. "Please tell me Kaylee is a woman. It's about damn time."

His former father-in-law was okay with Reed being in love with another woman?

"She is," he began cautiously, "a woman I've been seeing. I told her about me and Julie."

"Of course you did," Sonny agreed, getting up to refill his cup and offering more coffee to Reed. "Does she agree with your assessment?"

Reed shook his head and held his hand over his cup. "No, not at all. She said Julie asked me because she knew I would say no. That I would never do it so it was safe to talk about it. Kaylee said that Julie was angry with me because she was so secure in my love. She knew I would never leave her."

"Sounds like good logic. Julie did know you loved her." Sonny leaned forward. "You need to know that she bragged on you all the time. When anyone asked about her husband, she would tell them how you took care of her and how devoted you were. Real pride in her voice. Even before she got sick she talked about you that way. I think she just stopped saying it to you."

"She was scared." The words came out choked as his eyes filled with tears. "She was so damn scared of dying, Sonny. And I couldn't fix that for her."

The older man's eyes were bright as well, his hands shaking as he clasped them together. "I couldn't either and I was her father. She was my one and only little girl and I was helpless to stop what was happening. We tried everything we could to bring her comfort but Julie didn't want to die. Plain and simple. It was only the last day or two when she was so sick that I think she finally accepted it to some degree. But you didn't fail her, son. Never that."

"I want to believe that."

Sonny closed the journal and pushed it across the table. "I think I can help you. Ellie kept a journal from when Julie was diagnosed until the funeral. Some of the entries have Julie's thoughts as well. I think you should have them." He patted the notebook. "There's several more. I don't need them anymore, but you do."

Sonny stood again and went back the large desk, opening and shutting drawers before bringing back a stack of four more journals. "I honestly don't know whether this is going to help or hurt. Reliving all that might not be a good thing with you ready to start a new life with this Kaylee."

"What makes you think I'm looking to start a life with her?" Reed asked, looking up at Sonny with shock. He hadn't said a word to anyone that his thoughts were going that direction.

"You wouldn't be here talking about this unless you were."

Sonny set the books on the table next to the other journal. Reed reached out and leafed through them quickly. All hand written, his mother-in-law had painstakingly recorded every single day, down to the doctor's visits and what medication Julie had taken. Even how much she had slept or what she'd eaten.

"I don't know how to thank you." His eyes burned trying to hold back the tears that would surely come as he read through these notebooks.

Sonny grinned again, his face lighting up. "You already have. You loved my daughter, Reed. I couldn't have asked for a better man for her or a son-in-law for me." The older man scratched his head and sighed. "I think you know that we didn't want you and Julie to marry so young. It seemed like you both needed to live independently, grow a little before you settled down. But considering the way everything turned out I'm glad you did get married. You made my daughter happy and a father can't ask for more than that."

With that endorsement ringing in his ears, Reed gathered up the notebooks and bid goodbye, his throat tight with emotion he couldn't begin to express. Both men knew he was anxious to read them, even knowing how painful it would be.

"Don't be so much of a stranger, son. And bring your girl around so I can meet her. I don't get out much anymore but I sure like visitors."

Reed couldn't help but return the man's smile. He'd forgotten how much he liked Sonny's genial, non-demanding company. "If I can ever get her to come to Montana I promise you'll get to meet her."

"One of those long-distance things, huh? I think you're man enough to put an end to that and get her here."

Reed could only hope he was man enough to do what needed to be done. Deal with the past so he could have a future with the woman he loved.

Kaylee wrapped her hands around the mug of hot chocolate complete with mini marshmallows and sat down on her couch, tucking her legs underneath her. She'd gone overboard decorating the house this year but she'd been determined not to wallow in self-pity now that Reed was gone.

She had to admit the holiday décor had kept her spirits up through these past few weeks. Decorating the glittering nine-foot tree and hanging garland and lights from the mantle and the handrail on the staircase had kept her from brooding. The fifteen dozen cookies she'd baked hadn't hurt either. If she ignored the ache in her heart, the only thing suffering was her waistline.

She set the mug down and turned her attention to the package she'd received this morning. It was clearly her name on the label but it was the return address that had her on pins and needles.

Reed.

This was the first communication she'd had from him in weeks, and here it was Christmas Eve. Instead of opening it when she'd received it, she'd waited until almost midnight, knowing Reed liked to open his gifts on Christmas.

"Just open it. What's the worst thing it could be? A picture of his new girlfriend?"

Setting her mug on the coffee table, she picked up the scissors and snipped through the tape. The box was large and heavy so perhaps photos of his new, happy life without her were out of the question. Pushing back the cardboard, her breath caught in her throat and tears trembled on the tip of her lashes.

He'd remembered… everything.

There was a huge golden box of the dark chocolate Godivas she liked to eat while she wrote. Bars of the semi-sweet chocolate she used when making cookies. Several bags of the flavored coffees she loved to drink along with pretty fabric-covered notebooks and colored pens. A jar of pistachios. And last but certainly not least a hardbound copy of *Pride and Prejudice*. He'd listened when she'd told him her favorite book.

Hugging the book to her chest, she let the tears slip down her cheeks, the tree lights blurring. They weren't tears of sadness though. Kaylee was happy. Reed hadn't forgotten her. In fact, he hadn't forgotten a thing about her. It was the most wonderful gift she'd ever been given.

"I love you," she whispered. "I miss you. Keep fighting, Reed. Don't give in."

Reed halted the horse just at the edge of the creek that ran through his family's land. It was crazy to come out here, at least that's what his brothers had said when he'd saddled up for a moonlit ride on Christmas Eve. It was colder than hell and there was snow in the forecast but he'd been determined to make this trip.

This had been Julie's favorite place to ride. They'd spent many summer nights lying on a blanket staring up at the stars. Holding hands. Kissing and more. It had been…their place. He hadn't been there since she'd gone, hadn't had the courage to face it alone.

But he didn't feel alone. He had Kaylee in his corner even if they hadn't spoken. Strangely, his love had only grown stronger with the separation instead of waning. It was no here today and gone tomorrow emotion. He would love her forever.

He cleared his tight throat and blinked away the moisture that had already gathered in his eyes.

"Hi, Sunshine. We haven't talked in awhile and that's my fault. I thought you were angry with me. I thought I'd failed you. I had a long talk with Sonny and I see things different now." Reed had to clear his throat again, his voice shaky. "I'll always remember what we had. It was good, wasn't it? I know now how hard you fought to live. I know how scared you were and I hope you've found peace now."

The horse underneath him shifted impatiently in the bitter wind, wanting the warmth of the barn and a bucket of oats. But Reed had a few more things to say.

"I've met someone. You'd like her. She's a wonderful woman. Her name is Kaylee and she makes me really happy. She got me a Christmas present."

He pulled down the zipper on his heavy coat just enough to reach in and pull out the red and gold box he'd stared at every day since he left Illinois. It was Christmas Eve and there was no reason not to open the present.

Carefully prying up the ends, he slid his finger under the tape, revealing a plain brown box. Shaking the lid off, he smiled as he held a beautiful hardback edition of *To Kill a Mockingbird*. He ran his finger down the gilt-edged spine and smiled as he remembered that first day when they'd talked about anything and everything. They'd each shared their favorite book of all time. He hoped she enjoyed her gift as much as he loved his own.

Gently he placed it back in the box and under his coat again, zipping it closed to keep it out of the wind and the snow that was beginning to fall. He'd find a place of honor for it on his bookshelf.

"I want you to know that I'll always love you, Julie. Loving Kaylee doesn't take away from what you and I had. But I've wasted too many years feeling guilty. I hope you understand. If I can persuade Kaylee to come to Montana, I'll bring her here and tell her about you. She has such a big heart."

Reed gazed up at the twinkling stars, his hands tightening on the reins. Funny how he felt Julie's presence more these days but it wasn't a burden. It was a comfort.

"Merry Christmas, Julie."

He turned the horse back toward the ranch house, his head clear for the first time in a long time. His heart ached for what might have been but also for what could be. Had he waited too long? Did Kaylee still love him?

"Did you learn anything reading through your mother-in-law's journals?" Tanner asked Reed the day after Christmas while they finished the large pizza with everything between them. Reed had just finished telling the long and sometimes maudlin story to his friend in hopes of getting some good advice.

Tanner had been shocked by Reed's revelation. Apparently "widowed" had never even been on the list of possibilities for the secret that he had been keeping. They'd thought he might be a secret spy before a bereaved husband.

"Sonny was right. Julie did agree to the experimental treatment while I was here with my dad in the hospital. She just never got to try it. Somehow it was never mentioned to me since we were all worried about her. Anyway, it's good to know she did want to live."

"Just like you found out, the instinct to survive is strong," Tanner observed, pushing his empty plate away. They'd spent the better part of the last two hours talking and demolishing lunch.

"It was fucking exhausting reading those journals. Living through that time again, but dammit, I'm glad I did. The tumor messed with Julie's emotions and moods. She couldn't help herself and now that I have some perspective I can see that she did it with others too."

"But you most of all? It's like how a child will hit out at a parent. They know you love them and they're so secure in that love they'll tell you they hate you. Hurts like a bitch but deep down they don't really mean it."

"That's what Kaylee said. I don't know if that's what was truly happening but I think the theory is a sound one."

"So what happens now?" Tanner's brows were raised in question. "What about Kaylee?"

Reed had thought about Kaylee every single damn day since he'd left Illinois. Everything he did was centered around becoming the kind of man that she deserved. He'd thought leaving her had hurt like hell but it had nothing on being without her day in and day out.

"I've been seeing that grief counselor to help sort things out. I want to show Kaylee that I'm trying."

"There's nothing wrong with seeing a professional. I go to AA meetings every week and Madison doesn't think I'm less of a man for it."

Reeling as if he'd been knocked sideways by a two by four, Reed could barely speak. "You're an…alcoholic? I don't believe it."

Tanner laughed and wadded up the paper napkin, tossing it on the table. "Why, because I don't 'look' like an alcoholic? Because I don't act like one? I can assure you I had a drinking problem several years ago. It was bad but I finally sought help and got sober. I'm not too proud or macho to say that help saved my life."

Everyone admired Tanner because it looked like he always had his shit together, so to hear that there was a time when he didn't…

"And you still go?"

"I do. Hearing the other stories reminds me of why drinking sucked and being sober is good."

Come to think of it, Reed had never seen Tanner drink any alcohol. "I don't think I'll need to see this grief counselor forever. She suggested coming a few more times just to get on the right track."

"So I'll ask again. What now?"

"I'm going to call Kaylee and see if she might want to come visit here for a few weeks. I want to show her all the progress I've made. I just hope it's not too late. What if she's met someone else?"

He worried about that all the time. She was a beautiful, talented woman and any man would be proud to call her his own. Maybe he'd left it too long.

Tanner shook his head. "I think it's too late to ask her to come here and visit."

Reed's heart plunged to his stomach. Hell, even Tanner thought Reed had left it too long. "I should just let it go?"

"I said," Tanner replied patiently, a smile playing on his lips, "that it was too late to ask her to come here and visit. That's because she's already here. I saw her at the hospital today visiting Ava. She's staying at Logan and Ava's place."

Kaylee was here. *In Montana.*

As much as he loved her, it was amazing he hadn't felt her presence this close.

"I can't believe she's here," Reed said slowly still trying to wrap his mind around the fact that she wasn't over a thousand miles away. She was within driving distance and he could see her tonight if he wanted to.

Did she want to see him?

"She's here." The waitress dropped off the check and Tanner picked it up with a grin. "Dinner's on me. You're going to need all your money to buy her a diamond and pay for a wedding. Might be some good sales on rings the day after Christmas."

"You said you didn't think I was fit to be in a relationship," Reed reminded him.

"I did say that," Tanner nodded his head in agreement. "But you've changed and I think that Kaylee is the reason. You two will be very happy together."

"If I'm lucky."

Had everything that happened in Illinois been a fluke or could lightning truly strike twice? There was only one way to find out.

Chapter Thirty-One

Kaylee carefully watched the road signs as she drove back from the hospital to the lovely home of Logan and Ava Wright. Kaylee had flown in early this morning and was staying there despite her protests that she could check in to a hotel. She hadn't wanted to be a burden to Logan but Ava had insisted she wanted Kaylee at the house. She'd finally agreed thinking that she could be of use cooking and doing the housework so Logan wouldn't have to worry about it. Living there also had its perks. Kaylee would drive Ava's car back and forth to the hospital.

As they'd all feared, on Christmas day Ava's blood pressure had gone dangerously high causing a painful headache and starbursts in her vision. She was now ensconced in the maternity ward of the nearest large hospital with a neo-natal unit and not liking it one bit. Like Kaylee herself, Ava was a homebody and nothing made her feel safer or happier than to be in her own house. Tucked in Kaylee's purse was a list of things she would take to the hospital tomorrow to make Ava's stay a little more tolerable. Kaylee was already planning a few surprises not on the list including some of her homemade pot roast and maybe a coconut custard pie. Ava had complained that the food was horrid.

Kaylee was determined to keep busy and not think about Reed who was within driving distance for the first time in weeks. He was busy working on things and he needed his space. His Christmas gift had been enough to keep the hope alive in her heart.

She was still half an hour out of Corville when flashing red and blue lights appeared in her rearview mirror. She hesitated to pull over having heard horror stories about fake cops pulling over single women on dark, deserted stretches of road.

Roads just like this one, and so remote there weren't even streetlights to illuminate the pavement.

She had been speeding but barely at five miles over the limit. Sighing in resignation, she put on her right blinker and pulled smoothly off the road and onto the shoulder, deciding she wouldn't roll down her window until she got a good look at the officer.

Easing the car into park, she sat waiting for the cop to exit his own SUV. Impatiently, she tapped on the steering wheel as seconds stretched to minutes.

"Just give me the ticket already," she muttered under her breath.

The driver's door of the vehicle swung open and the officer stepped out. She could clearly see the outline of his body in her side mirror and it only took one look to set her heart galloping out of control. The closer he got the harder it was to breathe. She'd know those shoulders anywhere even in the dark on the side of the road with no light except his headlights and the moon in the inky black sky.

Reed.

He tapped on the window she hadn't yet rolled down, and she reached for the button with trembling fingers. It slid down until it disappeared and she was face to face with the man she'd thought about every single day since he'd left.

The cold wind whipped against her cheeks and tousled her hair. Damn, it was freezing in Montana this time of year.

"Can I see your license and registration, ma'am?"

Huh? He was actually pulling her over?

Confused, she stared up into his completely serious expression. "Um, what?"

"License and registration, please."

So he was pretending he didn't know her. Well, two could play at that game. Anger sprouted and she dug into her purse for her license before snagging the registration from the glove compartment. She handed them over and waited while he perused both items.

"Do you know how fast you were going?"

Asshole. Fucking asshole.

Kaylee didn't know why he was doing this but if he wanted to let her know he didn't give a shit anymore he couldn't have said it any clearer if he'd taken out a billboard in Times fucking Square.

"No," she answered stiffly. "How fast was I going?"

"You were exceeding the speed limit by four miles per hour, and you also failed to signal a lane change twice."

Pursing her lips in fury, she swallowed the bitter words she really wanted to say. "If you say so."

"I do." With one arm resting against the top of Ava's sensible economy car, Reed leaned down far enough that Kaylee caught a whiff of his aftershave. It brought back happy memories of Reed in the morning.

Forget them.

"Are you going to write me a ticket?" The question came out stilted and she wished she could put on a poker face the way Reed did.

"No, ma'am. I'm afraid I'm going to have to take you into custody."

His softly spoken words belied the steel and determination underneath. She'd heard that tone before and she knew it for what it was. He'd do anything to get his way.

And that's when she lost her temper. It was freezing outside but her indignation was keeping her warm. She'd bet her cheeks were crimson with anger.

"Are you serious?" she breathed in amazement. "You're arresting me? Reed, have you lost your mind? I was just coming from the hospital."

"Please step out of the car, then turn around and face the vehicle."

"I can't fucking believe this." Kaylee pushed the door open so hard it flew back on its hinges, almost knocking Reed over. He'd moved at the last minute but didn't reprimand her as she slammed the car shut and turned her back to him, infuriated beyond anything she'd felt before. "You're a total dick, do you know that?"

"Yes ma'am I do," he answered smoothly. "Now place your hands behind your head please."

He was going to cuff her? This was really going too far. She'd hire the best damn lawyer and sue his ass. His very fine, tight, handsome ass.

Placing her hands on her head, she waited as she heard the jingle of cuffs and then one hand was pulled behind her. The cuff wrapped quickly around her wrist and then the other. Perversely she pulled at the metal bracelets, but instead of the cold steel she'd expected they were padded with some kind of material.

Tugging again to try and figure out what he'd restrained her with, she watched as he reached into the car and retrieved her purse and keys before locking up the vehicle. His hand went under her elbow and he marched her back to his SUV but instead of placing her in the back, he sat her in the passenger seat and buckled her in.

He climbed into the warm truck and put the vehicle into gear, pulling back onto the road. Neither one of them said a word. Kaylee let her fury stew and build with each mile until they finally reached their destination.

"This is the police station?"

It looked like a house in the middle of nowhere. It was then that something clicked in her brain. This was Reed Mitchell, the only man she'd ever totally trusted. And he hadn't done any-thing—yet—to lose that trust.

He also hadn't said she was arrested.

She forced herself to relax and take a few deep breaths. She trusted Reed. He'd saved her life and he wouldn't hurt her.

Helping her from the truck, he led her into the house, the lights already on and a cheerful fire blazing in the fireplace. The table was set with a bucket of champagne, chocolate and straw-berries, and a large vase of roses.

Oh Reed. I didn't need this. I only need you.

After taking in the stage he'd set, she turned to him and shook her head. "I would have come if you'd just asked."

"I couldn't be sure," Reed said, his expression unreadable. "I needed to talk to you. I figured worst case scenario I would bring you here, we'd talk, and then I'd take you back to Logan and Ava's."

"And best case?" Kaylee held her breath, pulse racing with hope. Real hope.

"That maybe after we talked we could play sheriff and prisoner." Reed's dimples appeared and it almost took her breath away.

"I guess it depends on what you have to say," she said as he came up behind her and unlocked the cuffs. He rubbed her shoulders and a wave of longing so strong came over her she almost threw herself into his arms.

Almost. He needed to talk first. Had anything changed for him since they'd last seen each other? Had he come to terms with the past or at least started to?

"I've got a whole bunch to say if you're willing to listen."

She lowered herself to a large cushion in front of the fireplace and looked up at him. "I'm ready."

Coming to sit across from her, he paused to gather his thoughts. "I've made some progress. So much I was going to call you and then Tanner said that you were actually here."

"I flew in this morning."

Reed simply looked at her for a long time not saying a word, but there was a hunger in his eyes that matched her own.

"I love you, Kaylee."

She took a long, shuddering breath and felt relief sweep through her body. Finally.

"I know. I love you too, Reed."

His lips turned up at the corners and her heart pounded in her chest for this one man. "I know that too. If you didn't I wouldn't have the power to hurt you. And you trusted me. Even tonight. I could feel how angry you were and then suddenly you weren't mad. You remembered how you felt."

She couldn't deny it and didn't want to. "I did. I remembered how you saved my life and how you protected me. I knew you wouldn't hurt me."

He looked down at the floor and then back up. "But I did hurt you by walking away, didn't I?"

She shook her head, not wanting him to beat himself up over something he couldn't control. "It hurt because I loved you, not because I thought I'd done something wrong or not been enough. I knew you had work to do and I couldn't help you with it. You had to do it on your own."

He nodded. "It's not done but I've made progress. I talked to my father-in-law about things we'd never discussed before. I'm also attending a grief counseling group."

Kaylee tried to hide her shock but didn't quite succeed by the grin on his face. She'd suggested he see a counselor but never in a million years did she think he would do it. He'd been serious about getting better and that fact made her heart squeeze painfully.

"Do you still believe you betrayed Julie?" she asked softly, scared of the answer. Their entire future hung in the balance.

"No, I don't. After talking to Sonny, my father-in-law, I think you're right. Julie wanted to live, ultimately. She was angry and scared and she took it out on me mostly, but now I see that she took it out on others when I wasn't around."

Tears of relief, love, and hope slipped down her cheeks. "I'm so glad. I think Julie was a lucky woman to have you love her that much."

He hadn't touched her yet, not really. But he reached out and cupped her face in his hands so she was looking deep into his hazel eyes, almost gold with passion.

"Yes, I loved Julie. As much as a man can love when he's a callow, untried youth who doesn't know shit about life and death. But what I feel for you...dammit Kaylee, it goes so deep...so painfully rooted...aww hell, I just love you so damn much that it hurts. I want to build a life with you if you'll have me. I want my future to be you. If I can have that, I'll be happy for the rest of my life."

More tears but these were most definitely joyful. "Damn, cowboy, you have a way with words. Yes, I want a future with you. Yes, yes, yes. I've waited for you not just these last weeks but my whole life."

He dug into his pocket and pulled out a tiny black velvet-covered box. She sucked air into her lungs and tried to calm her racing heart.

It was actually happening.

He flipped open the lid and pulled out the ring but to her surprise only half of it came out. "I saw this in a jewelry store this afternoon and knew it was perfect. The ring is made in two parts that fit together, each one a gold band with a diamond. The two can be soldered together so it makes one seamless ring. No one would ever know that it had been in two pieces." He slid the ring on her finger and her heart fluttered in her chest. "I'm offering this as a promise and a vow that I'm going to do everything in my power to lay to rest the past and be worthy of you. When you feel ready, you can wear the second part and we'll consider ourselves engaged. But in my heart we're already husband and wife."

Two parts brought together as one. It was perfect.

Emotion too powerful for words clogged her throat so she simply nodded as her vision blurred with tears. "I feel like I'm always crying with you," she laughed shakily. "It may not look like it but I'm happy."

"Are you angry with me for leaving, honey? I'm so sorry, but I had to."

"I know you did. It didn't make it any easier but I knew if we were going to have any chance together that I had to let you go."

He leaned back against the chair and tugged her into his arms, her head resting on his chest. Her favorite place to be. "You could have told me you loved me before I left, you know."

"You already knew from the looks of things," she teased. "I didn't want to burden you with all my emotions when you could barely handle your own. Besides, you didn't tell me either."

"Did you know?"

She stroked his arm and then clasped her hand in his. "You may not have said it but you showed it. It's what gave me hope all these weeks we were apart. I was beginning to get worried. When Logan called and said that Ava had been put into the hospital I jumped at the chance to come here. I was pretty desperate to see you, especially after the wonderful Christmas gift you sent."

"I know the feeling." His hand slid down her back, his touch urgent. "Now I'm just desperate."

Pressing her palms to his chest, she straddled his thighs and bent to capture his lips with her own. There was no sound but their ragged breaths as they explored one another, his hands urgently delving underneath her heavy sweater. Her tongue traced his chin and then along his jaw before pausing to nibble on his earlobe.

"I'm pretty desperate myself," she whispered. "I missed you, Reed."

With one tug her sweater came off and she was rolled over onto her back with a grinning, gorgeous man on top of her, his weight delicious. "I missed you too, baby, and I'm fixin' to show you how much."

She could feel how much, his cock hot and hard against the softness of her belly, even through the thick denim of his jeans.

Her fingers moved to the buttons on his shirt, plucking them open one by one to reveal golden flesh stretched taut over muscle.

Sliding his shirt down his arms, she yanked at the fabric tucked into his pants. He laughed and tossed the shirt away before reaching down to unbutton his fly, his gaze never wavering from hers. Down to his boxers, he did something she didn't expect. He levered to his feet and padded over to the table where the strawberries and champagne were laid out and waiting.

She was wriggling in anticipation as he grinned wickedly. "This is one of my fantasies. But first we need to get you totally naked."

Jeans slid down her legs and her bra and panties disappeared into a clothing pile right after. "Lie down and put your hands over your head."

With a shuddering breath, she lifted her arms over her head only to be shocked when he snagged the cuffs she'd worn earlier from his jeans pocket and snapped them on her wrists again fastening her to the leg of the couch.

"Not too tight?" he inquired, those dimples making another appearance. She shook her head, too excited and aroused to speak. He lifted a strawberry from the plate and dipped it in the bowl of chocolate that was kept liquid by the flame underneath. "Stay very still."

Reed ran the chocolate covered tip of the fruit down her abdomen and up her ribcage before dipping it again and making perpendicular lines across her belly. His tongue snaked out and lapped at the sweet confection making her arch and sigh in contentment.

Dipping the berry again, he let the chocolate dribble into a pool in her belly button, the elixir warm as a drip tickled her sensitive skin. She giggled and he rewarded her by licking and sucking the chocolate from her quivering flesh and then finally biting into the fruit. The red juice was cold on her skin but he dashed it away so quickly with the warmth of his tongue all she could do was gasp in response.

He continued teasing and tickling her until she was panting with arousal and begging for relief. He reached out a callused finger and ran it around a puckered nipple. "I'm just getting started on this fantasy and you want me to go faster. Don't you like this?"

She loved it and hated it all at the same time. Apparently it was a rhetorical question as he didn't bother to let her answer, instead dipping another strawberry in the liquid chocolate and bringing it to her lips. Biting into the firm flesh, the flavors burst on her tongue and she hummed in appreciation even as the juice ran down her chin.

"I'll get that for you." He lapped at the sticky skin before pressing his lips to hers in a long kiss that seemed to go on forever. He tasted sweet and tart and all Reed. She whimpered when he dragged his own mouth from hers even as he drizzled chocolate on her nipples, the heat only serving to make them harder. He dabbed at her quivering rose-tipped breast until she was squirming underneath him.

"Now, Reed," she urged but he had already turned his attention to her other breast, giving it the same torturous treatment that left her gasping for air. Her thighs were covered in her own honey and he positioned himself between her legs so she couldn't close them, leaving her open to his gaze yet again.

"Reed," she moaned, wondering if she would ever get used to his molten expression when he looked...there. So intimate but so hot too.

This time he didn't bother with the strawberry. Dipping his finger into the chocolate, he painted the folds of her pussy before bending his head and licking it off in long strokes of his tongue. Flames rippled over her skin and a tight bar of arousal filled her belly. Her hands tugged at the cuffs and he had to pin her legs to the floor as his mouth closed over her clit and sucked gently.

She cried out his name as she tumbled over the cliff. Wave after wave of pleasure suffused every pore as he kissed his way up her body and ensnared her lips with his own. The room was still spinning when he pulled away and rolled on a condom he'd fished from his pants pocket.

His large, muscular body hovered over her own as he pressed forward slowly, taking his time and drawing out the bliss. It had been weeks since she'd last been filled by him but her spirit remembered the pleasure he gave so lavishly. Her hips swayed as his thrusts sped up, his breathing coming in harsh gasps. Moving quickly back to the pinnacle, she whispered hot dirty suggestions into his ear that only spurred him on to fuck her harder and faster.

"Now, baby." Reed's voice was deep and dark, triggering her climax. The world bubbled and sparked as Reed's orgasm overtook him as well. His body strained and his head was thrown back; he was so incredibly beautiful. Masculine yes, but there was tenderness as well.

There was love.

Chest heaving, he rolled onto his back when it was over, eyes closed as he dragged air into his lungs. She lay next to him feeling peaceful and content knowing that tonight was the first of many nights they would share. She wasn't alone anymore.

Eventually the sweat on her body cooled and Reed reached up and with a click her arms were free. He massaged her shoulders and planted kisses on her ears and cheek until she giggled and batted at his fingers that were tickling her tummy.

"I love you, baby. Thank you for saving me."

Kaylee rubbed her palm against his stubbly jaw. "I didn't save you, you saved yourself. But you're welcome anyway." She looked around the comfortable living room and smiled. "Does this house have a back porch where I can write? Or maybe a room with a big window so I can see outside?"

Reed smiled and her heart danced with happiness. "It does, but if it didn't I'd go out there in zero degree weather and build you one. Are you really okay with moving here, honey? I'll move if you don't want to."

Smiling contentedly, she shook her head. "I know you would but moving here means I get not only the sexiest man alive but also my best friend. Ava's going to need a hand when the babies come."

"I'm going to want it all," Reed warned. "Marriage, babies, a dog, and a picket fence. And those cookies you bake too. Run away now if that's not what you had in mind."

"I can't think of anything I want more."

All her stories and heroes paled in comparison to this man. He was everything and all she could ever want. She couldn't wait to build their future together on the firm foundation of love.

Epilogue

Reed slid several cans of soda down the table before popping open his own. Sunday morning at the roadhouse for the sheriffs' monthly meeting. It had been hard to get out of a warm bed with an even warmer and very willing body in it this morning. Hopefully the snow would hold off long enough to get this meeting over with and get home. While he was here Kaylee was tapping away at her laptop trying to get as much done as she could so they could spend the rest of Sunday together.

"Has Kaylee sold her house yet?" Tanner asked as he sat down at the head of the table.

"Not yet, but winter's a tough time to make a sale. We're hoping spring and summer will be better."

The other men nodded in agreement and that's when Reed noticed there was an empty chair. Again. Logan was either working or with Ava, the doctors closely monitoring her blood pressure. It was stable at the moment but according to the doctors that could change at any moment.

Reed couldn't imagine how scared Logan must be right now, worrying about his wife and babies. It was good that Kaylee was here as she visited Ava almost every day and took some of the stress off of Logan.

"Anything to report on Kaylee's stalker?" Seth chugged down half his soda and then reached for the bag of pretzels in the middle of the table.

"Cheryl Hill's lawyer asked for a psychiatric evaluation. I guess he must be going for the insanity defense but she knew what she was doing. Just like Presley's sister knew. Jealousy and greed are nasty things."

"Since Logan isn't here you may not have heard that Wade Bryson was ruled competent to stand trial," Evan offered. "That courtroom is going to be standing room only. The attorney immediately asked for a change of venue of course due to pre-trial publicity."

"If I were him I'd just plead out," Dare scowled, but then he was always unhappy about something. "They have a mountain of evidence against him."

"Don't mean shit if the jury never gets to hear it," Jared replied, his usual smile missing and a deep frown taking its place. "Damn lawyers could get him out on a technicality."

"I don't think there's a technicality that will free a serial killer," Griffin observed mildly. "At least I hope not."

"What's going on with Gordon?" Reed asked. "They were talking about a plea, weren't they?"

"He took a deal." Griffin looked calm but a muscle ticked in his jaw and Reed knew why. Gordon had tried to murder Griffin's wife-to-be and had almost succeeded. "I guess it's for the best. This way Jazz won't have to relive everything and testify."

Tanner pounded his fist on the table. "Let's call this meeting to order then. Any more old business?"

There was silence around the room. "Fine, we'll move on to new business. I don't know how many of you heard but DEA Agent Jason Anderson has gone missing. He was investigating a drug cartel and hasn't been seen or heard from in weeks. I say this to ask that you keep your ear to the ground with any of your snitches. They might mention an agent hostage being held as currency for trade."

Griffin groaned and shook his head. "If he's been taken hostage he'd be better off dead. I've seen what these guys will do. It's not pretty."

Reed had seen it as well and had to agree with Griffin. If Jason Anderson had been taken hostage by a drug kingpin he'd be praying for death before too long. Reed could only hope that Jason was okay wherever he was. He was a good man and a good agent.

The meeting continued with news from each town, nothing too violent or egregious. The lull before spring when things seemed to liven up again. Jared didn't speak much, his entire body tense and his expression a mask of some painful emotion. A few months ago Reed wouldn't have recognized the signs of a man trying to cover up something he didn't want to feel.

But now he was an expert.

"You want to get some lunch or something?" Reed asked Jared as they headed out to their vehicles, the cold wind a shock to the system even after all these years in Montana.

"I can't." Jared shook his head and opened the driver's door of his truck. "I promised my mom and dad that I would have Sunday dinner at their house today. It was practically a royal command."

Jared was trying to make a joke of it but Reed could easily detect the tension in the words.

"Another time then. And listen, thanks again for your help when I was in Illinois. I know you're busy but you took the time to do those background checks for me. I really appreciate it."

Jared grinned, looking happier than Reed had seen him all day. "You know I like that stuff. It's the gravy on the mashed potatoes. But you're welcome." Jared climbed in the truck with a quick salute. "See you next month."

The chilling wind seeping under his collar, Reed jumped in his own truck and fired up the engine. He turned the heat on full blast before backing out of the parking lot and heading down the road and away from the roadhouse. He had someone at home waiting for him and damn if that didn't feel better than anything in the world.

Reed wasn't afraid to feel, to love, to hope. Kaylee had saved him from a life wasted and he would never be able to love her enough in return.

The End

Cowboy Command
Cowboy Justice Association
Book One

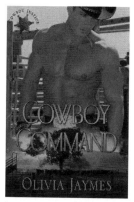

Sometimes you have to die to be born.

One minute Katie is eating lunch with her sister, the next she barely escapes a car bomb meant to kill her. If that wasn't enough, someone sets fire to her home and burns it to the ground. Luckily, Federal agents are going to give her a new identity until she can testify against the man who wants her dead. They change her name to Presley, her hair color to brown, and her shorts and sandals to jeans and cowboy boots. She's not thrilled about being sent to a small town in Montana to hide, but she wants to stay alive.

Sheriff Seth Reilly is doing a favor for an old Army buddy. He's promised to watch over a woman whose life is in danger, but he didn't plan on her being so young and beautiful. He's tempted, but she's a bundle of trouble. Seth likes his women calm and sedate. Presley is the kind of woman who would keep him up at night and make him crazy. Too bad he's starting to enjoy it.

Passion flares between Seth and Presley, heating up the cold Montana nights. Knowing they only have a short time together, they vow not to fall in love. But when danger finds Presley, Seth will risk everything to keep her safe until she can testify. Will Presley get her old life back or start a new life with Seth instead?

Justice Healed
Cowboy Justice Association
Book Two

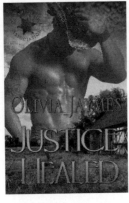

You can't go home again, but if you do, pretend you want to be there.

Dr. Madison Shay has left Chicago and moved back to her small town roots to take over her father's medical practice. She's not the skinny, gawky red haired, four-eyed girl any longer but it sure feels that way. She still remembers the painful teasing from her classmates and always feeling like she didn't belong. She wants this time to be different but deep down she knows she'll never be part of the cool crowd.

Sheriff Tanner Marks might have been the captain of the football team years ago but things aren't as rosy now. He has a son who hates him, and an ex-wife who is about to marry a man Tanner thinks might be a criminal. He doesn't really have time in his life for a woman. Considering the things he's done in his past, he's not sure he deserves one either. He can't help but feel envious of his friend, Seth Reilly, though. He found the love of a good woman. Is it too much to ask that fate send him someone as well?

Madison and Tanner aren't looking for love but it feels like the town has other plans. They keep finding themselves thrown together and it's not unpleasant in the least. In fact, they're starting to enjoy themselves. There just might be a future for them after all.

When a drug war between two cartels breaks out, their little town is caught in the crossfire. Tanner will call in every favor he can, from the five cowboy cops he trusts most in the world, to keep his town and the woman he loves safe. He's going to show the bad guys what cowboy justice really means.

Cowboy Truth
Cowboy Justice Association
Book Three

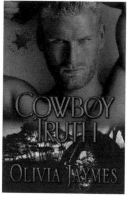

People will do desperate things to keep the truth dead and buried.

Sheriff Logan Wright might be the sexiest bad boy Ava Hayworth has ever seen but she's not interested in the least. He can have every other woman in town and probably already has. All she wants is to help him solve the murder of a prominent local citizen by a mysterious vigilante serial killer. A fling with a smokin' hot cowboy cop isn't in her plans.

Logan doesn't need a mystery writer who thinks she's a detective, trailing after him while he tries to do his job. She's smart and cute, but he doesn't want her to get hurt. By him or the investigation. He enjoys the pleasures of women – many women – and that's not going to change.

But as painful secrets are revealed, Logan begins to depend on Ava for more than just friendship. She's the first woman he's known who has kept her promises. It shakes him to his very core, challenging long held beliefs.

Everything Logan wants, but never thought he could have, is within his grasp. With the help of Ava and his friends, he's going to have to fight the past if he wants any kind of a future.

Cowboy Famous
Cowboy Justice Association
Book Four

Sheriff Griffin Sawyer likes his town quiet and his life uncomplicated. Fishing – alone – on a serene and sunny afternoon is one of his favorite things to do. So is coming home to a place that isn't littered with cosmetics, clothes, and panties. After growing up one of ten children, sharing his bathroom, his closet, or his thermostat is not high on his to-do list. Women have their place. Just not his place.

Jazz Oliver wants to be a star. Unfortunately, Hollywood hasn't been kind. The day she loses out on the part of a lifetime is also the day she gets fired from her crappy waitress job. Down and out and deep in debt, she's desperate for money and a big break. It's the only reason she's allowed herself to be signed up as a contestant on a reality show in some backwater town in Montana.

From their first meeting, the attraction simmers between the sheriff and the Hollywood starlet. Jazz knows Griffin needs his space, and he knows she will only be in town a short while. The one thing they both want? More of the hot, sultry nights they've been sharing. When they're together their differences don't seem to be any problem at all.

But when casual, naughty fun turns into something more, Griffin is stumped as to what to do. Having spent most of his adult life keeping women at arm's length, he doesn't know how to get one to stay. He needs to find a way to convince her – and himself – that he's finally ready to share everything. Even the remote control.

Cowboy Cool
Cowboy Justice Association
Book Five

Sheriff Reed Mitchell is a workaholic on a forced vacation. To make the best of a bad situation, he points his pickup truck toward Florida and some great fishing with an old buddy. He just has one quick stop on the way. He promised Logan Wright he'd check on Kaylee Blue who has been receiving creepy emails from a stalker.

Kaylee thinks Ava and Logan are worried over nothing. As the writer of erotic romance, she gets strange mail every now and then. She'll let Reed check her windows and doors, feed him dinner, and then send him down the road so she can get back to her writing.

But nothing goes as planned…

Kaylee's stalker raises the stakes and Reed is forced to put his vacation on hold. Despite Kaylee's protests that she can handle things on her own, she's relieved Reed is determined to protect her. Thrown into each other's company twenty-four-seven, the two find they have much in common, not the least of which is a heated passion whenever they're in the same room.

But living out the most naughty scenes from Kaylee's books is rapidly turning into something else. Something real. Reed hasn't cared about a blessed thing in the last fifteen years except work and he's not planning to change. Will he be able to turn and leave this woman when it's time to go?

Publisher's note: This book contains smoking hot scenes with a bossy alpha male cowboy cop, an erotic romance author, and some steamy fun between the sheets.

The Deputies
Cowboy Justice Association

Second chances. Unrequited crushes. Brand new love.

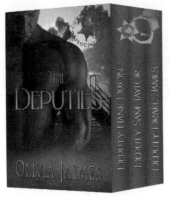

Deputy Hank Dixon:

When Hank's estranged wife shows up ready to mend their broken marriage, he has a hard time believing she's sincere. She's hurt him badly in the past and he's not sure he's ready to let her stomp on his heart all over again.

Alyssa has learned from her mistakes and is ready to do whatever it takes to get her husband back. She wants to spend the rest of her life showing Hank that he'll always come first for her.

But this stubborn cowboy cop isn't going to trust so easily. He wants more time but fate has other plans. When tragedy strikes, can Hank put the past behind him and embrace a future with the woman he loves?

Deputy Sam Taylor:

Sam's been alone a long time and that suits him just fine. On a night he plucks a scared woman from a car accident during a snowstorm, he finally realizes he's been missing out. Tabby is everything he's ever wanted in a woman. Too bad she's just passing through town.

Tabby's life is busy and complicated. The last thing she has time for is a sexier than hell cop that makes her weak at the knees just by smiling. She shouldn't get involved with him but she can't help herself. He's just so damn perfect.

When it comes time for Tabby to leave, Sam knows she's changed his life forever. And forever is a long time. Can this handsome deputy convince Tabby that he's worth changing her life for?

Deputy Drake James:

Tori Saunders has been in love with Drake forever. At least it feels that way. Now she's back in her hometown and she's determined to make the hotter than sin deputy her man. She's got it all planned. All she needs is a little cooperation from Drake.

Drake takes one look at Tori and decides some steamy nights between the sheets sound like just what the doctor ordered. The sexy pastry chef seduces him with her sweet desserts and sweeter curves. Together they really cook in the kitchen.

But when Drake finds out that Tori's planned out their entire lives together right down to the names of their kids, he ends the relationship then and there. It's not like he'd fallen for Tori. Or thought she was wonderful, and smart, and sexy. Nope, this cop is just fine without Tori Saunders. Except he's not. Looks like Drake has some work to do to win back the love of his life.

Publisher's warning: This book contains sexy scenes including some hot lovin' on the kitchen counter, up against a tree, and in front of a roaring fire.

Note – While these novellas are part of the Cowboy Justice Association series, the stories stand alone and may be read out of order.

About the Author

Olivia Jaymes is a wife, mother, lover of sexy romance, and caffeine addict. She lives with her husband and son in central Florida and spends her days with handsome alpha males and spunky heroines.

She is currently working on a series of full length novels called The Cowboy Justice Association. It's a contemporary erotic romance series about six lawmen in southern Montana who work to keep the peace but can't seem to find it in their own lives.

Visit Olivia Jaymes at: www.OliviaJaymes.com

Printed in Great Britain
by Amazon.co.uk, Ltd.,
Marston Gate.